Legacy

~ ~

Elizabeth Flaherty

www.flahertybooks.com

From Little B's Briefcase

DEDICATION

For my mom,
who taught me there was
nothing I couldn't do
and that real success
is simply doing your best.

LY

~ 1 ~

Serena Marlowe patrolled the streets of Whitefield the same way her father had done before her and his father had done before him. As long as there'd been a sheriff in town, there'd been a Marlowe on the job.

She'd spent her whole life fighting for her place in that storied history, but the reality of life in her new job left Serena with more than a few doubts. Voter turnout at the last election suggested that voters in Whitefield felt the same way.

Maybe family dynasties were out of vogue. Maybe they thought she was too young. Hell, maybe they just didn't like her all that much.

Whatever they thought of her, the town had elected her because they had no choice. When her father's heart had started giving him trouble, he'd had to resign. He chose his successor. That was the way it was done. The way it had always been done. But Serena knew that habit could only take her so far.

Most days she knew public opinion was something she shouldn't worry about. At thirty-five, she was the youngest person who'd even held the job, but that didn't mean she was inexperienced. She'd been a deputy since her high school graduation. Even more importantly, she had good judgment and an instinct for seeing problems coming, which was buttressed by her near obsession with finding and utilizing every training resource she could get her hands on. There was every reason to believe she'd be a great sheriff, if given enough time to grow into the job.

But being sheriff was as much about perception as it was about arresting people. And that was where she was having most of her trouble. She was expected to be more available to the public. More approachable.

Quiet nights were a constant reminder of her deficiencies. That meant stopping in at the local bar, swinging by the gas station, wandering into the convenience store. She didn't mind the patrolling – the slow cruise through the streets, keeping an eye out for anything that might be just a little off – but Serena had no natural talent for the stopping, the chatting, the handshaking. Nights like this she longed to go back to the way it had been when her father was in charge. When taking over her role in the "family business" was a happy dream and not an unnerving reality.

She glided her car through the town's main street. Most of the storefronts were dark. Only the bar and grill was still open. Through the massive plate-glass window, she could see her brother working the taps and a couple regular customers sitting at the bar. Everything looked in order. Liam even smiled and waved as she drove by.

She eased her foot off the gas, tried to force herself

to stop, but she took another loop through the back streets and finally climbed the hill to the site of the old hospital.

The hospital had closed down ten years earlier. And it was the last place she would find hands to shake or citizens to greet.

It was a crisp fall night and the almost full moon shone brightly against the black sky, illuminating the shadowed woods that surrounded her. She was hiding. Of course, she knew that. Still, a childish part of her insisted this could be enough. That if she just put her head down and worked hard the town would respect the police work. Respect her. And the rest of it would fall away.

Serena pulled into the crumbling parking lot, shining her spotlight around the silent building that screamed with sinister possibilities. One of her deputies had found some kids using the back parking lot for a keg party only a week earlier. Buildings like this were more than just blight. They provided opportunity.

She was grumbling to herself about the effects of decay when she saw it. The beam of her spotlight ran across a series of boarded windows, and then across a window where the wood was tilted at an odd angle. She stopped her patrol car and focused the light more precisely. Every board was perfect – every board, but one.

She called into the station. "Hey, Hayley, it's Serena, you there?"

The cheerful voice of their dispatcher crackled through the line. "What's the sitch, Sheriff?"

"I'm looking at a loose board at the hospital site. I suspect some of those kids came back around. I'm going to have to bring a couple of them in. Call their parents. I wanted you to know where I was headed."

"You sure, Sheriff? Maybe another warning? Shane seemed to think he'd gotten through to them. He's not on until morning, but I bet he'd be willing to come in."

Serena smiled a little at her enthusiasm, knowing she was right; Shane would be happy to do the follow-up.

"I'll take care of it. I'll update Shane when he gets in," Serena replied. A second offense meant it was time for a different approach.

She signed off and headed in. With her most intimidating expression firmly in place, she pushed the board aside and climbed through the broken window.

It was darker than she'd expected. The inky blackness concealed graffiti, crumbling tiles, and God only knew what else. The strong beam of her flashlight revealed moldy furniture and crumbling equipment in some of the rooms.

She'd only barely gotten inside when a scream echoed through the halls. Gun drawn, she raced toward the sound. Serena shouted her name and identification as she ran. She wasn't sure if she did it to assert authority or to give the promise of help, but either way, it seemed like the thing to do.

As she turned a corner, the sounds of hysterical chatter told her she was close. It was two people. They sounded young, frightened.

On her right a door stood open. Serena swung her flashlight and gun into the room, illuminating Andi Sinclair and Lucas Denton. There was a flashlight at their feet.

Though the high schoolers were the first thing Serena noticed, they didn't hold her attention for long.

In the center of the room was an operating table. The chrome reflected the beam of her flashlight back into her face, but the glare did not obstruct the truth. In the middle of the table was a human heart.

~ 2 ~

Serena barely remembered how she managed to remove Andi and Lucas from the crime scene, but she knew they'd been taken down to the station by Shane Gilbert, the same deputy who had warned them to stay away from the old hospital only a week before. Serena suspected they wished they'd listened.

She still wasn't sure if it was good fortune or bad that they hadn't. Without their trespassing the heart could have gone undiscovered for months, maybe forever.

Hayley had called all of the deputies in, but that wasn't saying much. With Shane back at the station, it was just Riley Scott and his brother Jake to assist her at the scene. Jake was the most junior of her staff, which was why he was doing a general search through the hospital. Riley was with her.

Almost ten years her senior, Riley was the most experienced deputy she had. Serena knew she had to respect his experience. She also knew he was going to love showing off his skills.

Riley had borrowed battery-powered floodlights from the high school and set them up on the edges of the room. A click turned the monochrome world into brilliant Technicolor and she saw the scene again for the first time.

Their killer had taken his time here. The chrome table and white tiles shone with a cleanliness that was absent from the rest of the hospital. It almost looked like an operational operating room.

In the middle of the room was more blood than Serena had ever seen, and, of course, the centerpiece – a human heart. Despite the mess, Serena felt the heart looked like it had been placed with care. Possibly reverence.

Swallowing her horror, Serena raised her camera and slowly worked the room, snapping as she went, making sure she captured every detail.

Riley was leaning up against the wall, investigating in his own way. Serena had worked with him long enough to understand he was thinking just like her, but his method was far less formal.

"Do you seriously think that's a human heart? You sure it's not a pig's heart or something?" Riley asked.

Serena knew how he felt. It should be a pig's heart or a cow's. It shouldn't be a human heart. Couldn't be a human heart. It was too horrible to even consider.

"Biology was not one of my best classes, but I'm pretty sure it's a human heart. The size and shape are wrong to be anything else," she replied without stopping.

She heard Riley pull a cigar out of his pocket. She knew he wouldn't light it. He'd just chew it while he tried to figure out what they were really looking at.

"So you're thinking that's human blood," he continued. It wasn't a question. He knew what she thought. They both knew he agreed. There was just something clarifying about saying it out loud.

Serena had made her way closer to the table now. Careful not to step in any of the blood, she snapped another shot. The pool was deeper than she'd initially thought.

"I think I'm seeing bone fragments here too," she said.

Riley cracked his knuckles and Serena could feel his anger rising. The brutality of the scene was starting to influence him.

"So, we're thinking some fucking monster cut somebody up?" he asked.

Serena looked around the rest of the room. It was empty. No tools, no other equipment.

She answered calmly, hiding her own stress and anger. "Where else would all this blood come from?"

Riley cracked his knuckles again. Though she didn't look at him, she knew he'd roll his neck next.

His voice held less agitation when he spoke, more resignation. "What the hell did those kids walk into here?"

Finished with the photos, Serena set her camera aside. "You want to collect blood or fingerprints?"

"I'll take the blood," Riley replied. "I'd like a closer look anyway."

Serena nodded and began to scan for surfaces that were likely to have prints. She'd deal with the table last.

As she scanned, she was again struck by the condition of the room. It had been prepped for this. Whatever the hell this was. Serena felt entirely certain someone who'd clean the place like this wouldn't leave prints.

She was powdering the doorknob when Riley spoke again. His tone betrayed his doubts about her abilities.

"Serena, if this is really a human heart and this is really human blood, you're gonna have a hell of a time keeping this in house."

She'd been thinking the same thing. Last time the department had a murder investigation, the state police had been called in to provide support. They'd cut the department out completely and bungled things entirely. The investigation dragged on far longer than it should have, threw the town into turmoil and practically destroyed her family.

No. She had no interest in the state police and no need for their help.

She said none of that to Riley. Her voice was stronger than she would have expected when she replied, "We do this by the book. Perfectly. That's how we keep it in house."

He was staring at her, judging her. She could see it from the corner of her eye. She could sense the weight of it, but she refused to react.

When his silence didn't get any response, he prodded, "Doesn't always work, you know."

She knew. She also knew she didn't have a better answer. "Are you suggesting we should call them in?"

Riley's eyes grew wide and it became clear that he hadn't expected that she'd call his bluff. Of course, he wasn't suggesting the state police were a good option. He'd worked with them. He knew their presence only gave false hope.

"I'm just saying they may try to inject themselves," Riley replied.

Serena kept her attention on her work, never letting him see her eyes, never letting him see the fear, the worry that they were in over their heads.

After a few moments, Riley continued, "You call the coroner?"

Serena wondered if she should be annoyed he'd think she wasn't competent enough to know the scene called for a coroner, or if this was just Riley's way to engage in a conversation about just how much he didn't like the town's new doctor. Clay was successful and good-looking. Riley preferred to believe he'd cornered the market on both those qualities.

Since the conversation was likely to quickly wear away her veneer of calm, Serena kept her answer short. "He should be here soon."

Sounds of footsteps in the dark hallway spared her further discussion, as did the familiar voice that called her name.

Clay Drayton, police-issued flashlight in hand, peered into the room. "Is this where you want me?"

Even as he asked, his expression changed. His eyes darkened. His jaw tightened. Serena straightened up and watched him carefully. On his face she saw many of the emotions she'd already experienced. Revulsion. Fear. Anger. But they all passed in an instant. When he met her eyes, Clay looked calm, serious, ready to proceed.

"I guess this is the place," he said, answering his own question.

Serena gave him another moment to get his legs under him. "I suspect when we hired you on as the local coroner you figured you'd be doing autopsies on natural deaths."

Clay gave her a weak but comfortable smile. "I guess I just figured there'd be a body."

Never one for bedside manner, Riley's voice was gruff and impatient. "She thinks this here is a human heart. Is it?"

Clay turned his focus to the table, slowly walking closer.

"Don't touch anything yet. It's a crime scene," Serena warned.

He nodded and moved a few steps closer. "I watch CSI like everybody else, Sheriff. You're right, by the way, that's a human heart. I'm going to need a closer look, but it looks like somebody cut that out with a scalpel or some similar instrument. Those are very precise cuts."

"What do you mean, precise cuts?" Serena asked.

Clay stepped back from the heart to explain. "If you were to cut into somebody with a kitchen knife or something, that would look different than this."

"You saying this guy is some kind of doctor?" Riley asked.

Serena glared at her deputy, hearing the accusation in his voice.

Clay was either oblivious or didn't particularly care that Riley was suggesting their killer was a doctor, like him.

"I couldn't possibly say if he's a doctor. I'm just saying it looks like whoever did this used a scalpel. Or something like that."

Serena looked back at the table. The heart. The blood. A scalpel? She wasn't sure what that told her about all of this.

Before she could say anything more, her attention turned to the dark hallway. The sound of shoes on linoleum. Someone was hurrying toward them. Serena eased Clay behind her, and both she and Riley drew their weapons.

Her heart was racing as the figure appeared in the doorway. Before she could order him to freeze, he stepped into the light.

Serena expelled the breath she'd been holding when she saw it was Jake Scott, her deputy, in the doorway. It was a moment before she realized something was wrong. His usually tanned skin was pale as death.

"What is it, Jake?" she asked.

"Sheriff, Riley, you guys need to come. It's bad. Really bad."

Riley started out, his gun leading the way, before Jake stopped him.

"You won't need the gun," he explained. "It's not like that."

The look on Jake's face told Serena that not needing a gun was somehow worse. She allowed Riley to follow Jake out before she turned to Clay.

"Doc, I'm going to need you to come with us."

Clay smiled. "Don't worry about me. I'm okay. I can stay here."

Serena only shook her head, knowing in her gut that they were going to need him down the hall just the same as they did here.

She didn't try to explain. Instead, returning his smile, she said, "It'd make me feel better if you came along."

Clay hesitated only a moment, seeming to try to read her expression. When he failed, he quickly followed behind.

Back in the hall, Serena was again overwhelmed by the darkness. Ahead she could see the lights that Jake and Riley held were already halfway down the hall. Her own light, even when joined by Clay's, did little more than reflect off the decaying floors.

As they walked on, the flashlights were enough to reveal that the colors of the tile had changed. She knew from the days before the hospital closed that the tiles changed colors between the different wards. Experience told her that the bright red and blue tile meant they were in the old children's ward. In case memory was not enough confirmation, they turned another corner and were met by a huge mural of children playing in the park.

Serena's nose told her they were getting close to something she was sure she didn't want to find. The scent actually made her realize something she hadn't before; there'd been no smell of decay in the other room. The scene must have been fresh.

The smell grew stronger and she had to resist the urge to put her hand over her nose. As the only woman among men, she'd learned long ago how important it was to be the toughest guy in the room. Today, of all days, that seemed essential.

Jake stopped in front of a door and pulled his sleeve over his hand, and then placed his hand over his face. "It's pretty bad in there," he advised. He opened the door for them to see, without making any move to enter.

Serena stepped past him, ignoring the stench. Inside, her flashlight beam found piles of corpses, all of them animals. The sheer volume was dizzying. The small bodies cast aside with no care, no discernable ritual. The scene was so unimaginable that a desperate part of her insisted it was a trick of the light, that in the long shadows she was seeing something that wasn't there.

But even in the dim light, she had to admit she knew what she was seeing. Cats. Dogs. There might have been a lizard in one corner.

There was one dog toward the front. His eyes shown brightly, reflecting the beams of their flashlights, demanding answers. His chest was cut open, sliced down the middle. Serena knew she should check to see if his heart had been removed, but she couldn't quite bring herself to do it.

Serena ignored the pain in her own chest. Her voice all business, she asked, "Have you checked the other rooms?"

Jake shook his head. "I knew you'd want to see this right away."

Clay looked confounded by her question and more than a little disturbed by the massive amount of death. "Why the other rooms?"

Riley, however, was with her immediately. "This is a storage room."

Serena suspected they would find another operating room somewhere in this section of the building. Though she figured it would be close to the storage room, as Riley called it, she knew the practicalities of the smell would have forced their killer a bit further down the hall.

Riley started checking the first few rooms, but Serena walked past them. She followed the hallway to the end and turned the corner. Only then did the stench begin to abate. That was when she began her search. The second door she tried revealed another prepped operating room.

This room had once been a basic hospital room. Shelves that had housed televisions hung unevenly on the walls. There no longer were any beds, but there were several tables and a silver cart that would have been used to wheel equipment into an operating room. Pristine tools were laid out on the cart – everything from scalpels to what Serena figured had to be a bone saw.

Unlike the other items in the room, the tools looked new. These were not cast-offs from the defunct hospital. These were the killer's own.

Serena was surprised when she heard a voice behind her. "Why the hell would somebody cut up animals?"

Serena turned to face Clay and, for a moment, she saw him that way. Just Clay. Not the local coroner, but the new town doctor, the guy whose primary job was taking care of the living. The guy she so enjoyed running into on the street, whose smile always put her in a better mood. God, she hated to do this to him.

"I'm going to need you to look at those animals in there to help us figure out why."

His eyes grew wide. "I'm not a vet!"

She placed a gentle hand on his shoulder. "They don't need a vet anymore, I'm afraid, but I'll ask Dr. Skylar to assist you on the autopsies. I imagine a vet would be helpful."

Serena wondered if it would make him feel any better to know she'd thrown her best friend into this maelstrom with him. Either way, she was certain it wouldn't make Missy Skylar feel any better.

Clay stared at her.

"Doc," she said as calmly as she could. "He was practicing. Had to have been."

"Practicing for what?"

Serena sighed. She wished she knew. "I think we're going to find out pretty soon, whether we want to or not."

~ 3 ~

Serena was sitting in her office staring at the ceiling when there was a knock on her door. She intended to call out that they should enter, but the noise she made was something more like a grunt.

Her father's voice filled her ears before she saw him. "I figure you can probably use this."

The smell of coffee was welcome, and only served to remind her how much she stunk of death.

She rubbed her eyes and greeted him with what she knew had to be a very tired smile. "Thanks, Pop."

William Marlowe drank his own coffee and slid into the chair in front of her desk. He gave her a moment of quiet. Not pushing. Not asking. Just waiting, while she drank her coffee.

After a while, he said, "The look on your face tells me the rumors are true."

Serena wasn't entirely surprised. How could she be? She'd known the moment her father appeared in her office. She looked at her watch. It was barely eight a.m. She'd just finished processing the crime scene.

"There are rumors already?"

William laughed. "Of course there are rumors already. They started about five minutes after you had to drag Coach Fletcher out of bed so you could commandeer his flood lights."

Taking a long drink of her coffee, Serena considered what the hell she was supposed to do next. "What do you already know?"

"Well, the word is you found a bloodbath at the old hospital, but you've got no body."

Hearing someone else say it somehow made it sound even worse. Trying to sound calm, detached, Serena replied, "Pretty good early release. In one of the operating rooms we found a whole lot of blood, no body, just a human heart sitting in the middle of the table as nice as can be."

William shook his head. "That's a truckload of crazy."

"There's more. We also found another makeshift operating room. Somebody's been cutting up animals. There had to have been close to thirty in there, just rotting. I asked Doc Drayton to autopsy them. I'm pretty sure he thinks I've lost it."

Now it was her father's turn to take a deep drink of his coffee. Though William was no longer the sheriff, Serena consulted with him on things. He'd seen a lot more than she had. She would have to be a fool not to take advantage of that.

"Practicing?" he asked, after a minute.

"That's what Riley and I both suspect. But, practicing for what?"

"For cutting somebody's heart out, I suppose."

Serena rolled her eyes and turned her attention back to her life-sustaining coffee.

William stood and began to pace the room. "Any prints?"

"A couple, but not many. My guess is that Lucas and Andi left them, not our killer. It looks to me like the killer wiped down the rooms before he started, cleaned the place up, then wore gloves inside."

Seeing the questioning look on her father's face, she added, "It was a hospital once upon a time. If he hadn't wiped it down, there'd be prints."

"Couldn't he have wiped it all down after?"

"Could have, but I don't think so. He didn't really clean the place up after he was done. There's blood at the scene. And his storage room was a mess. Also, there's something about the room. It looked specially prepared somehow. It's hard to explain."

"You think he wiped the rooms down ahead of time to sterilize them?"

Serena was pleased to see the realization in her father's eyes. He was thinking the same thing she was. "Sort of like he thinks of himself as a doctor," she replied.

William nodded. "Yeah. That's what you'd do, right? Clean and prep the room. Then wear gloves for the procedure."

"The doc says it looks like the killer used a scalpel on the heart."

Her father only shook his head and continued pacing.

Serena gave him a moment to digest before moving on to the next problem in her day. "I think we need to talk to the paper about the heart, but I'm going to keep the rest in-house for now."

William sank back into the chair. "You haven't talked to Norton yet? That boy may be the only person in town who's happy something like this is going on. You should be expecting he'll stop by sooner rather than later."

Serena suppressed a shudder. Dealing with Norton Finwick, ace reporter, was a nightmare on her best day. She didn't even want to think about how awful it was going to be today.

Her father offered a supportive smile. "I know what you're thinking, but there's no avoiding him. And trying will make it worse. You control the story as best you can, but, honey, things are going to come out. This is a small town. Somebody's gonna tell their wife or their momma or something. It'll get out. Don't get too upset when it does."

Serena stared at her father, unable to shake the feeling that he was sitting on the wrong side of the desk. She'd never wanted to switch places with him so badly in her life.

But she could see the years on his face now. The last heart attack had taken a lot out of him. Though he'd been watching his diet and taking his medications religiously, Serena wondered if she should be holding back information from him as much as everyone else.

"Stop looking at me like that, little girl," William growled. "I can still run rings around you."

"It's been twenty years since you could outrun me," Serena replied, referring to the race that she'd challenged him to years earlier.

"You were fifteen! Fifteen-year-olds can outrun anybody if they put their mind to it. You'll have one of your own someday, and then you'll see."

Serena laughed. At this point, there wasn't a whole

lot of chance of that. Maybe Liam would manage to give their father some grandkids.

The thought of her potential nieces and nephews reminded her of Missy. "I'm going to ask Missy to help Drayton with the autopsies – or whatever you call them – on the animals."

Her father's face shadowed with the same concern she'd been feeling herself. Missy and Serena had been best friends since they were little kids. Though Liam didn't have the sense to propose like a reasonable boyfriend, Missy was like a sister to Serena and a daughter to William.

Serena watched carefully, gauging his reaction, using it to assess her own judgment. Part of her wanted him to challenge her, tell her she was wrong. They both knew how hard this would be for Missy.

The darkness faded from her father's eyes and he only offered a sympathetic smile. "I'm afraid that sounds like the thing to do. I'm awful sorry for Missy, but you have to," he replied. "You talk to her yet?"

Serena shook her head.

William smiled in that knowing way of his. "You have a job to do, honey. So does Missy. Liam and I will look after her."

The words helped. Not a lot, but enough to get her up and moving again.

Serena stood, steeling herself for the day. She gave her father a hug before he could leave, as much out of a need for human contact as anything else. Though she couldn't let the pain in, it was there. This whole mess was horrible, violent, and pointless. And she was going to be standing in the middle of it until it was over.

William's large arms swallowed her narrow frame and the contact did, somehow, ease the pain a little.

When she finally stepped back, she was standing taller than she had been a moment earlier. She wasn't just giving the impression of being confident and in control, she felt the part.

"Thanks for the coffee, Pop. I'm going to have to go talk to the mayor in person."

"You know that bum's still in bed."

Serena laughed. "Have no doubt. That's why I'm going over to his house to break the news."

~ 4 ~

It was a beautiful morning, prettier than it should have been with all that had happened. A gentle breeze stirred the brightly colored leaves. The sky was a perfect blue with white clouds that looked painted on.

Serena saw none of it. The glare from the sun was giving her a dull headache and the chill in the air felt like more of a threat. A cold, dark winter was coming. There was nothing that would stop it.

Her visit to the mayor had been predictably pointless. It was an exercise in politics and a reminder of her weaknesses, her inexperience. Even if she was competent enough to lead this investigation, she was certain she didn't have the personality to calm, cajole and generally charm the populace into believing that everything was going to be all right. God knew she'd done nothing to convince the mayor.

As she turned onto Missy's street and pulled up to her house, Serena's mood only darkened. She was about to add being a terrible friend to her growing list of deficiencies.

It wasn't unexpected when Liam answered the door. But on a day like this, the last thing she wanted to face was her perfect brother.

"You know, it's kind of stupid to pay all that money for your house when you're here all the time," she said.

Liam stepped aside to let her in. "Well aren't you little miss sunshine and happiness this morning. By the way, you look like hell. Rough shift?"

She shot Liam a cold look. Though he'd clearly just tumbled out of bed, even his disheveled hair somehow looked casually tousled. William Marlowe the fourth. The golden boy. He'd been destined for her job. Everyone knew it. Everyone except for Liam, who'd never wanted any of it. On mornings like this, Serena couldn't help but resent him for it – at least a little.

He held up his hands in surrender. "I have no idea what I did to deserve that look, but I promise, I didn't mean it. Christ, Serena, what's wrong?"

Serena closed her eyes and settled herself, wishing she didn't already feel this exhausted. "Is Missy still here?"

"In the kitchen."

She motioned for him to join her. "Something went down at the old hospital last night. I need to fill you both in."

He stopped her before she could go any further. "Is Dad okay?"

Serena put a hand on her brother's arm, feeling bad that she was being such a bitch. "He's fine. It's nothing like that. It'll be easier to tell you both at once."

She found Missy leaning against the kitchen counter, coffee cup in one hand, paper in the other. She looked up when they entered, giving Serena a big smile. "Hey, you stop by to catch breakfast with us?"

Unlike Liam, Missy had clearly already showered and dressed for the workday. Like Liam, she looked perfect. She had long legs and a perfect figure to go with the serious brains that had gotten her through college and vet school on scholarships. Serena was certain that if she hadn't known Missy since they were kids, she would have hated her on sight.

"I guess neither of you heard what happened last night?"

Their expressions made it clear they didn't have a clue what she was talking about. Serena sat down at the kitchen table and began to go through the events of the night before. As she spoke, both Missy and Liam sank into the chairs next to her.

She had been planning to tell Liam about the animals, and now, watching Missy's face, she knew that she really didn't have any other choice. There was no way Missy could handle this without his support.

When Serena finished, the silence in the room screamed their horror.

Liam spoke first. "Holy God. That's insane."

Serena wished Missy didn't look so pale. "I'm afraid there's more. Missy, I'm going to...."

Missy stopped her. "You're going to ask me to help with the animals, aren't you?"

"I'm sorry, I wouldn't ask if...."

Missy offered a sad smile. "Of course not. Does Clay have the bodies?"

Serena nodded.

Liam leaned between them. "Um, excuse me, over here. What's this about the animals? What's Missy going to do?"

Knowing Liam was going to be far less understanding than Missy, Serena braced herself. "I asked Clay Drayton to examine the bodies of the animals. I'm asking Missy if she'd please help him."

Her brother stiffened. His eyes darkened into a glare. The affable Liam Marlowe didn't get angry easily, but when he did he had the same steely edge that served Serena so well in her work.

His eyes locked on Serena, he growled, "You're dragging Missy into this?"

Missy laid a hand over his. "I need to do this. It's my job."

The gesture did nothing to distract him. "You're really going to make her work with the state police? After all that happened? You, of all people, should understand that."

Serena took a deep breath. He was right. She knew he was right, but she had no other choice.

She tried to explain, knowing it was pointless. "There's no state police this time. Just me, Riley, Jake and Shane. We're going to figure this out on our own. We do this right, do it quick, there'll be no state police."

"Oh, Riley. Right. Your judgment is always at its best when it comes to Riley," Liam snapped.

It was like a slap across the face.

Missy hesitated only a moment, looking as surprised as Serena, before placing a protective hand over her friend's and glaring at Liam. "That was totally out of line and you know it."

Liam's head dropped and he rubbed the back of his neck, clearly trying to calm himself down.

Serena was helpless to do much more than watch. Liam's dislike of Riley was well known. When Serena and Riley had been dating, outbursts like this weren't uncommon from Liam. But it'd been more than five years since their breakup.

Liam met her eyes. "I'm sorry. That wasn't fair."

Missy squeezed Serena's hand. "It wasn't fair at all. Serena, he's worried. You understand."

Serena nodded. She knew that. Of course she did. But if her own brother didn't trust her judgment, it was hard to believe anyone else would either.

Serena rose. "I need to get back to work. I just wanted to update you both on things."

Missy walked her to the door, leaving Liam in the kitchen. "He didn't mean it," she repeated, once they were alone.

But he had. They both knew that. Serena hoped her smile didn't look as fake as it felt. "He's protecting you. I get it."

"Riley was a mistake. We're all entitled to a mistake every now and then. Serena, it was a long time ago. You're past it."

The look in Missy's eyes told Serena that her calm façade was not as opaque as it needed to be. So, she changed the subject.

"Are you sure you'll be okay helping Drayton with the animals?"

Missy put a hand on Serena's shoulder. "You don't need to worry about me. I'm sure Liam and your father will be taking care of that."

Now Serena did smile. She wished she didn't have to drag Missy into all of this, but wishing and hoping weren't worth much in situations like this. Missy, of all people, knew that.

~ 5 ~

The Whitefield police station was tucked between the barber shop and the local pharmacy. The only reason it looked any different than the shops on the town's main street was the presence of police cars out front.

There'd been talk a few years back about reserving parking spots in front of the station for police vehicles, but the general consensus was there was never enough traffic in town to worry about that sort of thing. The compromise had been the decision to reserve a single spot for the sheriff.

Despite that, people in town always left the spots open. The exception to that rule, and so many others, was Norton Finwick. As the town's self-proclaimed investigative reporter, Norton believed he was entitled to whatever access he wanted. Anything less was a clear violation of his rights and the rights of the town.

Serena should have expected to find him waiting for

her, but somehow it still caught her off guard.

He was actually standing in her reserved spot. Waiting. As if it was the most normal thing in the world.

Serena wished she could drive on, pretend she had some other pressing business elsewhere, but her father's warnings echoed in her mind. She couldn't avoid this. Norton wouldn't allow it.

She pulled into the spot slowly, allowing Norton time to step out of her way. She reminded herself that this wasn't about Norton. This wasn't about her. This was about the town. People needed to know what was going on. And it was her job to tell them.

Norton was talking from the moment she stepped out of her cruiser. "Sheriff, I'm going to need a statement."

For a conversation with anyone else, Serena would have taken off her sunglasses. It was rude not to. But at that moment she clung to subtle slights.

"Look, Norton, I'm not ready to give a full statement. Why don't you come on inside? Hayley will get you some coffee. I can be out to talk to you in about ten minutes. I have to check on a few things here first."

It wasn't a lie. She did need to check on her men. Make sure everything was in order. Everyone was all right. But mostly she wanted a moment. This morning, of all mornings, she needed a moment.

"Just like you, I have a job to do. We're doing a mid-day issue of the paper. I'll go to print with what I have, if you can't find the time."

It was difficult to be calm and reasonable around Norton. He was so pretentious, so officious.

Norton was only about ten years older than Serena. He'd covered the news in Whitefield since he was in high school. Like her, his job was inherited. His father had put out a weekly paper for the town. Norton had expanded it to a daily. These days the paper was more about Norton's ambition than the news.

But none of that mattered. Not really. Her personal opinion of the man couldn't change the way she did her job. Serena leaned up against the side of her car and slipped off her sunglasses.

"We have an on going investigation. There really isn't a lot I can say."

Norton pulled his notepad out of his pocket and a pen from behind his ear. "Can you confirm there was a massacre at the old hospital?"

If the term hadn't been so distressing, she might have laughed at its flamboyance. "There was not a massacre. We found a good deal of blood. Enough that we believe someone was killed there."

She wasn't really sure the amount of blood indicated death, but the heart sure as hell did. So, it seemed close enough to the truth to pass for now.

"You have no body?"

Serena hated to concede it, but her father had already told her the word was out. "No. There was no body."

"There was just a human heart."

"That's correct."

"No idea whose it is?"

She chewed on her tongue, trying to avoid a sarcastic retort. How the hell would they know whose heart it was if they didn't have a body? She successfully kept her answer to one syllable. "No."

Norton stared at her for a moment, tapping his pen on his notepad. "Anything else the town needs to know?"

The question caught her off guard. He knew something. She could see it in his eyes. But for the life of her she couldn't imagine what it was.

"Other than the heart?" she asked, stalling, waiting for him to say something more. "I think the heart's pretty big news, Norton. What more do you want?"

He smiled a little, just enough to confirm he had something. "Did you search the hospital?"

And there it was. She hadn't even made it through the morning without a leak.

"Of course we searched the hospital and the area around it. It's a murder. We've undertaken a complete investigation," she replied.

She had no way to know what he did or did not know. She was helpless to do anything other than pretend there was nothing else to say.

He shook his head slowly, the way a condescending adult might chastise a child. "If there was more information at the crime scene that could tell the town what's really going on, then people need to know."

"People need to know there's been a murder. People need to be cautious and they need to call the station if they see anything suspicious. And people need us to complete our investigation."

Norton radiated a smug confidence. "It might be helpful for people to know there were dozens of animals found at the hospital. It might help them understand the type of suspicious activity they should be watching out for. Why would you keep that from them, Serena?"

He used her name purposely to make the crack personal. He wanted her to know he wasn't attacking the office. He was attacking her.

No matter what she said now he would print a story that made it clear she was covering up the truth and he was looking out for the community. It wasn't even ten a.m. and she'd already lost the first major battle of her day.

She slipped her sunglasses back over her eyes. "It's an active investigation, Norton. I have no further comment at this time."

Turning to leave, she added, "There's a town meeting tonight. The mayor is going to be announcing it later. Why don't you call his people for the specifics on the timing? He'll be organizing it."

Norton peered at her through his thick glasses. "I'll do that. I have one last thing. Will you be bringing in the state police on this, Sheriff?"

His tone was obvious. He didn't think she was up for the challenge. Though Serena was already thinking that could be true, she had no intention of letting him know that.

"Not at this time. No."

Taking advantage of his distraction as he wrote down some notes, she stepped past him and opened the door. "That's all I have for you, Norton. You can call the station if you need me."

Though she managed to escape, the damage was done. They were going to eat her alive at the town meeting. Norton would ensure nothing less.

~ 6 ~

Serena found Riley in the conference room setting up a whiteboard to track their progress with the case. It was a ridiculous notion at this point. They didn't even know who their victim was.

Riley looked up when she entered. "You catch a break at home for a couple hours?"

As was so often the case with Riley, the question was belittling and dismissive. The idea that Serena wouldn't be giving this her undivided attention was infuriating.

"I had to give a report to the Mayor and bring Missy up to speed so she can help Drayton this morning."

Serena wished the explanation sounded more authoritative and less like a series of lame excuses.

Not surprisingly, Riley just shrugged. "I figured you'd had a long night, needed a break. Skylar's on-board for the autopsies?"

Serena nodded. "What'd I miss here?"

"I sent Jake home," Riley replied.

Jake had looked like hell when they finally made it back to the station. They both knew he was the last guy who could handle the horrors he'd stumbled upon in the hospital.

Serena sat down. "Is Kim home? He'll need somebody with him."

Happy to discuss his brother, Riley said, "When she heard all that was going on, she knew he'd need her, so she took the day off. She and the baby will be home all day."

Serena was relieved to hear it, but it reminded her of her father's warning from earlier in the day. Leaks were inevitable. Jake would tell his wife. Then God only knew who she would tell. They'd both need someone to talk to about all of this. Of course they would. Wasn't that why she'd told Liam all Missy would be dealing with?

It was understandable, but it also meant Norton was probably going to know everything about the case two minutes after it happened. Maybe sooner.

Serena shook it off. She couldn't worry about things that were beyond her control. Looking up at the board, she surveyed what they had so far. "Shane's still compiling a list of local missing persons?"

Riley nodded. "Yeah. Not much use right now, but it'll give us something to compare to eventually."

Serena closed her eyes a moment and she could see the scene again. The sterile room. The blood. The heart. It was going to be tough to figure out who the killer was without any real information about the victim.

Focusing on the only evidence they had, Serena turned her attention back to Riley. "The doc's looking over the heart. He'll send it out to the state lab when he's done."

"I wanted to talk to you about that."

She'd been waiting for this. One thing she could say about Whitefield, certain things were expected.

Riley leaned toward her, his most reasonable expression pasted on his face. "I've been giving this some thought," he began. "All of a sudden we've got some nutcase who likes to cut out people's hearts. By my count there's only one new guy in town. And I'm none too happy to have him processing my evidence."

Serena sat back in her chair and met Riley's stare. His dark eyes smoldered, his square jaw was tight. She hated that she was still intimidated by that look. The expression that insisted he was right, she was wrong, and her stupidity was only further evidenced by her decision to ignore the truth according to Riley.

Digging deep, she met his stubbornness with her own. "Would you rather we call the state police and let them take over?"

"Look, I'm not saying…."

She'd intended to keep her voice even, calm, but her temper edged through. "You're saying you think Clay Drayton should be a suspect because he's new in town. I'm saying if he's a suspect then he damn well shouldn't be processing evidence. And if he can't process evidence then we're gonna need a state medical examiner. And you know as well as I do that state police come with state medical examiners."

"Now, Serena, come on, you're overreacting."

His tone was dismissive, patronizing, and designed to put her in her place. Experience taught her not to back down.

"You want me to consider Drayton our number one suspect because he's new in town. I'm not overreacting, you're overreacting."

Riley's voice softened. "Look, I'm just saying. New type of crime, new guy, makes sense. And besides, this looks like a medical person, don't you think? Cutting people's hearts out and all."

"You think this looks like a medical person? Really? Clay Drayton is a coroner. Do you think that sounds like a person who needs to *practice* on animals to figure out how to cut somebody's heart out? Do I need to explain what happens during an autopsy?"

Riley glared for a minute before he cracked his knuckles and rolled his neck. He was forcing himself to calm down. Maybe his anger management classes were good for something.

Serena stared at her deputy long enough to wonder if they should be questioning who was processing the evidence in the case, and it wasn't Drayton she was worried about.

Finally, Riley said, "I want to make sure we're looking at all the angles."

Riley wanted a simple solution to their complicated problem. The angles were not his favorite part. They both knew that.

Serena took a deep breath and tried to be rational. "I can't see how all those animals were anything other than practice. Can you?"

Riley cracked his knuckles again. "Nothing else makes any sense really."

"Then we agree?" she asked.

Riley nodded, his eyes still shining with skepticism. Serena took the gesture as the closest thing she'd get to an agreement.

She turned her attention to the board. There wasn't much, but it did note Lucas and Andi's presence at the crime scene.

"Have you read their statements?" she asked.

"They were in the hospital on a dare and happened upon the scene."

"You believe that?"

"Do I believe two healthy teenagers weren't trying to use the old hospital as a fucking motel? No."

"Did Shane ask them if they saw anyone around the hospital in the past month or so?" she asked, suddenly wondering if Riley had accidently made a good point.

Riley shook his head. "Not as far as I know, why?"

"We've got a creepy old hospital, with a solid roof and some reasonably accommodating furniture. Maybe somebody took up residence there and we didn't know?" she suggested.

Riley's eyes almost glowed with hope. "You think some crazy homeless guy did this?"

It was false hope, Serena suspected, but it was a theory. And it felt a hell of a lot better than thinking one of her neighbors was a psycho. "I think it's worth asking some questions."

"Maybe we swing by the school?"

Serena smiled. Now they were getting into territory where her manipulative deputy could be quite useful. "I think we'll have a bit more luck talking to them when their parents aren't around. You want to come with me?"

"That sounds like a plan. Besides, I have to tell Coach that we're going to need his floodlights for a few more days."

The floodlights needed to be moved from the interior of the hospital to the exterior. They all knew it was going to prove impossible to adequately patrol the hospital in the dark. The biggest problem was a lack of manpower, but Serena hoped the floodlights would make the process somewhat easier for whoever would be patrolling the scene.

Of course, her lack of manpower was a reason to turn this whole thing over to the state police. They had a heart, no clues and no suspects. Her working theory was that a psychotic transient attacked their unknown victim. It was ridiculous.

But she couldn't hand it over. Not yet. Not ever. She couldn't let that happen again.

~ 7 ~

At first glance, the regional high school didn't look any different than it did most days. But Serena could sense that the rumors had spread as quickly here as they had in town. Possibly faster. The air was electric.

It was plain from the glances and whispers as they passed that the crime had instilled more excitement than fear in the students. She wondered if it was a generational thing or just the invincibility of youth.

Either way, the buzz was disconcerting. It was going to be difficult to convince the kids to be cautious and alert if they thought of the crime as little more than a funhouse prank.

Serena and Riley were escorted through the halls by Claudia Daly, the school principal. Claudia and Serena had graduated in the same tiny class, but they were never what anyone would have mistaken for friends. Claudia had been a cheerleader. Her hair was as bouncy as ever, though she now walked the halls with an air of intelligence she'd strategically hidden as a student.

They gave Claudia some of the details from the night before, most specifically that Andi and Lucas had been at the scene. It looked to Serena like Claudia had already heard the rumors, but she didn't let on.

"You're sure they aren't in any trouble?" Claudia asked. "I don't want their parents getting angry that you're talking to them."

Riley, who'd been a star basketball player in his day and therefore far better equipped to talk to Claudia, handled the response. "We just want to make sure they didn't leave out something crucial because they were embarrassed in front of their parents. I mean we all know how many innocent secrets we kept back in high school. They might've left something out that'll prove important later."

The answer seemed to satisfy Claudia. Though, Serena found it hard to see anything other than the doe-eyed cheerleader who used to fawn all over the basketball team.

Claudia led them down the hall to a small office that was used by the school psychologist once a week. Knowing Claudia would be more than happy to be left alone with Riley, Serena slipped away, promising to meet them in a couple of minutes. She had a source she needed to meet.

The small library looked different than it had when Serena was in school. Though books still lined the walls, most of the tables were taken up with computers.

One thing hadn't changed. Sitting at the library's main desk, looking every inch the librarian, was Mrs. Betty Tinsdale, reading glasses perched on her nose as she reviewed some periodical. Serena allowed herself a moment to absorb the comfort of the space and the woman who had turned this room into a place of hope for Serena so many years earlier.

While Serena's grandfather tried to convince Liam to join the family business, Serena relied on Mrs. Tinsdale and her endless patience to help her find every resource available to learn about law enforcement. Serena read and studied, and with Mrs. Tinsdale's guidance, she learned how to think like a cop. By the time her father noticed her interest, she was already fluent in everything from crime scene investigation to the psychology of criminal behavior.

This was where she'd found the confidence to tell her father what she really wanted and the skills to convince him she was serious. Mrs. Tinsdale had started her down the path she was on today. Most days she felt blessed by the decision.

Mrs. Tinsdale looked up as Serena approached, offering a sweet smile that had the same soothing effect it'd had when Serena was fifteen and feeling even more awkward than she did wearing her father's badge now.

"Good morning, Sheriff," she said, her voice church mouse quiet. "What brings you here?"

Serena spoke in a similarly soft voice. "I had a question or two about some high school gossip. I thought I'd go right to the source."

Mrs. Tinsdale heard everything. Her quiet demeanor and easy presence made people forget she was close enough to listen.

Serena didn't miss the glance she cast to the other side of the room before she answered. Following her eyes, she saw Mrs. Tinsdale's granddaughter, Lori-Ann, sitting among the students tapping on the computers.

"I assume everyone's heard what's going on," Serena said. "How's she doing?"

Mrs. Tinsdale shook her head and focused her attention back on Serena. "You don't need to worry about us. You just need to figure out who did this."

The words didn't ease Serena's worry, despite the obvious intention. They only reminded her how many people needed this thing solved.

So Serena focused on her questions. "I was hoping to find out if you knew who – other than Lucas and Andi – has been hanging out around the old hospital."

"You don't think the kids are responsible for this, do you?"

Serena took a deep breath and offered a silent prayer that this was the work of some transient, because people in this town did not take kindly to accusations directed at their own.

"I don't think much yet," she replied, avoiding the question. "I just want to know who's been around the crime scene. Maybe they saw something useful, something that'll lead us to more information."

The answer seemed to put the librarian at ease. "From what I've heard, a group of them have been going up there since spring."

"Lucas and Reece Henderson are the ringleaders I assume?" Serena asked.

The librarian hesitated long enough that Serena prodded her. "What am I missing?"

Mrs. Tinsdale smiled a little. "I knew you'd be good at this, Serena."

She glanced back over at her granddaughter before she continued, "From what I hear, Andi really runs the group."

Serena considered the answer. In her experience, Andi never seemed interested enough to be in charge of anything.

Wondering if there wasn't something else to the story, she asked, "Are you getting this from Lori-Ann?"

"I know what you're thinking. Lori-Ann has been teased by Andi and her friends since they were kids. They never liked her. She's never liked Andi. But I don't think that's what this is about."

Serena knew Mrs. Tinsdale would have preferred to leave it at that, but Serena wasn't ready to dismiss it so quickly. "What has Lori-Ann told you?"

"It's not really what she's told me. It's more what she doesn't tell me. There are times when we're talking that I can see there are things she's leaving out. Typically, those things relate to Andi."

"You haven't seen it?" Serena asked.

Mrs. Tinsdale shook her head. "Not a thing. Andi's the same as ever. Distant. Disinterested. Simultaneously intelligent and vapid."

Serena glanced over at Lori-Ann, who was completely oblivious to the conversation they were having. Part of her felt compelled to find out more, but Serena pulled herself back, at least for now. There was no reason to believe Andi was a part of any of this. More likely she was a dumb kid who ended up in the wrong place at the wrong time. That was all.

"Either way, you've heard that Andi, Lucas and Reece have been up at the old hospital?" Serena asked.

The librarian seemed to relax a little as the questions turned. "And the rest of the gang of course."

"That'd be Stu Foley and Brad Cooley, along with Tracey Golden and Marcy Crimple?"

Mrs. Tinsdale nodded. "And whoever Brad is dating in any given week."

Serena smiled at that. "Right. Who's the lucky girl this week?"

"Suzy Martin's been attached to him for a couple weeks now."

Serena nodded and scanned the room.

Mrs. Tinsdale chuckled again. "Oh, none of them would ever wander in here. No cell phones allowed. No garbage on the computers."

Serena grinned. The library might look different, but some things would never change.

"Are you working with Riley on this one?" Mrs. Tinsdale asked.

Serena wished she could pretend the question was as mundane as the librarian made it sound. "Working with all the deputies on this. I'm afraid it's going to take all we've got."

"You know, I was working here when Riley was in school, too."

Serena nodded.

"He didn't spend much time in here. Occasionally, he'd pass through. He was rough around the edges back then, too. But there was something about him. People were just drawn to him."

Serena smiled at the description. Riley was good looking and charming. He always had been. The rough edges somehow only added to the draw. She'd spent most of her twenties caught in his web. And it was starting to feel like it would take most of her thirties to extricate herself.

"Mrs. Tinsdale, trust me, it's over. It's okay. It's been okay a long time now."

The smile Serena received in response told her that her declaration wasn't as convincing as she'd have liked.

Mrs. Tinsdale nodded knowingly. "You remember that."

~ 8 ~

The room where Claudia had left Riley was tiny and windowless. It was clearly set up to be an office, with a small table tucked in one corner and an even smaller desk tucked in the other, but Serena found it hard to believe that the space hadn't been originally designed to be a closet. It was too small to be anything else.

Riley was sitting at the table, his long legs stretched out to the side. Though he looked too big for the room, he somehow didn't look uncomfortable. It was a quality Serena had admired in him once. Now it was a reminder of how well Riley concealed what was really going on in his head.

He looked up when she entered.

"Claudia went to track down Andi and Lucas," he explained. "She thinks Lucas is in Math right now. Didn't want him to miss that. Apparently he's not much of a math guy."

Serena found it hard to believe that Lucas was much of a student generally. She quickly updated Riley on Mrs. Tinsdale's report, leaving out the parts about Andi. The whole conversation had made the woman so uncomfortable that Serena decided she wouldn't use the information unless she had to.

"You want to talk to the whole group of them while we're here?" he asked.

Serena had been asking herself the same question. Parents didn't like it much when you talked to their kids without them knowing. The trouble was, kids tended to omit crucial details when their parents were around.

She knew what she had to do. "We'll wait. Talk to the rest of them with their parents."

Riley nodded.

Before either of them could say anything more, Andi Sinclair entered the room. She looked entirely perky and refreshed. The horror she'd seen the night before didn't seem to have even dented her armor.

It was disturbing, but Serena tried not to make too much of it. Teenagers were expert at keeping a cool and unflappable demeanor. It was entirely possible that there was more going on beneath the surface.

But Andi was all about the surface. She was a bright, bouncy brunette, whose big, brown eyes were painted with a faux innocence.

When she turned her attention to Riley it was immediately clear that the look was a fabrication. There was nothing innocent about the way she looked at him.

"Andi," Serena began, "we wanted to ask you a couple more questions about last night."

The girl didn't take her eyes off of Riley when she said, "I'm happy to help in any way I can."

"Can you tell us how you got into the hospital?"

Andi glanced Serena's way for a moment. "It was like we told Deputy Gilbert. We went in through that window with the loose board. The same one we went out through."

"Was the board loose when you got there?"

"Yup," she replied. Clearly bored, Andi turned her attention to her perfect nail polish.

"And you guys went down there on a dare?"

"Yeah, like I said already, Lucas thought it would be fun."

Riley leaned toward Andi and said, "That was the only reason you two were out there?"

His movement pulled the girl's eyes from her nail polish. "Yeah, that was the only reason."

Riley smiled flirtatiously. "I mean, I was young once too, and there's a lot of reasons I'd want to take my girl to a place like that, but a dare sure isn't one of them."

She met Riley's smile with a coy flutter of her eyelashes. "Lucas said it'd be like going to a haunted house, you know? He was totally right."

Serena couldn't help but notice the way Andi kept shifting the focus to Lucas and away from herself. "Was this the first time you guys went to the hospital?"

Andi nodded.

She was a little surprised at the girl's lie. Did she think Shane Gilbert had actually covered for them the night he'd broken up their party? "Weren't you there about a week ago?"

"Oh, you mean the party. Yeah, a bunch of us were there, but that was outside, you know in that covered space, by where the ambulances used to pull up."

"So, you didn't go in that night?" Riley asked.

Andi shook her head.

"Why not?" Serena asked, hoping the switching off might catch her off guard.

"What do you mean why not? We weren't supposed to go in there."

Serena shrugged. "But you went in last night."

Andi's entire expression changed. She was no longer the flirty, vapid girl. Suddenly, her eyes were sharp, her tone accusatory. "You're trying to trick me, aren't you? My dad said to watch what I said to you, because you might try to trick me. I'm not going to say things just because you want me to say them!"

Riley put his hands up to indicate surrender. "Nobody's trying to trick you. We're only trying to figure out if people were around the hospital before last night. Maybe they saw something."

It was too late. Serena could see that. They'd lost her.

Andi's eyes never moved from Serena's. "I don't want to talk to you anymore. My dad said I don't have to talk to you if I don't want to. I suffered a trauma last night."

Serena seriously doubted that, but there wasn't much she could do.

"Why don't you go back to class, Andi? We'll talk to you some other time."

Without another word, Andi stormed out.

Serena sat back and considered what they'd witnessed. She hadn't previously had a lot of contact with Andi. There'd been no reason really. She'd never seemed like anything other than the person who was standing near Lucas when he managed to get in trouble for some petty crime. Much like the keg party at the hospital.

Now Serena wondered. This hadn't been the harmless girl she'd expected. This was a woman who was used to getting her way. One who would force the matter if necessary.

Focusing on Riley, Serena asked, "Thoughts?"

Riley was leaning back in his chair. Predictably, he focused on facts, and not psychology. "She didn't know anything else. They went in for the first time last night. It never dawned on her to go in before that. Lucas might have checked things out though." He paused and then added, "She's scared of you, which is something we might be able to use in the future."

Serena hadn't noticed that, but it was consistent with the defensive response. She noted, "She thinks you're hotter than her boyfriend, which may prove more useful."

Riley shook his head. "She's a child."

"Yeah, but she doesn't think so. We can use that to our advantage."

Riley laughed. "Well, that's one way to look at it."

"You want to take the lead with Lucas?" she asked.

Riley nodded. "He should be an easier nut to crack."

~ 9 ~

Lucas Denton was a small town punk. Popularity deluded him into thinking he was a god. As the starting point guard for the basketball team, the only thing more important than his jump shot was the dense mane of hair that hung in his eyes with a sort of calculated messiness. Serena didn't doubt he spent an hour making his hair look like he didn't care what it looked like.

Unlike Andi Sinclair's parents, the Dentons didn't pay much attention to their son; they were too busy fighting with each other. Serena had long since lost count of the number of domestic violence calls she'd answered at their house. It was always a surprise who'd be the victim and who'd be the aggressor. She'd found Lucas's dad on the receiving end of a frying pan as often as she'd found his mom with an eye blackened.

That meant two things: Lucas's parents probably hadn't carefully informed him not to talk to her and

Lucas had far more freedom than most high school students. Serena wasn't ready to believe the latter meant he was involved in this mess, but she knew it probably meant he'd spent more time up at the old hospital than anyone else.

Serena sat back to watch, observe. Riley didn't say a word. Instead, he pushed a chair out with his foot and nodded toward it.

Lucas took his cue, sitting, eyes flitting between them. Unlike Andi, he looked tired, his eyes just a little too wide.

Riley started the questioning abruptly. "What made you think there might still be furniture inside the hospital?"

Lucas stiffened immediately, eyes sharpening. "We've never been in there before last night, I swear."

The look and his answer told Serena everything she needed to know about his guilty conscience.

Riley cast her a sidelong glance and suppressed a smile. "Was it the night Deputy Gilbert broke up your party or have you been back since?"

Lucas pushed his shaggy hair out of his eyes. "I told you, I've never been in there before."

"Of course you've been in there before, Lucas," Riley insisted. "I only asked how you knew about the furniture. There were a million ways you might have found that out. Hell, you might not have even known. You're the one who said you knew about it because you went inside."

Lucas looked directly at Serena, as if he was appealing to a higher court. "I didn't say I was in there."

Serena shrugged slightly. "No, but you denied it before we asked you. That's good enough for me."

He kicked his feet out and rocked on the chair. "Fine," he said. "I was in there. Once," he added emphatically.

Serena raised an eyebrow to suggest she was still skeptical.

Lucas continued to plead his case. "I noticed the loose board the night of the party. I didn't have a flashlight or anything. I went back yesterday and checked it out. It was a pretty crazy place – all that old hospital equipment. That room with the blood was empty yesterday afternoon. I went in there and left a sleeping bag and some candles. You gotta believe me. I had no idea about the rest of it."

Serena was pretty sure she did believe him. If he was telling the truth, they were working with a reasonable timeline. And it did make sense. There hadn't been much decomp with the heart. It might have been there only a few hours.

"How'd you pick the room?" Riley asked.

Lucas shrugged. "Go in through the window, go straight back and you get to a dead end. I turned right. Went in the first door on the right."

"You sure?" Riley asked.

Lucas seemed irritated by the question. "What do you mean, am I sure?"

"First door on the right?" he prodded.

Lucas's eyes darted to Serena's. She didn't offer him any reassurance, so he turned back to Riley. "Of course it was the first door on the right. The heart was in that room. You know that. First door on the right."

They'd found a sleeping bag and candles, but not in the room with the heart. They'd been across the hall, first door on the left. It probably didn't matter, but details were important.

Now Serena did offer him a lifeline. "You said you left a sleeping bag, right? You left it in the room where we found the heart? Are you sure?"

Lucas turned his attention to Serena now. He looked less annoyed, more confused. "Yeah, I'm sure. I mean, I guess so."

Riley pressed him further. "I'm going to need something more than, 'I guess so.'"

Lucas's eyes darkened. "Of course I'm sure. I left the stuff there yesterday."

Riley shook his head. "There was no sleeping bag in that room, Lucas."

Lucas tensed. "What do you mean there was no sleeping bag? You saying that guy stole my stuff? Why the hell would he steal my stuff?"

Again, Serena tried to diffuse the tension, give them room to build it up again. "It was across the hall, Lucas, first door on the left. Any chance that's where you left it?"

Lucas seemed unaffected by her tone. "Obviously, the guy moved my stuff."

Serena was pretty sure that wasn't obvious at all. "Why would he do that, Luc?"

"I don't know. I mean, the guy's crazy."

"You sure you aren't remembering wrong?" Serena asked.

Lucas shook his head. "I'm sure I put my stuff in that room. Totally sure."

Serena wondered about that.

Certain this was going nowhere fast, Serena asked, "Did you look around the rest of the hospital?"

"That afternoon, nah. I just checked the one room. It seemed cool. It was kinda creepy, but plenty of space

– you know?" The "plenty of space" reference was clearly directed at Riley.

"Why not check the other rooms? Look for a better spot?" Riley countered.

Clearly feeling more relaxed, Lucas tilted his chair back and rocked with amusement. "It's a freaking abandoned hospital. How the hell is one room gonna be any different than another?"

"You guys spend a lot of time up by the hospital?" Riley asked.

Lucas's eyes darkened. "We had that party in the ambulance bay. Thought it'd be a laugh, you know. But that was it. Nothing's up there. No reason to hang there."

"I don't know, seems like a good place to me. Remote. Isolated," Riley suggested.

Lucas put his feet square on the floor and met Riley's eyes. "I got no interest in isolated."

"In my experience, girls like isolated," Riley replied.

Lucas leaned forward a little more. "I guess we don't like the same type of girls."

There was an aggression building between the two of them. It was odd how quickly it had turned. Serena was torn between her concern that the situation would escalate further and her professional need to see if this could expose Lucas for who he really was.

Riley didn't seem to have any of the same concerns. His own temper seemed disturbingly close to the surface.

"We're hearing you guys spend a bunch of time up by the hospital," he accused.

Lucas's neck was tight, the muscles in his jaw tense. If Riley hadn't been a deputy, Lucas would have been throwing punches. Serena was sure of it.

"You don't know what you're talking about," Lucas growled.

The fire in Riley's eyes was what caused Serena to intervene. She had enough trouble without Riley creating more.

She leaned between them, hoping to break the focus. "Lucas, we only want to know if you guys saw anybody hanging around the hospital. Maybe someone who shouldn't have been there," she suggested.

His head swung to face her, but none of the anger dissipated. "How would I know if anybody's been lurking around the hospital? I just told you I've only been there the two times."

Serena stared a moment. And she began to wonder if she could be looking at something far worse than a punk teenager.

~ 10 ~

Before she could say anything more, there was a cheerful knock at the door. After waiting only a beat, the door swung open and Coach Garth Fletcher poked his head in.

"I hope I'm not interrupting. The principal said you guys were in here."

Knowing their conversation with Lucas was over anyway, Serena sent him back to class and offered the coach a seat.

At about sixty, Coach Fletcher looked half his age. Coach of the men's basketball team and fall and spring track teams, Fletcher was a virtual celebrity in town. In case his coaching prowess wasn't enough, his flamboyant teaching style and gift for storytelling made him everyone's favorite history teacher. He made ancient cultures fascinating. Wars were vivid, brutal. Rulers were dramatic, human. By the time he was done with you, you could see the past better than if it had been projected on an IMAX screen.

Serena didn't want to waste too much of his time. "Coach, I have to thank you for letting us use your lights. I hope it's okay if we use them a bit longer?"

He smiled. "I think the team can do without them for a bit. It's starting to get dark earlier, though, so we will be needing them back eventually."

She knew how hard he'd fought the school board for the money for those lights. And frankly, since Liam had been a high school track star, she'd listened to him bitch about running in the dark for long enough that she knew how important they were.

"We'll get them back to you as soon as we can. Liam will probably make sure of it himself."

Fletcher sat back in his chair, crossed his legs. "I haven't been down to the bar in a couple weeks. How's that boy doing?"

"You know Liam, he's good, having more fun than all of us combined."

"How's Missy?"

It was a loaded question. Melissa Skylar had had eyes for Liam Marlowe for as long as anyone could remember. Liam had been oblivious for years, but eventually had seen the light. And in the years since, everyone, Missy included, was waiting for Liam to get his head out of his ass and ask her to marry him. It seemed everyone but Missy figured hell would freeze over before that happened.

Serena decided not to take the bait. "She's good. She found an injured cat in her backyard the other day. She's nursing it back to health."

"One of these days that brother of yours is gonna use the sense God gave him." More seriously, he looked between her and Riley and asked, "You aren't thinking Andi and Lucas are involved in all that stuff up at the hospital, are you?"

"We're just looking into things, Coach. That's all," Serena assured him.

"Are the rumors true?"

Serena tried to appear casual. "I guess that'd depend on what the rumors are."

"I'm hearing somebody drained the blood out of a body and left you only the heart."

Riley guffawed at the description. Serena hoped she was the only one who heard the fear under his raucous laugh.

"You and your stories, Coach. This isn't some crazy Aztec ritual or tribal spirit exchange. Just some nutcase who left a bloody mess."

He grinned. "Actually, hearts were more of a thing for the Mayans. They would use the heart as a sacrifice – a plea for eternal life."

Serena shook her head. "And here I thought the best way to make sure you live a long life is by keeping your heart inside your body."

He laughed at that. "You don't have the spirit of an anthropologist."

Serena thought back to junior year – Ancient History with Coach Fletcher. All the boys loved it. He brought the pages of the history book to life with colorful images of ancient cultures. The color of choice, unfortunately, was typically red – blood red. He made the past look like a Stephen King novel gone awry. To his credit, they learned their history.

The coach's penchant for drama aside, Serena felt compelled to tone down the color in this story. "I'm still thinking modern day murderer and not Mayan, but I'll be sure to keep a look out, Coach."

He smiled and stood. "Claudia announced there's going to be a town meeting tonight, is that right?"

Serena nodded. "I guess we'll be seeing you and Lauren there?"

Fletcher's smile faded. "Lauren's been a bit under the weather. With all that's been going on, I worry about leaving her alone."

The coach's wife had been cancer-free for a couple years now, but her breast cancer treatment had seemed to take a lot out of her. "I didn't know, Coach, is she okay?"

He shook his head. "Oh, no, it's not like that," he said. "She's got this nasty little stomach bug. I suppose it's possible she'll be feeling better tonight, but she wasn't looking too great this morning."

Serena was relieved to hear it. Before he could leave, she said, "Make sure you keep your doors locked, okay?"

Fletcher gave a weak smile and a little salute as he went on his way.

Again, the true weight of what they were investigating began to settle over Serena. This was a murder investigation. A murder investigation with no leads. And worse still, it was the type of crime that had all the marks of a serial offender. They needed to find something and they needed to do it fast.

~ 11 ~

Serena allowed herself a quick trip home at lunchtime. Her dog greeted her with his usual enthusiasm when she walked in.

Buster was an adorable little mutt whose legs were far too short for his frame. Missy wasn't sure what breed Buster was, but she hypothesized he was some kind of Labrador, Rottweiler, Corgi mix. The result was her ridiculously strong, wonderfully loyal dog, who was the love of Serena's life. Though some might have thought that a little sad, Serena believed she could have done far worse, especially in this town.

The note she found on her kitchen counter told her that her father had already been by to take the dog out.

She managed to tackle canine entertaining, a decent shower and a quick lunch within thirty minutes. Then she headed back out with a freshly brewed cup of coffee for the road.

She grabbed an extra cup as a bribe. There weren't too many people as bone tired as she was today, but since she was about to visit one of them, a cup of coffee seemed an appropriate offering.

She found Clay Drayton's office closed. A large sign indicated he was "in surgery" and all appointments would be rescheduled. "Surgery" was an awfully pleasant word for what was going on in the basement of the doctor's office.

The job of coroner in Whitefield wasn't a busy one. It usually left plenty of time for Drayton to run his own medical practice in town. People went to him for everything from the common cold to treatment for their significant chronic conditions. None of them gave much thought to the fact that the facilities for the town coroner were just downstairs.

Though the only other options for a general practice doctor were about an hour away, Serena had chosen not to use him as her primary doctor. She'd thought up several extremely unpersuasive reasons to justify her decision, but a small part of her was well aware that her attraction to him would have made that encounter more than a little awkward.

It took about a minute before Drayton answered the bell. He was drying his hands, seemingly having come from "surgery." He was wearing scrubs, which were still surprisingly clean. He looked every bit the doctor.

Serena ordered herself to ignore the shadow of stubble on his face, and she refused to acknowledge how well he wore the exhausted look. His hazel eyes were glowing a sort of dull blue, like a stormy sea.

She extended her lame bribe as she joined him in the room that typically served as his patients' waiting room.

Drayton offered her a tired smile. "Sheriff, I've got to say, I'm having a hell of a time getting used to this place."

It was impressive he was still managing to smile. "What makes you say that? The grisly crime scenes? The animal autopsies?"

Sinking onto his waiting room couch, he laughed. "No, that doesn't seem all that strange to me. The coffee. The general politeness. People treat each other pretty well around here. It's weird. Nice."

Serena thought about the fights she'd broken up over the years, the domestic disputes that occurred and reoccurred. "Yeah, I think it's possible you may just be getting to know us all. Trust me, all that glitters isn't gold."

Drayton had a distant look on his face. He sipped his coffee and stared at an invisible spot across the room. "Sometimes it's nice to see there are things that still glitter."

It was an innocent remark, the sort of thing a person says when they're too tired to filter themselves as they normally would. It made her wonder about their doctor. This was a man who'd left everything behind to start over in their town. Serena wondered what would make a person do something like that.

"I talked with Missy this morning about the animals. Did she call you?"

He took another sip of his coffee. "I'm impressed, this is even good coffee."

Serena sat back and drank a bit of her own coffee. She sometimes forgot that other people didn't process the way she did. She moved quickly, coldly through scenes. Frankly, through most of her life. Normal people weren't like that. That's why she got along with Buster better than she did with most people.

It didn't take Drayton long to gather himself and deal with the matter at hand. "Your deputies brought everything over. As you can imagine, the exhaust fans are working overtime downstairs. Sheriff, I'm going to be honest with you. I took some classes before I started this job. Kind of like autopsy 101."

Serena nodded and let him continue.

"You give me a body, I have a checklist of things you're supposed to do. You gave me a heart. I don't have half a clue what the hell I'm supposed to do when there's just a heart."

Though she didn't know what landed Drayton in their little town, she did know his resume. He was smart enough to figure this out – that is, if there was anything helpful in the evidence they'd recovered.

"I have confidence in you," she said honestly.

He snorted at the prospect. "You shouldn't. I'm processing the heart the same way I would in a general autopsy, but I think it has to go to the state labs when we send the blood for analysis."

"That sounds right. Even if you were the greatest medical examiner of all time, I doubt you'd be able to do much here. Our equipment sucks."

He looked a little relieved that she wasn't expecting miracles. "Preliminarily, the incisions are very precise. They look like they were made with something like a scalpel. Though after what we found in that other room, I suppose that's less of a surprise than it otherwise would have been. Superficially, the tissue decomposition appears minimal. I'm guessing this person hasn't been dead for too long."

"Any way to tell exactly how long?"

Drayton laughed. "There should be a way to figure out an estimate based on the decomposition of the tissue in the heart, but that's beyond my skills."

Serena had been afraid of that.

"Dr. Skylar called me this morning. I'm expecting her in the next few minutes, actually. Did you tell her what she was getting into?" he asked.

"I can't imagine she's prepared for all of this," Serena admitted.

Drayton shook his head. "I can't imagine there's any way anyone could be prepared for all of this."

Serena agreed, but she tried not to think too much about it. Instead, she focused on trying to put him at ease with the situation. "She's a very good vet. We were really lucky she came back to town after she got her degree."

"She's a friend of your family's, right?"

He probably meant nothing by the question. He wasn't the type of guy who would. But it was a loaded question whether he realized it or not. And it was a reminder of the curse of life in a small town. Everyone knew everyone's business. It didn't matter if you'd just arrived or if you'd grown up there.

"She was our neighbor. Her family had some troubles. So, she spent a lot of her time with us."

Of course "troubles" was a kind word for it. She'd once pulled Missy's father off Missy just long enough to get a black eye of her own – she and Missy had been thirteen at the time.

There was something in Drayton's eyes that told her he knew there was more to the story, but he had the good sense not to say anything.

"Missy went away to college on a full scholarship and managed to put herself through vet school. We were all a little surprised she came back home."

Serena had been certain she'd keep running away — no one could have blamed her.

"I met her in passing once, over at your brother's bar, she seemed nice, quiet."

Serena, again, credited Clay's decision not to remark on just how gorgeous Missy was. There was no way he hadn't noticed.

"I think you'll find her easy to work with."

Before Serena could say anything more, she was interrupted by a voice from the doorway.

"Find who easy to work with?" Missy asked.

They'd left the front door ajar and only a screen stood between them and Missy. She looked somewhat amused, clearly having overheard just enough of their conversation to know that it made sense to interrupt.

Serena laughed. "I was telling Dr. Drayton here how impossible you are to work with."

Missy joined them. She offered Clay a hand and introduced herself. "We haven't really met yet. I'm Melissa Skylar. Call me Missy, everyone does."

Feeling her work there was done, Serena stood. "I have about a thousand things to do. So, I'm going to head out. Can you give me a call whenever you finish up your day? Just to give me a sense of what you have so far. I'm going to need to keep things moving pretty quickly."

Before Serena could leave, Clay stopped her. "There's one other thing. I was thinking about all that blood on the floor. I know Riley gathered samples of everything, but could he gather up all the blood that's there?"

The thought of her telling Riley Scott that he needed to mop up blood was almost laughable. "I'm sure we can get someone to do that. Why do you need it?"

"We don't really know yet if the blood's even human. If it is, that was an awful lot of blood. If the blood is not from the same person as the heart, we could be looking at two victims. The amount of blood could give us a sense of how badly hurt the other person is."

Serena wanted to dispute the assumption – two murders were too horrible to even consider.

Feeling a headache coming on, Serena gulped down some more coffee. "You have to send the samples out to the lab for DNA. So, that'll take a while, right?"

"Yeah, I imagine. I can do blood typing here and I'll be able to confirm if the blood is human."

Serena sighed. "Doc, the blood is human. That was his human operating room. He sliced up the animals on the other side of the building."

From the corner of her eye, Serena saw Missy wince.

Clay nodded slowly, considering the comment. "You're right. That makes sense."

"I'm not sure how much sense it makes, but it looks like the pattern we've got."

As she considered the patterns, Serena was struck by an idea. "How are you with psychology?" she asked.

"I am not qualified to be the town psychiatrist, too. I assure you." Clay laughed.

"You must have done a rotation in psych, right?"

His eyes narrowed. "What are you getting at?"

"Do me a favor, Clay, when you're researching how the heck one does an autopsy on various animals, could you look into a little criminal profiling?"

"Oh, now it's 'Clay'? You and your coffee are barking up the wrong tree, *Serena*."

Serena couldn't help but notice that he didn't look as put out as he wanted to sound. And besides, she was pretty sure she was going to need somebody to talk the psychological stuff through with. And there was no chance at all that Riley or her father were going to be that person.

~ 12 ~

When Serena finally made it back to the station, she found Shane Gilbert leaning over the front desk, flirting with Hayley, the dispatcher. They were both young. They were both single. And, frankly, flirting was pretty much the norm with them, but Serena was in no mood.

"Deputy Gilbert," she barked, before either of them even realized she was back, "if you aren't too busy, I need you in my office to talk about the party you broke up last week."

Shane straightened up so fast he tripped over his feet and almost fell on his face. He babbled something that sounded like an apology and immediately followed Serena into her office.

Once he was seated, he managed to speak more coherently. "I'm sorry, Sheriff, I was just taking a five-minute break. It's been a long day."

The first of many, no doubt.

"Shane, it's fine. I'd like you to run through with me what you saw the night you broke up the party at the hospital."

"I was doing the regular patrol, and when I pulled around back by where the old ambulance bay was, the spotlight on the car swung right over the whole group of them."

"Did you notice anything strange before that? Were all the boards still over the windows?"

Shane ran a hand over the top of his head, gliding over his blond buzz cut. "I wasn't really looking too closely at that. I didn't notice any loose boards though."

"Okay, tell me who was at the party."

"There were eight of them. All couples it looked like. Two ran off before I could see who they were. Then there was Reece Henderson, Tracey Golden, Marcy Crimple, and Stu Foley. And, of course, Lucas and Andi."

The names matched what Mrs. Tinsdale had told her.

"Any guesses on who the other two were?" Serena asked.

"Well, I didn't see them well enough to really say. You know how dark it is over that way." He met her eyes, clearly unsure if she really wanted him to guess. He took her silence as a sign. "Knowing that group, it was probably a couple – which means it'd be Brad and his girl of the week. Probably Suzy. It's been Suzy for a little bit now."

There was something on his face. Something behind his eyes.

"Shane, any information is valuable right now," she urged.

He met her eyes with a look that confirmed her suspicions. "You aren't going to like it."

Serena shook her head. "I haven't liked much in the last twenty-four hours. You may as well tell me."

"Lori-Ann Tinsdale was tutoring Brad this summer."

Serena sat back in her chair, hearing the unspoken suggestion, thinking of the librarian's granddaughter. "You're suggesting Lori-Ann had a thing with Brad?"

Shane rubbed his hand over his neck. "I'd rather not suggest anything. You know Lori-Ann, she's a good girl, from a good family."

Shane didn't say anything more. He didn't need to. Considering the story, Serena asked, "Could she have been at the hospital with Brad?"

Shane shuffled his feet. "I don't know. I didn't see. I mean, I'm pretty sure he's dating Suzy now, but you know…."

Lori-Ann's presence in this mess was just about the last thing Serena wanted to consider. "Thanks, Shane. I'll look into that myself."

She wasn't sure about much, but Serena was certain they'd get more out of the Tinsdale family with her asking than with anybody else.

"I talked with Mrs. Tinsdale this morning when we were at the high school," Serena explained. "She told me that group's been hanging out around the hospital all summer."

Shane straightened in the chair. "Hell, really? How'd we miss that?"

"The woods around the hospital are pretty dense. My guess is they've got a spot in there where they've been hanging out. If they were out in the open, I think we would have seen signs of their presence."

"You think it's possible they've been hanging inside the hospital?"

Thinking back to her interview with Lucas, she replied, "I don't think so. Lucas was pretty persuasive on that. More importantly, we searched the whole hospital. No indication they've been hanging around there. There'd be trash – beer bottles, fast food wrappers – no fun in having a party spot if you can't trash the place."

Shane nodded.

"We know our killer hangs around the hospital a lot. The room full of animals told us that."

Shane cut her off before Serena could say anything more. "Sheriff, you don't think these kids are involved in all this mess, do you?"

She almost dismissed his concern as quickly as she had with Mrs. Tinsdale, but she stopped herself. The truth was – she was worried. The more she thought, the more worried she became.

"Shane. We don't know anything at this point."

He stared at her with a look of complete bafflement that reminded her just how young her deputy was.

"They were there. They've been there. Lucas is lying about it and Andi is being evasive. That's all we know. It's not much, but right now we need to consider all we can. That means they may be involved. It also means they may have seen something that will help us. Either way, we need to keep an eye on them."

He seemed to consider this for a moment and then said, "So, we start with the connection to the hospital. See what they know. Then proceed from there?"

It was nice to see him keeping up. Shane had always seemed like he had potential. An investigation like this one, it could make or break him. Hell, that could be said for all of them.

Serena glanced at the clock on her desk. The kids should be home by now. "They like you, Shane. I'm hoping they'll be more likely to tell you their secrets. If I go talk to them, or even Riley, I think they'd start worrying they were in trouble."

Shane nodded. "I'll keep it friendly. Don't worry."

"Riley and I talked to Lucas and Andi this morning. We didn't get anywhere."

Her deputy stood and chuckled. "The secret police couldn't get anything out of those two. I guess you'd rather I talk to the others with their parents around?"

"I wouldn't rather, but I think it's the best approach at this point."

With a nod and a smile, Shane left her alone to think about what she had to do next – question one of the smartest, nicest kids at the high school, Betty Tinsdale's granddaughter.

~ 13 ~

The Tinsdale house sat on a fairly substantial plot of land, a little apart from the main section of town. Betty Tinsdale's son, Jack, made a very good living doing something with computers. Not great with computers herself, Serena had never entirely understood the details.

Whatever it was, it brought in a very good salary. He bought the family house right around the time Lori-Ann started elementary school. About a stone's throw from the main house was a fairy-tale style cottage where his mother lived.

Serena was relieved when the librarian answered the door. She didn't have any problem with Jack or his wife, but this seemed more comfortable.

"Twice in one day, Serena, how come I'm so lucky?" she asked with a smile.

"Mrs. Tinsdale, I was hoping to talk with Lori-Ann."

The woman's face darkened, but she opened the door. "Why don't you come in?"

Serena followed her into the large open kitchen in the back of the house. Mrs. Tinsdale offered her a glass of iced tea, before she asked, "Is Lori-Ann in trouble?"

Serena's stomach tightened as she spoke. "I don't think so. I'm hoping she might know some things about the comings and goings of Lucas and his friends over the past few months."

Mrs. Tinsdale's face grayed a little. "Jack is out of town. My daughter-in-law is running errands. I can try to reach her on her cell phone, but she never remembers to turn it on."

Serena nodded and waited. She hated to do this. Hated to use tactics on a friend, on the person who'd given her the confidence to learn those tactics.

The strategic thing to do at this point was to lie a little. Tell her there was nothing at all to be concerned about. Get the girl alone. But she couldn't.

"I can wait," Serena suggested.

Mrs. Tinsdale sank into a chair next to her. "You think those kids have something to do with this whole mess?"

Again, the truth was not her friend in this situation, but Serena felt compelled to be as honest as possible. "I hope not. But you told me yourself they've been spending time up around the old hospital. That tells me they could be involved. More importantly, it tells me they might have seen something – or someone – that could shed some light on the situation. I'm not going to lie to you, I'm really hoping it's the second one. I don't want to find out a kid is involved in all this."

Mrs. Tinsdale nodded slowly.

Serena continued, "I don't think Lori-Ann is involved. I find it hard to even believe she'd spend much time with those kids. But I need to ask. I need to talk to her."

Rising, Betty Tinsdale picked up the phone and dialed a number. A moment later, she tried a second number. Clearly getting no response on either, she replaced the phone on the cradle. She leaned back against the counter, steeling herself, locking Serena in with one of her trademark stares that motivated even the most indolent high schooler.

"Both her parents have their phones turned off," she said. "I imagine you're in a rush."

Serena said the only thing she could in the situation. "I can wait," she lied.

Mrs. Tinsdale shook her head. "You're going to want to talk to her alone, aren't you?"

The weight of the librarian's stare was almost too much. "I think it would be better, yes," she almost stuttered.

Silence hung between them for an interminably long time. Finally, Mrs. Tinsdale spoke, "I'll get her."

Without another word or another look, she disappeared into the house. Moments later, Lori-Ann appeared, alone, looking confused.

"My grandmother said you wanted to talk to me?"

Serena forced herself to focus and push the guilt from her mind. She didn't think Lori-Ann had done anything wrong. There was no reason to get so worked up about all this.

"Please, sit. I just want to ask you a couple questions."

She slipped into the chair across from her. Everything in her manner looked open, honest. The girl sincerely had no idea why Serena wanted to talk to her.

She paced her questions accordingly. "I wanted to talk to you about Brad Cooley."

Her face immediately tensed. "What about Brad?"

"Are you two friends?"

She shook her head a little too vehemently. "Why would you think that?"

"You were tutoring him this summer, weren't you?"

"I tutor a lot of people. My grandmother says it'll help me learn it better if I explain it to other people."

Serena smiled and took a chance. "Lori-Ann, it's important for you to tell me the truth. Really important. I know you were tutoring Brad this summer. I know there was something between the two of you. I'm not the relationship police, but I do need to know more about Brad, about his friends."

Lori-Ann's eyes glistened with what were probably old tears she'd just as soon have forgotten. "Brad's a jerk."

Serena's smile broadened a little in sympathy. "There's something about jerks. I've been there myself."

"He seemed different with me, you know?"

They always did. In Serena's experience, they never actually were. "Yeah, I do know."

"When did you stop tutoring Brad?" Serena asked.

Lori-Ann smiled a little at the word choice. "About a month ago. Right before school started."

Serena calculated back. That would have been before the keg party at the hospital. "Did you spend time with Brad's friends – Lucas, Reece, Andi?"

Lori-Ann shook her head. "No. He never brought me around the rest of them. They don't like me, never have."

It was pretty clear from her tone that she didn't like the rest of them very much either.

"What did you and Brad do together?" she asked.

Lori-Ann smiled a little, as if she suddenly understood what was going on. "The hospital. You want to know about the hospital? Of course. That makes sense."

Serena nodded, waited.

"He never took me up there. He said it was a stupid place to hang out. Honestly, I think he wanted to avoid them."

"Can you tell me what you know about the hospital?"

"They have some spot they go to. In the woods up there. I never really heard the details."

Serena raised an eyebrow. "In the woods? Not in the hospital?"

Lori-Ann seemed to think about that for a moment. "It always sounded like the woods. Like a campsite or something. I don't think it was actually in the hospital. Though, I guess that's where Lucas and Andi were last night, so maybe, I guess."

Unfortunately, this conversation was quickly degrading into the kind of vague innuendo that had been plaguing Serena all day. Unless they got somebody talking she'd never get to the truth.

"Do you know when this whole gathering up at the hospital thing started?" Serena asked.

Lori-Ann shrugged. "Like I said, I don't really get along with any of them. Andi isn't going to be telling me her secrets, if you know what I mean." She paused, and then added, "I started hearing things about them hanging out up there last spring. I don't know when exactly. Right around when the nice weather started."

"You were never up there?" Serena pressed.

Lori-Ann shook her head, her eyes earnest. "I swear to you. Brad and I never hung out with them. We avoided them."

Not only did Serena see the truth in her eyes, she knew the story made sense. Smart girl starts hooking up with cool kid. The rest of the gang isn't just going to invite her into their crowd. They'd stay on the outside. They'd have to. Serena suspected it was no coincidence their breakup coincided with the start of the school year. Frankly, it was inevitable. One of life's universal lessons – high school sucks.

"You think Lucas was giving Brad a hard time?"

Lori-Ann shook her head. "Not Lucas. Lucas wouldn't have bothered to get involved. Andi would have taken care of things."

~ 14 ~

In any interrogation the things people didn't say were usually more important than what they easily volunteered. Though Serena didn't really view this conversation as an anything that formal, the change in Lori-Ann's tone immediately caught her attention.

Thinking about Mrs. Tinsdale's comments about Andi earlier, she asked, "How would Andi have changed anything?"

Lori-Ann glanced away, her eyes now firmly focused on her hands. "You know," she said vaguely, "Andi and Lucas are always doing stuff together."

"That's not what you said, Lori-Ann. You said, Andi. Why Andi?"

Lori-Ann met her eyes. There was a silent fear there. The kind of fear Serena typically saw in the eyes of crime victims who were hoping to convince her to drop a case. They all hoped that pretending nothing was wrong would make the nightmare go away. The fear came out when they finally realized it couldn't be that simple.

Serena sat silent, waiting for the girl to talk, knowing she would.

"You know Kylie Fulton?" Lori-Ann said, eventually.

Kylie should have started her first year of college that fall, but she'd missed most of her senior year after a suicide attempt.

Still not sure where all this was heading, Serena replied, "What about Kylie?"

Lori-Ann took a deep breath and then met Serena's eyes. Her voice no longer sounded afraid when she spoke. The anger was too apparent. "Andi did that," she said.

Serena only stared. The accusation made no sense. Kylie had taken pills. A lot of them. Serena had been at the scene when she was found. There'd been a note. There was no doubt it was a suicide attempt.

Lori-Ann seemed to see the confusion. With a slightly calmer voice, she explained, "I don't mean she literally did it. I mean she may as well have."

When it became clear Lori-Ann wasn't going to say anything more, Serena said, "You're going to have to explain that for me."

Lori-Ann nodded. "Last summer, Kylie and Lucas hooked up. It was a thing. A big thing. Everybody knew. People were saying Lucas was going to break up with Andi. The rumors spun for a couple days. Andi never seemed to react. Not really. She almost seemed smug about it. I didn't understand it at first. When everything happened, things became pretty clear."

Lori-Ann paused in the story. It might have been for effect, but Serena saw something different. Again, it felt like the girl was hoping Serena would tell her that she could stop. That the story wasn't important. When Serena didn't, Lori-Ann continued.

"It happened really fast. Suddenly there were pictures of Kylie everywhere. Horrible pictures. There were rumors about her and a bunch of guys on the track team. It all sounded so credible. So perverse. Even though I saw what was happening, even though I knew it probably wasn't true, I can understand why people bought it. Andi's just that good. Within a day, the damage was done. Lucas was back with Andi. And Kylie was a pariah. Andi destroyed her."

Serena couldn't believe what she was hearing. How could all this have happened and no one knew?

She wanted to ask more questions about these pictures, the rumors, but she realized there was a more important question that needed to be asked, "How did the pictures get out?"

"There were emails. Some mass text messages."

"Did they come from Andi?"

Lori-Ann shook her head. "Of course not. They came from different random emails. You know, those free providers. I'm betting if you checked now, the email accounts wouldn't exist anymore."

"Do you have the emails?"

"I deleted them. I could see what was happening. I didn't want any part of it."

"Why didn't you tell anyone?"

Lori-Ann looked away. "I couldn't. If I had, it would have been me next. I knew that. I'm just trying to get through, you know? Next year, I can leave for college. I can leave Andi and the others behind. I never have to come back."

Serena thought it all made a certain amount of sense. That said, it was a lot of innuendo and absolutely no proof. Anyone could have sent those emails. Lori-Ann admitted this wasn't her crowd. It was entirely possible she was mistaken about the whole thing.

Serena wondered how it was possible all this had happened and she'd never heard a peep about it. Could it be that everyone was that afraid of Andi?

Serena did have one last question. "If you were so concerned about Andi, why'd you get involved with Brad?"

Lori-Ann smiled sadly. "He promised to protect me from her. Turns out I should have been more concerned about who was protecting me from him."

Serena leaned forward and placed a hand over Lori-Ann's. "I'm guessing you kept this from your mom and dad."

Lori-Ann nodded and met her eyes. The tears were back, brimming at the surface. "You aren't going to tell them are you?"

"I'm not going to tell anyone anything, but can I offer you a little advice?" Serena paused, giving her what she hoped was a maternal look. "Talk to your parents or your grandmother. They just want to know you're okay. They're going to worry that I had to talk to you. They're going to think it's far worse than it really is."

A vigorous nod sent one rogue tear sliding down the girl's cheek.

Serena stood and gave her a hug. In a soft voice she said, "You are not the first person who was fooled by a guy. Smart girls find their way out. That's exactly what you did. There's no shame in that."

It was a lesson Serena had learned the hard way and an explanation that she hoped the girl believed more than Serena did herself.

~ 15 ~

Back in her office, Serena tried to write up her interview with Lori-Ann. She wished she could shake the girl's tears from her mind. She couldn't focus on things like that. Not today. The clock was ticking and with each passing hour it felt like they were getting further from the truth, not closer to it.

A knock brought her out of her deep thoughts. She looked up to see Liam leaning against the door jam.

Serena shook her head. "Hayley just sent you back? Really? We have an intercom. We're in the middle of a murder investigation."

He laughed and dropped a paper sack on her desk. "You want to eat some fries before they get cold or do you want to complain that this is your dispatcher's first murder investigation?"

Serena took out the paper plates she kept in her desk for moments like these and Liam pulled out a container revealing still steaming french fries.

They were both settled in eating before Liam said anything more. "It's not *her* first murder investigation, you know."

They both knew he wasn't talking about Hayley anymore. "She's my best friend, Liam. I know what I'm asking."

"She still has nightmares. Not every night, but a lot of them."

Serena knew that too. Knew it had been a miracle Missy made it out of the house alive. Knew that miracle was the reason she was the state police's number one murder suspect.

"She's our only vet, Liam," Serena explained, knowing it didn't matter. "The town needs her help."

"This town turned on her like a pack of wolves. She doesn't owe the town shit."

And that was one more thing Serena knew all too well. She sat back in her chair feeling the weight, wishing her father was still in charge.

Eventually, she said, "Somebody's dead. Somebody killed them in a vicious and very strange way. Vicious and very strange is a bad combination. Usually means it's not a one-time thing. There are some people in this town who aren't worth much, but there are good people here, too. Are you willing to risk the good because you're still pissed at the stupid, ignorant ones?"

"They didn't believe he did those things to her," Liam growled.

And that was the worst part. Serena knew that. But she said the only thing she could. "He put on a good show."

"They thought she killed him for the insurance money," he continued.

Serena sat forward, looking her brother dead in the eye. "It's over, Liam. People will believe what they'll believe. We've got a real live problem right now. And I've got to figure out what the hell is going on before someone else gets killed."

Liam shook his head. Running a hand through his hair, he focused his attention on the floor. His breathing was deep, as if he was trying to gather himself.

When he finally spoke, his voice was soft, sad. "You ever notice she's the only one who doesn't get mad about it."

Serena let out a breath that would have been a laugh on any other day. "Missy doesn't get angry. In more than thirty years, I've never seen it. Sometimes I think that's why she needs us. Marlowes get angry."

Liam met her eyes with a weak smile. "Bet your ass we do."

Serena returned her attention to the fries. After a moment, Liam did the same.

"Has Pop been by?" he asked.

"First thing this morning. He brought me coffee."

"We Marlowes are big on food," Liam joked. Then he added more seriously, "Don't let him sign back up and help."

Serena shook her head. "We have an arrangement. We talk things out. He gets to help, which is great for me, but none of the physical strain."

They both knew William would send himself to an early grave if they'd let him. It wasn't until he'd actually had a heart attack breaking up a fistfight that he'd agreed to retire, and even then they both knew he'd conceded the point only because he refused to be anything other than perfect at his job. It had nothing to do with his own well-being.

It was a moment before Serena realized her brother was staring at her. "What?" she asked.

He offered her a half smile. "I was just thinking. We covered Missy and Dad. I was wondering who was going to look out for Doc Drayton. I mean, all this has to be a terrible strain on him."

Serena rolled her eyes. "You are unbelievable. You want me to use a murder investigation as a way to flirt with Drayton?"

Liam shrugged, his eyes bright with sarcasm. "I'm telling you, the guy is always asking about you. God knows why. I'm trying to be a good brother. Also, a good Drayton story will put Missy in a much better mood," he added with a wink.

When Serena refused any further response, Liam laughed. "Oh, come on. You have to have noticed the way he looks at you. Frankly, it makes me a little uncomfortable."

She threw a french fry at her brother's head. "You have an overactive imagination."

"I'm actually a little disappointed in the guy. A couple times there I thought he was going to man up and ask you out, but nothing yet."

Serena snorted at the suggestion. Of course the brilliant, good-looking doctor was after her – the average-looking, emotionally stunted, overworked sheriff. It was ridiculous.

But before she could object, Jake Scott appeared in her doorway.

"Sheriff, I just got back on duty, like ten minutes ago, and Hayley transferred a call to my desk. It's Mrs.

Roman. Claudia Daly stopped by her house to bring her some dinner and she wasn't there."

Daisy Roman was a shut-in. There was a group of people in the community who brought her meals on a rotating basis. She relied on them for survival.

Had they figured out who their heart belonged to?

Liam stood. "You go. I'll clean up here."

Serena nodded to her brother and headed out of her office. "Jake, come with me."

~ 16 ~

As Daisy's house came into sight, Serena saw a woman sitting on the front steps. Though her head was resting in her hands, Serena knew it had be Claudia. She thought back to the woman's demeanor earlier in the day when she'd seemed mostly unconcerned about the case. It proved what Serena had suspected. People were less afraid of the crime scene than they should be. A heart was something too abstract for them, too unreal. Now a person missing – that was another story.

Claudia's head bobbed up as the cruiser approached. She jumped to her feet and hurried to the edge of the driveway, clearly not wanting to waste a second.

She was talking from the moment Serena opened the car door. "She isn't in there. Dear God, she's dead, she must be. Serena, you have to do something."

It was a sentence Serena was already beginning to hate. She tried not to think about how many times she'd hear it at the meeting that night. Of course she had to do something. The question was – what?

Despite her inner turmoil, Serena placed a gentle hand on Claudia's shoulder and led her back to the porch. She urged her to take a seat on one of the aging porch chairs.

"One step at a time," she said. "First, tell me what happened."

Wide panicked eyes told Serena that the principal wasn't soothed by her words, but she did sit down.

"You know a bunch of us bring Daisy dinner a couple nights a week. Tonight was my night. I was bringing her a pan of baked ziti. I used the key like I usually do. She wasn't in the living room. She usually is, but she wasn't today. I didn't think much of it. I put the ziti in the oven and called upstairs, but she didn't respond. Well, that's when I started to worry. I mean, I thought maybe she was hurt or sick or something. I looked and I looked and…" her voice broke, and Claudia lowered her head into her hands.

Serena motioned to Jake to sit with Claudia and she went inside, her heart heavy. She knew there was no chance Claudia was mistaken, but she found herself hoping she'd find Daisy inside, sitting in her recliner watching television.

Hope was stolen from the moment Serena stepped in the house. It was deadly still. Oddly, there was no sign of a struggle. Next to the recliner was a dog-eared copy of the TV Guide, where she figured Daisy had left it. The rest of the ground floor looked undisturbed. The click of the oven and the smell of pasta told her Claudia's ziti was still warming.

Upstairs was a little different. The bed was unmade and looked like it was in a bit of disarray, but not so much that it couldn't have just looked slept in. In the bathroom, she found a tube of toothpaste and a toothbrush that was dry. Again, it didn't tell her much. It was dinnertime, even if she'd been there that morning, the brush would have dried by now.

In the small office, there were bills stacked very neatly next to a perfect checkbook. A glance inside the register told her that Daisy was meticulous in her records. In a back corner of the desk was a page-a-day calendar that hadn't been turned in two days.

Jake's voice interrupted her calculations. "Sheriff, Coach Fletcher just pulled up to his house next door. Miss Daly told him what had happened and he took her over to his house for some tea. I figured you might need my help."

Serena nodded. "We need to check the basement and the attic, but I think Claudia's right. It looks like somebody took Daisy."

Jake looked unsteady as he placed his hand on the wall for balance. "Jesus, Sheriff, I didn't think that horrible heart could be somebody in town, you know?"

Of course it had been most likely that it would be somebody from town, but Serena understood his distress.

More comfortable discussing crime scenes, she explained, "I think somebody must've taken her from her bed. Probably overnight, not last night, the night before."

Jake looked around the room, clearly looking for the clues he was missing.

Serena explained. "She seems really neat – so I doubt she would have left the bed unmade. We'll have to check with Claudia on that to see if she knows if that's true, though. And the calendar is up to Saturday, so she most likely was here until at least Saturday morning."

"Why the hell would somebody do this to Daisy? She never did anything to anybody."

Somebody who'd do this to poor harmless Daisy sounded like the type of person who would cut up animals for practice. They had a mess on their hands. That was increasingly clear.

Serena left Jake to check the attic and basement and went next door to collect Claudia. She needed her to look through the rooms with her, see if she saw anything askew.

She grabbed her camera from the trunk on her way. Serena wasn't sure what good the photos would do, but she had to be thorough.

She found Claudia sitting on Coach Fletcher's porch, clutching a mug, eyes focused unblinkingly on Daisy's house.

The coach looked resigned, having clearly figured out what must be going on.

His voice was calm when he spoke, "You know, they believe it was the Chinese who first embraced the custom of drinking tea. Even today there are those who believe it has healing benefits. The ritual of drinking it was said to soothe the spirit and revive the heart."

Serena wondered if it might be a good idea to serve tea at the town meeting. At this rate, they could use all the help they could get.

Unfortunately, it didn't look like Claudia had embraced the healing attributes of tea. Her eyes didn't leave Daisy's house when she spoke. "She's gone, isn't she?"

Serena leaned against the porch railing, blocking their view of the house for a moment. "Nothing good will come out of jumping to conclusions. She's not there, but there are no signs of struggle. So, we really don't know anything."

Claudia snorted. "She hasn't left that house in twenty years. Hell, I'm not sure she could leave the house even if she wanted to."

The coach patted Claudia's hand soothingly, and asked, "What do you think happened, Sheriff?"

Serena didn't even consider answering that question. "I'd like you both to walk through the house with me. See if there's anything that looks out of place to you. I noticed a couple things that looked off, but you know her better than I do."

"Like what?" Coach asked.

"Her bed wasn't made."

Claudia jumped in. "Daisy was compulsive about tidiness. The obsessive compulsiveness is part of what kept her in that house. She used to joke that she made the bed before she got up in the morning. She would never leave it like that."

Serena supposed she should have been happy to have found the likely victim in the case. The timeline was near perfect. Unfortunately, it only made her feel worse.

"Was anyone scheduled to drop dinner last night?"

Claudia shook her head. "We only come by every other day. Somebody would have stopped by Saturday night. I don't remember who."

Serena was confident it didn't matter. Daisy had still been there Saturday night around dinnertime. And since she'd clearly been taken from her bed it really didn't matter who it was that had seen her hours before. But they'd look into it.

She turned her attention to Coach. "Did you notice if she was around last night?"

Fletcher shook his head. "Daisy's living room is on the other side of the house. Those are really the only lights that are ever on at night. I don't think it would catch my eye."

Since there was no neighbor on that side of Daisy's house, it was pretty unlikely it caught anyone's eye. Serena would have Jake canvass the block, but she was not optimistic. And that was what bothered her most of all. This seemed very planned, very strategic, very *not like* a transient who had been hiding out in the old hospital.

Before she could say anything else, her cell phone rang. Seeing the readout, she excused herself. Lowering her voice, she answered the line on the other side of the porch. It was Clay.

"I wanted you to know I've done what I can with the heart and I've got the other samples ready for the state lab. I'm going to drop them at the station if that's okay."

"Doc, I hate to have you dealing with transporting evidence. I suspect you have better things to do. I'll send one of the deputies over in a little bit to pick it up."

Clay laughed. "I have plenty to do. Not much of it's better than getting the hell out of the autopsy room for a little while. Seriously, though, Missy and I found some interesting things already. I'd like to talk to you about it, if you have the time."

"That sounds perfect. Why don't you wait before you head over? I should be back at the station in about an hour. I can talk to you there before the meeting tonight."

Before she disconnected the line, Serena realized there was something more that he might be able to tell her. "Can you tell anything about the person whose heart it was by looking at it?"

Clay hesitated. "By looking at it? I can maybe make some guesses. Why? Do you have a thought about who the victim might be?"

"It may be Daisy Roman."

Though Serena heard the expletives he muttered to himself, Clay's voice was more calm than she'd expected when he finally spoke. "I went out to see her once, for a check-up. You know, basic stuff. I can check on her health generally, it might give us some clues. Her cholesterol wasn't good, if I'm remembering right," Clay continued, talking more to himself than Serena. "I'll look at the heart again. I won't be able to say for sure it's her, but I may be able to tell you if it's not."

Serena figured that was better than nothing and reminded him to drive safely when he transported their precious cargo. She disconnected the call, and again she was alone on the porch with two concerned citizens who were most likely eavesdropping.

She ignored their unspoken questions. "Why don't you two come with me? You can tell me if you see anything I don't."

Inside the house, Claudia led the way, flying through rooms. Serena hung back with Coach Fletcher, who was far less frenetic.

"Did you get a moment to check in on Lauren?" she asked.

He offered her a sweet smile. "I did. She was up in bed, watching some talk show. I caught her up on things while the teapot came to a boil. Serena, this is an awful, awful mess."

Serena smiled, trying to look confident and competent. "It's been less than twenty-four hours. We're still gathering information, but we're moving the case. We'll figure it out."

Fletcher seemed to see through her bravado. "You know, they say Sherlock Holmes' character was based on a real person – a physician, actually."

Serena was impressed with how well he put people at ease. "Holmes wasn't a doctor."

"Conan Doyle wanted to make it more exciting. Life isn't anywhere near as exciting as books. In life, you just have to pick through – one piece at a time. Eventually, you'll get down to the real story."

She paused for a moment and placed her hand on his shoulder. "Thanks, Coach. Liam always told me you were great with pep talks."

He smiled. "It's going to work itself out. I hate to see you beat yourself up."

Serena thought of Claudia, thought of all the others who would be demanding her attention, demanding answers in the coming days. Fletcher was right. She didn't need to beat herself up. There'd be plenty of people lining up to do that for her.

~ 17 ~

Serena was in the conference room, staring helplessly at the whiteboard when Riley joined her.

"Tell me you have something," she said without preamble.

He sunk into the chair opposite her. "They really took Daisy? Really?"

Serena leaned back and stared up at the ceiling. "She's gone and it looks like somebody took her."

"How?"

"Her bed was unmade and the sheets looked messier than I'd expect. Hard to say what happened. Maybe somebody knocked and she let them in."

Riley's voice was vicious when he spoke, "Or somebody used that fucking key she kept under the mat and let themselves in."

Exhaustion was starting to creep in already. She was going to have to make sure she got some sleep tonight and order Riley to do the same. The lack of sleep was only increasing the sense of desperate resignation.

"I don't think there's a person in town who didn't know about that key."

They sat in silence for a while, both calculating what they had, both realizing it wasn't much.

"I was looking through Shane's reports. These kids won't even admit they've been hanging out by the hospital," she said.

Riley nodded. "Shane said it was pretty clear they were lying. He thought Reece Henderson seemed like the most likely one to crack."

That sounded about right. "Reece is a good kid. A smart kid. If we press him we may get somewhere."

Since she refused to lift her head off the back of the chair, Serena could sense more than see Riley's cold examination of her.

"You're really pushing with the kids," he said finally.

Serena could feel her anger rising. She sat up and met his eyes. "Yeah. You have any other leads you'd like me following up on?"

Riley's expression was even more dismissive than his tone. "You can't possibly think any of them had anything to do with this."

She told herself she didn't, but really she did, she just didn't want to. She couldn't get mad at Riley for feeling the same way. And if she was going to succeed in this investigation, she was going to have to convince him that she hadn't fallen down the rabbit hole.

"Why would someone do this?" Serena said finally.

"Because they're a sick fucking lunatic," Riley spat.

It was an answer she should have expected. It was the reason she'd been planning to discuss the psychology with Clay instead of Riley.

She kept her voice calm, even. "It doesn't sound like a transient to me. I really wish it sounded like some guy who was just passing through. That wouldn't be as bad."

"Why can't it be some homeless guy?" Riley asked.

Serena shook her head and allowed it to tilt against the back of the chair, focusing again on the ceiling. "Doesn't fit. We'll know more when we talk to Clay and Missy. The stuff with the animals took time, I'm betting. The more I think about that, the less this looks like a wanderer. Really, the problem is Daisy. They picked the most vulnerable person in town. They picked her on Saturday when no one would be by again until Monday night. And they probably used the key she kept under the mat. How would a transient know all that?"

Serena heard the steady cracking as Riley worked his way through each of his knuckles. A small, weak part of her remembered he used to do that when they fought. The sound always made her feel insecure, somehow less, just like their relationship had.

"So you think this is somebody from town," he said.

"I don't see how it isn't."

The creak of Riley's boots told her that he'd crossed his legs. "Why would somebody in town kill Daisy?"

"So they could cut her heart out, I suppose." The reply had been sarcastic, but the words set off a light bulb.

She sat up in a flash. "You took ancient history with Coach Fletcher, right?"

"Of course. Best class ever. Junior year."

"When did he do the Mayans and the Aztecs?"

Riley shrugged. "What does that have to do with anything?"

"When?" she insisted.

He clearly thought she'd lost it, but Riley considered the question. "In the spring, I think. No, wait, late March. Had to be late March, actually, before April Fool's Day, because I bought this fake blood and stuff and I made this crazy altar thing to freak out my girlfriend. It was awesome."

Nausea churned in her stomach. She locked her eyes in on Riley and simply waited. He'd not only answered her question. He'd confirmed her suspicions.

"What?" he asked. But it was only a moment before he said, "No way. There is no way at all. I mean it's one thing to play, to make a joke of it. This isn't a joke, Serena. Not by a long shot."

No, it wasn't a joke, but that didn't mean it didn't make sense.

"You said it yourself. You thought it was a fun prank."

"No way," Riley repeated. "That's crazy."

Serena shook her head. "This whole damn thing is crazy. Can't start ruling theories out because they're crazy."

"You're thinking this is just some prank?"

She choked on the idea. "No, not a prank, not in the childish way you're thinking. This is the work of a sociopath, no doubt. I'm saying maybe our sociopath got some ideas from his high school history teacher, just like you did."

There was agreement behind his eyes now, even though he continued to fight her. "The timeline's wrong. Lucas and his friends, they had the class last spring. Why wait until now?"

"They didn't wait. They've been preparing all summer." According to Lori-Ann's story, they'd been hanging around the hospital since spring. It actually fit. Though it was the first workable theory they'd been able to conceive, it didn't make Serena feel better.

"We'll know more when we talk to Drayton later about the animals. I'm thinking the timeline is just about perfect," Serena said.

Riley didn't respond, didn't say anything, but his face said it all. For that moment, that brief moment, she had his respect.

Taking the win, she moved on. "It's too late in the day to search the woods and the river over by the hospital, but that's got to be the next step. Daisy's body has to be somewhere. We find it. It may tell us something."

"The body could be anywhere," he replied.

Serena met his eyes. "We've worked both crime scenes. We've got nothing. We could sit here and let the trail get cold, or we can get some tracking dogs out there looking. The worst thing that happens is we don't find her. I think we start early tomorrow in the woods over by the hospital. You up for it?"

Riley seemed surprised by her tone. "My dog and I'll be there. You want me to pick up some stuff from the house to help the dogs catch the scent?"

"That'd be great. I'll get the town involved tonight at the meeting. Tell them to meet at the hospital at eight a.m. Hayley can meet me there at seven-thirty to get things set up."

Before he could answer, Hayley's voice came over the intercom. "Sheriff, Riley, Dr. Skylar's on the line. She says she needs you down at Dr. Drayton's office right away."

Serena was on her feet and out the door in a second. Missy was not the type of person who called in anything short of a true emergency. Something was wrong, terribly wrong.

~ 18 ~

Missy led Serena and Riley back to the waiting room where Serena had shared her coffee earlier in the day. Inside, Clay was laying across a couch, his feet dangling uncomfortably over the arm. His head was turned to the side, two large ice packs across the back of his head and neck. He met her eyes with what looked like a combination of shame and remorse.

"Somebody jumped him," Missy explained, "whacked him across the back of the head with an old board."

Serena couldn't believe what she was hearing. What the hell was going on in her town? Now people were getting jumped for no reason?

Even as she thought it, she realized what must have happened. She should have figured out a way to send one of her deputies to transfer the evidence. This was her fault.

"What did they take?" she asked.

Clay began to shake his head, but stopped in obvious pain. "They took the heart."

"What the hell do you mean they took the heart?" Riley snapped.

"I mean, I was bringing the heart out to the car and somebody jumped me. When I came to, the heart was gone and I was laying by myself in the dark. Missy was still inside cleaning up for the night."

Missy stepped between Clay and Riley, taking over the story. "He came stumbling in and, before he let me help him, he told me I had to call you guys to tell you what had happened." She shot Riley a glare, daring him to accuse anyone of anything.

"Did they get anything else?" Serena asked, trying to ignore the tension.

"Everything else is still in the lab. I didn't have a chance to bring the rest out," Clay explained.

Serena turned to Riley. "I need you to get those samples to the state offices. Take Jake with you. Missy, can you show him what goes and what stays?"

Once they were alone, Serena kneeled next to the couch. "Can I see?"

Gingerly, she removed the ice packs, revealing a swollen purple bruise at the base of his skull that disappeared into his hair.

"You need to get to a doctor," she said.

Clay chuckled and pulled away from her. "I am a doctor and I diagnose me as fine."

"I don't need you to be a hero, Clay. From what I can see of this bruise it already looks nasty. How long were you out?"

"Not more than a minute or two. Missy didn't even have time to notice I was taking too long. It's nothing."

"Shouldn't somebody check this out? Maybe you need some kind of scan or something?"

Clay laughed and sat up to prove his point. "I'm fine. I'm the asshole who lost your evidence, but otherwise I'm fine. I'm not letting you take me to the hospital."

Before Serena could argue more, she felt Missy's hand on her shoulder. "He'll live," she said. "I checked him out while we were waiting for you. I don't see any signs of serious issues. He's oriented. His pupils are reactive and equal. No signs of blood in the ears or nose. No unexpected bruising."

Seeing Serena's skepticism, Missy added, "You know, vets aren't complete idiots. I do have some training."

"I'm not suggesting..." Serena began.

Missy smiled. "I was an EMT once upon a time."

Serena looked at Clay again. He looked a little pale. She suspected they all did after this day.

"Are you sure you're alright?" she asked again, though the question was more of a surrender.

Clay didn't even answer. Instead he handed the ice pack to Missy. "Would you mind putting this back in the freezer?"

Missy took it, and then looked sternly at her patient. "I want you to make sure you keep icing throughout the night. And, Serena's half-right, this is bad enough that I want you monitored. You know as well as I do what you need to be watching for – vision issues, dizziness, disorientation, slurred speech – if there's anything, you call an ambulance immediately. Your second call is to me. I can get here faster than the ambulance. Do not wait around. I don't want to be drilling a hole in your head to relieve the pressure."

Clay smiled. "Yes, Ma'am."

"I'm serious," she threatened. "As we already discussed, I'm not thrilled you're here alone."

"Missy, I'm fine. I swear. I'm fine. I barely lost consciousness."

"You know as well as I do that presentation of symptoms can be delayed."

Clay pulled a cell phone out of his pocket. "If I call you every hour or so for the next couple hours, will that appease you?"

Missy nodded. "That sounds reasonable."

Clay glanced at Serena and smiled. "Is she this tough with the dogs?" he asked.

Feeling fairly confident their medical crisis was passing, Serena allowed herself a smile. "Oh, she's far worse with the dogs."

Missy seemed satisfied with the agreement. She sat down in the chair next to the couch and gestured to Serena to do the same. "I told Riley to take the patrol car. I'll drive you to the town meeting from here."

"Aren't you getting bossy?" Serena joked.

Missy shook her head. "You dragged me into quite a little mess here. I think I'm entitled."

Serena sighed. "Seriously, I'm sorry. I didn't know what else to do."

Clay laid a hand on Serena's knee. "If you hadn't asked Missy to help out, I would have asked you to bring her in. I couldn't have done this without her today."

Serena was surprised by the gentleness of his touch, though she tried hard not show it.

"So what did you guys find?" she asked.

The doctors exchanged glances and seemed to come to an unspoken agreement that it would be Clay who told her what had happened.

"We got through preliminary examinations on a bit more than half of the animals. It's pretty much the same thing over and over. Chests cut open. Rib cage cracked. Heart removed. As you'd expect, on the older bodies the cuts are more jagged, ugly. The work generally isn't that good. But the fresher bodies, well, the cuts are expert. He's been practicing."

Serena cursed under her breath. She really hadn't wanted to be right about that.

"Can you tell how long he's been at it?" she asked.

Missy spoke up. "We thought it'd be better to process a lot quickly today. We'll try to focus in on more specifics tomorrow. There are some pretty broad variants in the decomp."

"Meaning it's been a while?"

"Meaning it's been a while," Missy agreed.

"Maybe spring, early summer?" Serena asked, again hoping to be wrong.

"Probably about that." Missy gave her a look, clearly wondering where the specifics were coming from.

"There's more," Clay explained. "I did check the heart again, before…."

"Before someone smacked you over the head and stole it," Serena suggested.

"I was going to say before I lost it, but I like your version better," Clay said. "Either way, I did take a closer look at the heart. I wish I had someone to consult with on this, but Serena, I'm afraid we have some bad news. I don't think there's any way that could be Daisy Roman's heart."

Serena didn't think there was anything Clay could have said that she would have found more surprising. "It's not her heart? It has to be her heart. She's missing."

"I could be wrong. I've observed surgeries, including open heart surgeries on people with bad arteries. This heart was clear. The arteries were pristine. With the levels of cholesterol in Daisy's body, I can't imagine that's her heart."

"Jesus, are you sure?"

Clay smiled. "I'm way out of my depth here. I'm not sure of anything."

But Serena could see he was sure, at least pretty close to sure. She glanced over at Missy.

Her old friend seemed to read her thoughts. "I think you may want to start figuring out who else is missing," she said.

The notion that they had two missing people in the community was so horrible it was practically incomprehensible.

At a loss, Serena asked, "I didn't ask originally. I assume you didn't see who hit you?"

Clay's expression was a mixture of shame and frustration. "I was walking to the car and then I was waking up on the ground. The heart was gone and there was a two-by-four lying next to me. Honestly, I don't even remember getting hit."

"Riley took a whole bunch of pictures and he took the board back to the station," Missy explained.

They'd test for blood and find Clay's. They'd test for fingerprints and get nothing. It seemed pointless, but it was necessary.

"He roped the area off. Said it was too dark to do much until morning."

Serena was beginning to think she was going to have to start traveling around with Coach Fletcher's floodlights in the back of her patrol car. The night was getting darker and more sinister by the minute.

~ 19 ~

Serena managed to skim through the special edition of the *Whitefield Witness* before heading over to the town meeting. It had been as bad as she'd expected. Norton's article had been gory, graphic and designed to incite panic. He'd dedicated a fair amount of space to the "butchering" of animals and Serena's formal "no comment" on the point.

He had the details of the scene right, more than he should have. Which left Serena with a very uncomfortable question – who was telling him?

Though the question nagged, Serena didn't have time to give it any real thought. The town meeting was packed. People were radiating an odd mix of curiosity and panic. It was her job to simultaneously reassure while conveying just how dangerous the situation really was. After the day she'd already had, Serena was sure she wasn't up to the challenge.

Clad in his spray tan and bad suit, Mayor Mario Smith opened the meeting promptly at eight. His introduction was classic politics, lots of gloss with pretty words that had almost no substance. If Serena hadn't known better she would have thought he didn't actually know what had happened. She couldn't entirely blame him. She would have far preferred playing stupid to answering the barrage of questions she was certain to face.

Despite saying nothing, the mayor managed to talk for fifteen minutes before he called Serena to the podium. She started with a very simple summary of what they'd found in the operating room. She felt it was best, at this point, to leave out the fact that someone had stolen their biggest piece of physical evidence. This was no time to make things sound worse than they already were.

She'd decided to avoid the issue with the animals entirely. There was no good spin and no purpose that could be served in letting people know more.

People had clearly already heard about the hospital, but the expressions changed when she explained about Daisy Roman's disappearance. Several gasps and whispers confirmed that the news hadn't traveled through the town yet.

She noticed Norton Finwick sitting in the front row scribbling notes in his little book. It looked like even pesky Norton had missed that one.

"I've decided we need to search the woods around the hospital. And that means we're going to need the help of anyone who is able. I'd like to break into teams to search different sections of the woods. Those of you who have hunting dogs should bring them. It can't hurt to have the help. I know Buster will be coming with me. We'll be meeting in the old ambulance bay at the hospital tomorrow morning at eight. Hayley will have a post set up there to keep things organized."

She watched as people began muttering among themselves about their ability to change their plans for the day. She could see from their faces that she was going to get the response she needed.

"There's one more thing," she added. "The evidence we have suggests there might have been another victim involved in the crime. My deputies and I can't reasonably go around town to do a head count, so I'm relying on you all to check in on your neighbors, make sure they're okay."

That brought the roar of questions she'd expected all night. She raised her hands. "Please, everybody. One at a time. We'll get to you all. I promise."

Avery Sinclair raised his hand like a shot. Andi's father was a pompous ass, but as manager of the local factory, he enjoyed a position of power throughout the town. Serena considered passing him over for one of the other hands in the audience, but she wanted to get the worst out of the way first.

"What the hell do you mean 'the evidence suggests there was a second victim?'" he snarled. "There was one heart on the table. I know that. My daughter saw the whole thing."

Serena almost laughed at the question. If that was the worst he had to offer she didn't have a lot to worry about.

"I can't comment on those kinds of details. To be as clear as I can be, let me say this. There's nothing definitive at this time. It may be there was just one victim. However, we have certain evidence that causes us to be concerned there's more to it."

Before she could move on to the next question, Avery snapped, "You don't have a clue what you're talking about. Tell me one thing in that room that makes you think there were two victims."

Though she was sure she could think of more than one thing, Serena replied, "Avery, I've spent the past twenty hours investigating and following up on leads. I know a bit more now than I did last night when we dragged Andi out of our crime scene."

With that, Serena moved on to the next question and transitioned from the aggravating to the inane.

Ollie Nelson wanted to know if it was true that cannibals were responsible for the crime. Yvonne Beech wanted to know if it was a satanic ritual, because she was certain the boys on her block wore a lot of black and didn't go to church, which concerned her. Though Serena had no specific evidence to the contrary, she assured them neither was possible.

Homer Tracy, who was still astonishingly spry for ninety-four, wanted to know if it was possible the hospital had forgotten to properly clean when they left. Serena thought of the old equipment that had been left behind, but she promised him the scene was, unfortunately, quite new. The smile she got in response told her that he thought she was sweet, but he was sure she was wrong.

It was Lucas's father, Albert Denton, who stood to ask the question she knew was inevitable. "Do you have one of the deputies keeping an eye on Drayton? Because he sure as hell ought to be your top suspect."

Serena took a breath before she answered, and tried to ignore the whispered agreement in the crowd. "I don't round up people because they're new in town. I guarantee you that we will look into him, just like we'll look into everyone. The truth is, Dr. Drayton was attacked this evening. Someone hit him across the back of the head with a two-by-four. It seems they were trying to get their hands on some of the evidence. Fortunately, he's going to be all right. It does make it seem far less likely he's the person doing all this."

Serena was pretty sure she heard somebody mutter it was a damn good thing somebody was protecting them from the outsider. She considered further reprimand, but thought better of it.

Instead she said, "Look everybody, whoever is doing this is very aggressive and very violent. I need you to look out for each other. If you see anything strange, call the station right away. Keep an eye on your neighbors. And I'm begging you, lock your doors. I know a lot of you don't worry about stuff like that, but I'm serious. Lock the doors. There's no need to invite trouble."

Norton waited until the end of the meeting to ask his questions. "Do you have a response for the people who are calling for the reappointment of William Marlowe until this is solved?"

She'd thought she'd been prepared for anything, but the question was a punch in the gut. She told herself people weren't saying those things – that it was just Norton attacking her – still, the question stung.

Torn between the answer she would give as William's daughter and the answer she would give as the sheriff, Serena hesitated. She needn't have worried.

Her father's voice boomed over the crowd. "William Marlowe is retired. He's been retired and he's staying retired. Serena Marlowe was the sheriff yesterday, she's the sheriff today, and she's gonna be the sheriff tomorrow. Anybody who suggests different is an idiot."

Serena looked out over the hushed audience. She let her father's words settle over them before she said very calmly, "If there's nothing else, I'd like to send you on your way."

~ 20 ~

The crowd dissipated quickly. Everyone clearly wanted to get back home behind locked doors. Serena couldn't say she blamed them.

Eventually, she found herself standing outside the hall with her father, Liam, and Missy.

Her father gave her a generous pat on the shoulder – a tender endearment for a Marlowe. "You did a good job tonight, honey."

Liam smiled. "You really did. They wanted to eat you alive, but you didn't give them the chance."

"Did somebody really knock Doc Drayton over the head?" William asked.

Serena nodded. "Yeah, he took a really nasty hit. I'm actually going to stop by there on my way home and make sure he's still looking okay. He refused to go to the hospital. Insists he's fine."

"You need to make sure you get some sleep tonight," Liam insisted. "You won't be any good to anyone if you go another day without sleep."

"Yes, Mom," Serena teased.

Serena went with Missy to pick up her car at the station. Before they left, she heard Liam say he'd meet her at her place in fifteen minutes.

Once they were alone in the car, Serena said, "I'm glad Liam's staying with you tonight. I feel safer knowing you aren't alone."

Missy glanced over as she pulled out of the parking spot. "Who's going to make sure you're not alone this evening?"

Serena laughed. "I think Buster has that covered. We have a game of fetch planned."

Missy shook her head and for a moment seemed to consider leaving it at that, but instead she said, "So, I spent the day with Drayton. He's a good guy, you know. A really good guy."

Serena laughed. "Seriously? My punishment for dragging you into this case is that you're going to give me a hard time about Clay?"

"Clay, huh?" Missy smirked.

"You're worse than Liam. I work with Doctor Drayton," she said, stressing the title. "There's nothing else to it."

"Well, there isn't yet, but that doesn't mean there couldn't be. He's cute, Serena. Really cute. I know you've noticed."

Of course, Missy was right about both points, but there were bigger issues. "I think you're missing the point. We work together. I made that mistake once. I'm not making it again."

Missy pulled her car behind Serena's patrol car and turned to her friend. "Riley? Really? You're worried about this because dating Riley went badly? Jesus, Serena, dating Riley went badly because you were dating *Riley*. Drayton is nothing like Riley. He's like the anti-Riley. You may need to date him so you can cancel out the fact that you dated Riley."

Serena shook her head. "It's not that simple."

"It actually is," Missy replied.

Serena didn't know if it was the stress or the exhaustion, but the words came out before she could stop them. "You can't possibly understand how it was with Riley. You weren't here. You left."

Missy sat back in her seat, clearly surprised by the outburst, momentarily speechless.

Serena closed her eyes and took a deep breath. "I'm sorry. That wasn't fair. I didn't mean that."

When Serena finally worked up the courage to meet her friend's eyes, she was surprised to see she didn't look upset. She looked more curious than anything else.

"You've been waiting a long time to say that," Missy observed.

Serena denied it immediately. "No. I haven't. I mean, I don't think that. How could I think that?"

"Why wouldn't you think that? It's true, Serena. I left and I didn't look back. Not really."

"You were in school. You were working. You were doing what you needed to do. I understand that. I've always understood that," Serena insisted.

"We're best friends. You spent our childhood looking out for me. The second I had the chance I left."

Serena shook her head. "That's not true. Sure you weren't around a while, but you would visit. You came back."

Missy smiled sadly. "You didn't know if I was going to come back. I didn't know if I would, if I'd ever be able."

She was right. That had been part of it. Her best friend was gone. They'd been inseparable since the day they'd met and then suddenly Serena was left behind. She had been starting out in a job that meant everything to her. Riley knew the job. He'd known her. He'd understood. Or so it'd seemed at the time.

Still wanting to explain, Serena said, "There were good times, too, you know. He wasn't always a jerk."

Missy laughed at that. "Of course there were good times. I was around enough to see that. Serena, you need to understand. It didn't work out because it was never going to work out. That's not on you. It's not a reflection on anything other than your ability to see the best in people. You deserve to be happy. Don't let what happened with Riley get in the way of that."

Serena knew her friend was right. Frankly, Missy was usually right about this sort of thing.

"Look," she said finally, "I appreciate the pep talk, but it's all a non-issue. However I feel about any of this, Clay Drayton has no interest in me. None. If he had I would have noticed."

Missy started to object, but Serena stopped her. "I am going to his place to make sure he's okay. That's all."

Missy rolled her eyes and smiled. "I don't believe for one second you're stopping by his house to check on the bump on his head."

"You said yourself there was a risk it could be worse than we'd initially thought and it was important to check in."

"I said it was important for him to keep an eye on things and to call the ambulance. We agreed he'd call me, which he has."

Serena decided to ignore the response. Instead she slipped out of the car. "Go home and deal with your own love life. And get your nose out of mine."

Missy drove off with a broad smile on her face. The kind of smile you only got when you knew you were right.

~ 21 ~

Serena had been telling herself she wasn't interested in Clay for so long she almost believed it. But, as she walked to his door, the lie was growing more and more apparent. She could feel it in her rapid heart rate, in the thoughts that were racing through her mind.

It was stupid. There was no reason to be nervous. She'd talked to Clay a million times.

But this was different. She was checking on him because she was worried about him. Worried she'd put him in harm's way. Not because he was their coroner, but because he was one of the few people in this town who she truly looked forward to seeing.

Every instinct she had was ordering her to turn around. To go home. To forget about all of it. Though she knew it was just fear, it was harder than she would have expected to find the courage to raise her hand and knock on the door.

It took Clay less than a minute to open the door, but it felt like several lifetimes.

He greeted her with a surprised smile. "I didn't really expect you'd have a chance to make it back here tonight."

Serena tried very hard to seem normal and totally unlike how she really felt. "I wanted to make sure you were doing okay."

Seeming to suddenly realize he was blocking the doorway, Clay stepped aside to invite her in.

"The place is kind of a mess," he said. "I had no idea there'd be this whole forensic nightmare, followed by me getting hit on the head."

Serena tried not to laugh. Clay kept the small apartment over his office far neater than her home. If nothing else, you didn't need to step over a pile of dog toys to get inside.

Instead of admitting to her own messiness, she said, "It's a nice place. Actually, it's bigger than I'd expected it to be."

Clay raised an eyebrow. "You must have expected something really small then. Let me give you the tour. This corner here with the couch and TV – that's the living room. That corner there – that's the kitchen slash dining room. And through that door there is an equally small bedroom and bathroom."

He was right. It was a small place, but he'd somehow made it seem so comfortable and cozy you didn't notice. There were framed photos placed artistically throughout the room, and several leafy plants were scattered about.

"Did you take these pictures?" she asked.

He seemed a little embarrassed. "They're all trips I've taken over the years. That's my favorite over the couch – the Grand Canyon. I know it's probably a little predictable to say, but it's the most beautiful thing I've ever seen. A relatively small river carved that. It's a pretty amazing reminder of the rewards of perseverance."

Serena found herself looking at Clay more than the picture. She wasn't seeing the town doctor anymore. She was just seeing him. The more he talked, the more interesting he became. She took a step closer without really meaning to.

She could see the bump on the back of his head now. It was visibly raised, even under his hair.

"I'm fine," he assured her, noticing her gaze.

"Are you sure?" she asked.

He sat on the couch and gestured for her to do the same. "Serena, this is not your fault."

Happy to sit, she joined him. "Of course it's my fault. It was my evidence you were protecting. I've got a psycho on my hands and it never dawned on me that he might go after the evidence."

"It's not your job to protect me."

"Actually, I'm pretty sure that's the definition of my job," she pointed out.

Clay raised his hands in surrender. "Okay, fine, it's your job and your fault. So I should thank you. I'm guessing half the town was ready to tar and feather me today. All of a sudden you've got a killer loose among you. Everybody's going to look at the new guy first. But if the new guy gets cracked over the head, then I guess he can't really be a suspect anymore."

Serena thought of Riley's earlier remark, thought of the comments at the town meeting. Clay was wrong. The type of people who would question him were going to need a lot more to be convinced otherwise.

But she took the quip in the spirit in which it was offered.

"Well, I'm glad to help in any way I can."

"You know, I've been a little surprised you didn't hand the evidence over to the state offices to cut me out of the investigation."

Serena sank back on the couch, thinking of all the history he didn't know, but not having the energy to enlighten him. She gave him the same answer she'd given the town. "I don't arrest the new guy any time something bad happens."

Clay shook his head. "I don't mean it that way. You know everything there is to know about most of the people in this town, but you really don't know much of anything about me. Wouldn't that automatically place me at the top of the list?"

There was an easy answer to the question – they had a killer who was apparently *practicing* to be a surgeon. As far as she was concerned that excluded the two doctors in town immediately. Unfortunately, the two doctors in town were her best friend and… Serena didn't really know how to define the reasons she might not want to believe their new doctor was a killer, but she was certain she didn't entirely trust her judgment on the topic.

Since she didn't want to get into any of that, she ducked the question. "I've known these people my whole life. But I don't assume I really know everyone in town – in fact I'm sure I don't really know more than a couple of them."

"You know them better than you know me," Clay suggested.

Serena shook her head. "I've seen people singing in the church choir on Sunday morning and beating the crap out of their wives Sunday afternoon. Hours earlier you would've never known the cruelty they were capable of. Nothing different here. Bigger. Scarier. But not different."

"All that glitters," Clay responded absently.

It took a minute to realize he was using her words from earlier in the day. Funny, it felt like it was years ago.

It was such a disturbing thought. They were one day into this investigation and it didn't seem like they were even a minute closer to the truth. Serena wondered how many days like this she'd need to endure before she figured this out.

But the exhaustion was outweighed by her worry. How many days did they really have before their killer did something new, something worse?

~ 22 ~

Serena shook off her dark thoughts and focused on Clay. His easy smile had a funny effect on her. It made her far more nervous than bizarre crime scenes and potential murder sprees.

Reminding herself that she was capable of having a normal conversation, Serena asked, "Has it been hard to get used to living here in the middle of nowhere?"

"Want to know a secret? I grew up in a place not all that different from Whitefield."

"You grew up in a place like Whitefield and you actually chose to come here?" she asked. "You did that on purpose?"

Clay laughed. "You joke, but you don't mean it. You love this town. Love these people. That's why you do what you do."

He was right, of course. She didn't always like life in her small town, but it was a part of her and she loved it the way most people loved family.

It was funny to realize Clay knew her better than she'd expected. "Don't tell them, alright? It'll go to their heads. Besides, I'm pretty sure we were talking about your secrets, not mine."

Clay smiled. "I was the first Drayton to go to college. The pride of the family. My mom died when I was in high school, and she made me promise to get out of our little town, to make something of myself. My dad encouraged me to go to medical school."

"From what I remember from your application, you didn't just go to medical school, you were Ivy League the whole way through."

Clay's expression grew distant with the compliment. "I wanted to be the best. I worked a lot. Didn't think too much about that part until my dad died. It was sudden, a brain tumor. By the time they found it he only had a couple weeks left."

"My God, I'm so sorry."

It was clear from his face that Clay had heard the words so many times they'd lost their meaning. "After he died, it all seemed so pointless. When I saw the ad for this job, I thought it'd be the perfect way to start over. It was like going back to the beginning."

"So, you gave it all up?"

"I gave up a hectic practice in a city where I didn't know anyone or care to. It really wasn't a sacrifice. What about you?"

Serena looked at him, confused. "What about me?"

"Town sheriff. Pretty big deal. How'd you end up doing that?"

It was so very strange to be talking to someone who didn't already know the whole story. There was the easy answer, of course, the obvious one everyone in town would have reported. The legacy. The family tradition.

There was no getting away from that, but it wasn't the story. Not really.

"Missy Skylar was our neighbor when we were kids. She spent most of her time over at my house. I didn't know it then, but her mom used to drink – a lot. My mom managed to quietly keep Missy with us as much as she could. Sometime before we started kindergarten, Missy's mom left, up and disappeared."

Clay's eyes were filled with compassion. "Jesus, what happened to her?"

"Nobody really knows for sure, but the guess is she just left town."

"She abandoned her kid?"

Serena shook her head. "I don't remember the whole thing very well, but honestly, I don't think Missy's mom would have given leaving that much thought. If she felt like going, she would have gone."

Clay simply stared, clearly unsure what to say.

"It gets worse," Serena assured him, with a sad smile. "After that, Missy pretty much became one of the family. She spent her days with us and she'd stay with us a few nights a week. When my mom died a couple years later, it was one more thing that brought us all together.

"As we got older, I noticed how much she really hated to go back to her house. On summer nights, when the windows were open, I could hear her dad shouting at her." Serena shook her head. "It was horrible stuff. You wouldn't believe the things."

Clay placed his hand over hers, and she realized she was happy she'd decided to tell him the whole story, the real story. "I asked Missy about it a couple times. She never said a word, always minimized it. I'm telling you, even though I'd heard the yelling myself, I believed her when she said it was no big deal."

"You were a kid," he said.

Serena shook her head. "So was she."

After a moment she continued, "Things went on like that for a while. I never noticed the bruises. My father did, or so he told me later. The thing with abuse is it's really hard to prove, and he had no better luck getting Missy to talk to him than I did. He knew he couldn't do anything until he was sure he could prove it, or he'd make things worse for her.

"We were about thirteen when everything changed. It was spring and Missy hadn't been to school in a couple days. I figured she must be sick, but it was pretty weird that she hadn't called or anything. I marched over there after school. I knocked, but when there was no answer I fiddled with the front window and climbed in."

Clay laughed. "You broke into her house."

"I didn't think of it as breaking in at the time. It was the same way Missy got in if she forgot her key. I was just checking in on her.

"Anyway, I found her in bed, like I'd expected, but not at all the way I'd expected. She was a mess. She had a black eye, her jaw was bruised, and she'd somehow managed to tie her arm into this sort of sling to immobilize it."

Clay shook his head. "Even as a kid she was thinking like a doctor."

"Yeah, I guess that's right." Serena had never thought of it that way. "You can imagine the story and, as you also might imagine, that was that. My dad came. They took Missy to the hospital. She had a broken arm, a cracked rib. Turns out it wasn't the first cracked rib she'd had."

Clay let out a breath that sounded more like a curse.

"She insists that night was the worst it ever got. I almost believe her. But her efforts to minimize things were always really convincing and now I know a lot of that was a lie too."

"And that's how you knew what you wanted to do?" Clay asked.

"Almost. Missy came to live with us, but her dad managed to get bail before the trial. As you might expect, the restraining order didn't stop him from coming into the yard when he saw me and Missy playing out back. He was really calm at first, nice. He told her how much he loved her, missed her. Eventually, he asked her to come with him. I informed him that my father had told us that we weren't even allowed to talk to him. That didn't go very well."

"I wouldn't imagine."

"He grabbed Missy by her arm and tried to force her to come. She fought him as best she could, but she was just a kid, and Missy was a skinny little kid. I'd been sitting on the top of the swing set when he got there. I somehow managed to jump down, landing square on his back. I poked at his eyes, pulled his ears, his hair, used every kid trick I could."

Clay's eyes were wide. "You managed to get him to leave?"

Serena laughed. "Not even close. But Liam had been in the house doing some homework. We caused enough of a commotion that he heard us. He called my dad at the station and then ran outside to help. Liam is only a couple years older than us, but he's always been a pretty big guy. And like most bullies, Missy's father had no interest in a fair fight. He let her go. By the time my father got there, the three of us had managed to take care of the situation."

Clay shook his head. "That could have ended a lot differently."

"Yeah, I know. I knew it then, too. That's why I wanted to be the person who helped, who protected people. I didn't want anyone to feel helpless and alone like that."

Clay smiled. "Does Missy know she was an inspiration?"

Serena laughed. "I think she'd prefer her father not get that much credit."

They just sat for a moment, and Serena began to realize they were sitting closer than they'd originally been. It was nice. Being here, telling stories, actually getting to know someone new, someone different.

"Do you remember the first time we met?" he asked.

She thought back to the day. It was in Liam's bar, she'd been sitting at the counter eating lunch. Clay had come over and introduced himself. They'd talked for a few minutes.

"Of course, we met at the bar. You'd gotten into town the week before, I think."

For the first time all night, that ever present calm was absent from Clay's eyes. They shifted away from her as he spoke.

"It was your day off, remember? I didn't realize at first that you were the sheriff. Liam just introduced you as his sister. Other than tonight, I'm pretty sure it was the only time you talked to me in anything other than an official capacity."

Before Serena could respond, Clay shook his head. "I'm sorry. That doesn't even make sense."

It actually did make sense. He was right about the first day they'd met. It'd been different, more casual. They'd talked about the baseball game on television, small town living as compared to city living, stupid things. The types of things you talked about with friends, maybe a date.

She'd spent every day since making sure she put her job between them. The more she thought about it, the more she realized she didn't really know why she'd done it. Was she letting an old mistake distort her judgment? Or maybe she was scared of getting hurt again.

She placed her hand on his cheek. "Can I tell you a secret?"

He smiled a little. "I think it's your turn."

"I'm new at this sheriff thing. It's pretty all consuming."

The statement darkened his eyes a little and she realized her words weren't coming out right.

"I'm trying to work on that," she added.

The smile returned now. "Do you think I might be able to help you?"

She should decline. She was in the middle of what was quickly starting to look like the first murder spree in town history. It was no time to be mixing business with pleasure – especially with the guy who was on top of the town's most wanted list.

But the words came out before she could stop them. "I think I'd like that a lot."

He grinned broadly. "Are you off-duty?"

The question caught her off guard. "Yes," she said, meeting his eyes. "Shane will call if there's a problem, but I'm done for the day."

Clay leaned closer, running his hand over her cheek, down her neck. "Good, because I've been dying to do this all day."

He moved slowly, giving her every opportunity to back away, but once his lips touched hers the experience was anything but slow. Serena's cluttered mind immediately cleared and all at once it felt as if there was nothing at all except for him, with her, in this moment.

She had no idea how long it had been when he pulled away, but she knew it wasn't long enough.

"I guess you're feeling okay," Serena said, clumsily, as she tried to remember how to stand up without help.

Clay laughed and took her hand in his. "This is totally the wrong time for this, but I had to."

She squeezed his hand tightly. "I'd be lying if I said I minded."

"Does that mean you'd say yes if I asked you out on an actual date?"

She couldn't remember the last time she'd gone on a date. In fact, she'd pretty much given up on the idea of ever going out on one again.

"I think a date would be fantastic."

He leaned in and kissed her again, this time more gently. "Is tomorrow out?"

The question was a reminder of what was really going on in the world, things that were far more important than her going out on a silly date. Clay seemed to see the change.

"Ah, there it is – the serious face that scared me so thoroughly that I couldn't work up the nerve to ask you out."

"I'm sorry…" she began.

He held up a hand for her to stop. "You have a murderer to catch. You should probably be focused on that."

"I don't usually…"

Again, before she could finish Clay stopped her. "You don't usually have homicidal maniacs running around town? Well, that's good to hear, because this is a pretty small town. I would hate to hear murders happen on a regular basis."

Serena searched his face for some clue that this was bothering him and was hugely surprised to see there was no anger or judgment there. "You're a pretty unique guy, Clay Drayton."

He grinned. "And you look like you think that's a good thing. This may be my lucky day."

Though it seemed an asinine thing to think, in light of the way her day had begun, Serena had to agree.

~ 23 ~

The cheerful voice of a DJ invaded Serena's dreams. He was telling her that it was another beautiful day with clear skies. The chill in her room told Serena that the voice was leaving out the fact that clear skies in the fall typically meant cold days. Clearly today was no exception to the rule. Knowing how cold her wood floors would be when her feet touched the ground, she longed to hit the snooze bar and pull the covers over her head.

As the voice gave way to an old song about lost loves and heartbreak, Serena wiped the sleep from her eyes and accepted reality. Buster, who was stretched out next to her, opened one eye in disgust and sighed dramatically when she climbed out of bed.

Serena ran her hand over his soft coat. "You're on duty this morning too, buddy, so you'd better shake the sleep off."

Buster ignored her and curled into a tight ball. He was snoring again within a minute.

When she was ready to head out, the dog reluctantly climbed out of bed, stretching the entire way. It wasn't until she told him they were going in the car that she got the response she needed. Despite the hour, Serena smiled at his exuberance. It was nice to see one of them was happy to face the day.

She arrived at the hospital site with several thermoses full of coffee and enough paper cups for anyone who might want a kick in the butt before they headed out. She wasn't surprised to see her father's car was there already, nor was she surprised he was walking the perimeter of the hospital, clearly looking for whatever they'd missed.

The moment he was given the chance, Buster bounded out of the car and directly for his favorite man in the whole world. If William hadn't heard him coming, Buster would have knocked him flying.

Leaving the thermoses in the car for now, Serena pulled out two thermal mugs – one black and one with sugar – and she joined him.

"You know, I could have you arrested for disturbing a crime scene. You aren't supposed to cross the tape," she pointed out.

William accepted the coffee she offered, but ignored the advice. "I'd love a look inside."

"Liam would kill me if he heard I let you into a crime scene, especially this crime scene."

"Come on. You got the place all cleared out, right? There's nothing there. Nothing to see. I think the old ticker can handle walking through an abandoned hospital."

Buster looked up at her with plaintive eyes, clearly making the case for his buddy.

"Strap him onto his leash. We go in quick and we're back out here before Hayley arrives."

William took his comrade's leash and fished a flashlight out of his coat pocket.

She glared at the flashlight. "Couldn't you at least pretend you didn't know I was going to let you in the scene?"

He laughed. "You showed up twenty minutes early. You were planning on this as much as I was."

"I have to set things up before people arrive. I had to be here early."

"Yeah," he challenged, "you don't have anything to set up until Hayley gets here. And if I know you, and I'm pretty sure I do, Hayley won't be showing up for another twenty minutes."

Serena smiled, despite herself. "I don't do everything exactly the way you did," she insisted.

William grinned at that. "Honey, you're doing plenty your own way. You really want to waste more time discussing it?"

Serena shook her head. Of course he was right, but she had no intention of admitting it. Without further discussion, she led the way through the loose board and into the dark hallway beyond.

They came to the end of the hallway about a minute later. "It's to the right here and then it's the first room on the right," she explained.

Before she could turn the corner, Buster let out a low growl. His eyes were fixed on the corridor to their right.

Serena had her gun out in an instant. She hadn't heard anything, but Buster had far better ears than she did. Using her flashlight to site the gun, she scanned the hallway, but saw nothing.

Knowing he was about to be ordered away from the situation, William firmly stood his ground, and tightened his hold on Buster. He leaned in and whispered, "If you think I'm leaving you in here by yourself then you're a moron. We'll follow you."

He switched off his flashlight and slid it into his back pocket. And as he did, Serena saw him reach beneath his coat and pull out a handgun.

"You brought your gun?" she whispered.

William's voice was muted, too low to be heard by anyone but her. "Of course I brought my gun. Now, move. Buster and I will hold back a little, but only a little."

Though she wanted to argue the point, Serena knew she would lose. Her father was the only person on earth more stubborn than she was. And, what was worse, he was right; she needed backup and he and Buster were all she had.

The beam of her flashlight lit only the middle of the long hallway. She swung it to the left and the right, chasing away many of the shadows, but she really couldn't see anything more than fifty feet away. It was lunacy to continue on, but she did. She didn't really have any choice.

Buster's growling had abated, but she could sense his continued tension.

When they reached the first door on the right, Serena was not at all surprised to find it closed. Of course, it shouldn't have been; they'd left it open. But that room was the key to everything, why wouldn't it be the key to this too?

She cursed under her breath and flattened up against the wall. Her father dropped back further, sensing what she'd discovered. She kicked the door open.

And waited.

After a full second, she swung her flashlight and gun inside. The light bounced back in her face, reflecting off the surgical table. It was a moment before her eyes adjusted, but even when they did she couldn't believe what she was seeing.

In the middle of the table was a human heart. Sitting. Waiting. Taunting.

~ 24 ~

Serena's brain screamed every curse she knew as she stared at the scene. Knowing now that they'd certainly scared off the killer, she called it in. The night girl was still on, and she wasn't thrilled to have to call the guys in early. Serena had to bite her tongue not to tell her off.

She signed off and looked at her father, who was standing in the room with her now.

"How's Buster?" she asked.

William looked at her as if she'd completely lost her mind. "You're really asking me about the dog?"

"I'm asking you if the dog, who seemed to sense someone was here, seems to still sense someone is here. Because I'm thinking the killer heard us coming and ran off. That's what Buster heard. That's why he growled. So, I'm asking, how's the dog?"

Serena swung the beam of her flashlight in Buster's general direction. Though his eyes reflected green in the bright light, he otherwise looked completely normal. Sitting, tongue hanging out, almost smiling, clearly proud of his ability to warn and protect.

She rubbed his neck and praised him.

"You want to check the rest of the hospital?" William asked.

Of course she wanted to check the hospital, but she couldn't, not without backup. Someone had been here minutes ago. He was either gone or lying in wait somewhere. It was suicide to go after him without support. She might have taken the risk herself, but she wasn't taking it with her father or Buster.

"We can't leave the scene until the others get here."

William knew she was lying, but he was respectful enough not to call her on it. It was clear that he, too, was unwilling to risk Buster's well-being.

"Shane was on tonight. He should be here in five, ten minutes. Riley and Jake will be a bit longer."

Not particularly wanting to discuss the matter further, Serena ran her flashlight over the room and then back to the table.

Now that she was able to look more carefully, she wasn't sure it was a heart on the table. It looked similar to what they had seen before, but the heart had been one single organ. The mass on the table now was something different. There were large pieces of tissue. At least a few of them. Collectively they looked about the same size and shape as the original heart. Frankly, they looked awfully similar. But without better light it was hard to figure out what she was really seeing.

"What the hell is that?" William asked.

Serena shook her head. "I wish I knew."

As she'd expected, Shane arrived quickly. Riley got there only a couple minutes later. Serena left Shane and her father at the scene, waiting for Jake. She asked her father to start processing the crime scene, while she and Riley searched the hospital.

It didn't take long. They were familiar with the halls now, the rooms. Serena couldn't remember all the details from their prior search, but at first glance, nothing looked any different. She wished they'd photographed everything after the original crime – then she could have really compared.

Not surprisingly, they found an empty hospital. That was it. She couldn't have been more pissed. She'd had him within her reach, and she'd hesitated. If she got the chance again, she wouldn't make the same mistake.

Though Riley didn't say much as they searched, his silence told her that she wasn't the only one who thought she'd screwed up.

When they returned to the scene, they found the coach's lights back in the room, illuminating everything she'd never wanted to see again. Jake was taking pictures, Shane was taking notes, and her father was supervising.

Knowing William had the deputies under control, Serena stood in the doorway and calmly surveyed. The scene was so similar to their original crime scene that it was difficult to see the ways it differed, but it did. Serena knew the difference might prove significant eventually, so she analyzed the scene slowly.

The table was glossy now, shining and reflecting the lights. No fingerprint dust. None of the streaks of blood that had remained the last time she was in this room. And unlike their first scene, there was no new blood. No pools on the table or the floor.

The psycho cleaned the table before placing this new organ on it. What the hell was that about?

William's voice brought her out of her thoughts. "Hey, Doc, thanks for getting here so fast."

Serena looked up to see Clay, who was standing in the doorway of the old operating room clearly trying to shake the sense of déjà vu.

"We've got another one," she explained.

He looked at her for a moment and asked, "Can I get closer?"

She nodded. "Go ahead. Please don't move anything yet."

Clay hovered around the table for a few minutes, looking at the organ from several different angles. Shaking his head, he indicated that Riley and Serena should join him in the hall.

In a low voice he said, "I don't know who knows about what happened with the heart last night. So, I didn't want to say much in there. That could be the same organ."

After the morning's surprises, she hadn't thought things could get any stranger. She'd been wrong.

"That's a heart?" she asked.

Clay nodded. "That's not just a heart. That's what a heart looks like after an autopsy."

"What do you mean?" Serena asked.

"I don't just check the exterior of the heart. It needs to be sectioned, cut into pieces. There's more to it, but essentially, what you're seeing there is a heart post-autopsy."

"So it's the same heart?" Riley asked. "Why the hell would somebody steal the heart only to leave it here again?"

Clay shrugged. "It may not be the same heart. I'm saying that's a heart. It's in the same condition as the heart that was stolen from me yesterday."

"Can you check to see if it's the same heart?" Serena asked, starting to feel more confident that it was.

"I can do a couple things with it. I may not be able to say for sure it's the same heart, but I may be able to tell you it's not. Obviously, the state labs can run DNA against the samples from the original heart that weren't stolen."

The idea that the killer might return the heart to its original spot as if the placement was some kind of a ritual was disturbing. But, unfortunately, it sounded exactly like the type of thing their killer might do.

"Once they're done with the scene, please take the heart and check it. I want Shane to stay with you at all times. I don't know what the hell this guy wants with this heart, but I don't need you getting jumped again."

Riley seemed bored with the whole conversation. It was clear to Serena that he was not at all bothered by the notion that some lunatic would steal the heart to return it to the same seemingly random abandoned hospital room.

She looked at Riley. "Can you check on things outside? We have people who have shown up for a search today. We still have to do that. I'll be ready to go in fifteen minutes."

Once she was alone with Clay, she said, "Do you think it's the same heart?"

"I'm not sure of anything. Once I get it back to the lab I'll be able to tell more. I'll check the measurements and compare the samples."

"Thanks." She glanced around, making sure they were alone, before she asked, "How's your head?"

"You are a mother hen, you know that?"

"I'm the sheriff. You have to keep me updated on your condition. It's important."

"So, you're asking in your official capacity?" he teased.

Serena smiled. "Not even a little."

"It's actually a lot better today," he replied.

"I'm glad to hear it." She allowed herself a moment to look at him, and a half a second to remember what it felt like to have him close to her, but it was all she could spare. "I'm afraid I have to get out there for the search. Buster's waiting with Hayley."

A look of confusion spread across his face. "Buster?"

It was going to be a little strange to have a relationship with someone she hadn't known since birth. She suspected she was going to like it. "My dog."

"The dog, huh? Big scary guy?"

Knowing Buster, it was the most ridiculous notion in the world. "Maybe you'll have to stop by sometime and meet him. I'm sure he'd be interested to know I was spending time with you last night instead of him. He's the jealous type."

"I may take you up on that."

"I hope you do." Knowing she'd spent more than her allotted minute on this conversation, Serena reluctantly stepped away. "I really do have to go. Clay, I am serious when I say be careful. I don't know what kind of crazy person does this, but I sure don't want to find out what they'll do to you if they try to go after the heart again."

He promised to be careful and Serena reluctantly left him in the dark hallway. She found her father still orchestrating the crime scene.

Reading her mind, he said, "I got this. You have to direct the search. We'll have everything laid out for you at the station when you get back."

"Thanks, Dad. I appreciate it."

In a low voice he added, "When did all that start?"

She stared for a moment, not wanting to believe she understood what he was saying.

"With you and the doc?" he added.

She glanced over at her deputies, who were completely focused on the crime scene.

William laid a hand on her shoulder. "They're good kids, but they aren't bright enough to realize I'm whispering stuff they can't hear."

"It's not really even a thing," she explained.

Her father shook his head. "Oh, it's a thing. You go on. We'll talk about it later."

"Dad, don't…"

He interrupted before she could finish. He cast a predatory glance Clay's way, before he said, "Don't you worry about me, honey. You take care of the search. I'll take care of the doc."

~ 25 ~

Serena's eyes were still adjusting to the brightness as she slipped under the old crime scene tape. That was why she almost ran into Norton Finwick.

Armed with a pad and pencil, he had no intention of letting her pass without answering questions. "What's going on in there, Sheriff?"

The question caught her almost as off guard as his presence had, but she thought she was mostly able to conceal her surprise. "It's a crime scene, Norton. I'm pretty sure you know that already."

His pursed lips and disgusted expression spoke volumes. "It's an old crime scene. You have two deputies in there and the town coroner. And I don't think I see your father out here anywhere, but isn't that his truck?"

Damn Norton and his attention to detail. "It's an active investigation. In fact, we're pretty much working 24-7 trying to figure out what's going on. That means

Riley and I are doing the search this morning, while Shane and Jake review the scene with my father. Riley and I worked the crime scene originally. I thought it might be a good idea to bring in fresh eyes. Maybe they'll see something I didn't."

Serena was surprised by how easily the story came to her. She was a far better liar than she would have expected.

"There's something else going on in there. I saw Shane pull up and run in. Something's going on."

"What the hell were you doing here at that hour?"

"I was doing my job. I watch. I report. People deserve to know the truth. What's going on, Sheriff? Are you covering something up?"

The accusation caught Serena completely off guard. "Covering something up? What would I be covering up? Jesus, Norton, we're reviewing the scene. That's all. Your overactive imagination is going to cause panic."

Without another word, Serena turned on her heel and joined the group gathered for the search. She knew she hadn't completely diffused things, but she knew people well enough to know that continuing the conversation was going to get her into trouble in the long run.

Hayley had already broken everyone off into three groups. Serena was impressed by her quick thinking, actually. The original plan had been four groups – one officer in each. Obviously that was no longer the plan. Without any instruction, she'd separated everyone out with Riley in one group, Serena in another, and Liam in the third.

She'd put Liam with a group that included Jack Tinsdale and his dog. Jack and Liam would make an excellent duo to lead that team.

It seemed Riley would have Norton with him, which spared Serena from being interrogated for the length of the search.

It looked like she and Buster were getting the all-star team of Lucas Denton and Avery Sinclair, along with Tom Henderson and his son Reece. On one hand she had her chance to talk to Reece with his father around; on the other, she could only do it under Avery's watchful eye, which pretty much cancelled out any potential benefit.

After the dogs had been given an opportunity to check the scent, they all headed out. Despite his odd stature and his dubious guarding skills, Buster was a champion tracker. He led them into the deep woods that surrounded the hospital.

They hadn't gotten far before Buster led them to the place that confirmed her suspicions about Lucas and Reece. With a bark of excitement, the dog crashed through some bushes and into the site of an old campfire. Beer cans and several used condoms littered the circle.

The smirks on Lucas's and Reece's faces were enough confirmation for Serena. She was wondering how she was going to deal with the situation with Avery Sinclair breathing down her neck, when Avery did the job for her.

"You boys know about this site?" he accused.

It seemed Avery was less opposed to interrogation when there was an issue of his daughter's boyfriend and used condoms.

"No, sir," Lucas said far too quickly.

Tom Henderson followed up. "Reece, this is no laughing matter. Is this your mess? Have you boys been out here?"

She watched as the smile faded from Reece's face and he dropped his head. "Yes, sir," he admitted.

Lucas spun on him, dumbfounded and clearly furious.

Reece only dug his hands deeper into his pockets. "We hang out here a lot. It's just a place to get away."

Reece's father kicked a beer can in the direction of one of the used condoms. "Hang out? Is that what you're calling it these days?"

Avery looked even more furious. He smacked Lucas across the back of the head.

But Tom was still in full control of the discussion. His eyes darted between Reece and Lucas. "Did either of you tell the sheriff about the time you spent out here?"

Serena didn't dare speak. She felt as if saying anything would only serve to remind them they might not want to have this conversation in front of her.

Reece looked between her and his father. "Sheriff, we came here a bunch of times, but I never saw anybody around but us. I would have told you if I saw anything. I swear."

"Were you only here at night, or were you around during the day, too?" Serena asked.

The look on Reece's face told her that he was so happy she wasn't yelling at him that he'd tell her anything she wanted to know. "A bunch of different times of day."

Serena nodded. "Why did you move the party up to the hospital? This looks like a pretty nice place back here."

Reece's eyes shifted to Lucas, and his hesitation told Serena all she needed to know.

Tom Henderson, however, demanded a more complete answer. "Answer the question," he commanded.

"We all, um, we all talked about it and we thought it'd be a fun time," Reece replied.

The eyes of every adult turned to Lucas, all wondering if he'd tell the truth. No one was surprised when he didn't. He merely stood silently.

Serena looked between Tom and his son. This was probably her last chance to get an honest answer to this question. "Reece, was that the only time you were up at the old hospital?"

He shuffled his feet. "Lucas and I went up there the afternoon before you guys found that heart. He'd seen a loose board on one of the windows, and we wanted to go inside to check it out."

"What did you see inside?"

Reece met her eyes. "It was crazy dark in there. Like a haunted house. I didn't really see much of anything. We, um, walked around a little. And that was it, we came back out. I was glad to get out of there."

"That was the only time you were there?" she asked, though she felt certain she knew the answer.

Reece nodded.

Her final question was the least likely to generate an honest answer, but she had to ask. She needed the whole story.

"Who's been out here with you boys?"

Reece's expression was plain – it was one thing to tell the truth, it was another to sell out your friends.

His father saw the same thing Serena did. He was less sympathetic.

"I'd worry less about your friends and more about how much trouble you're already in. I'm thinking one week for every beer can out here. Care to add to that?"

By Serena's count, Reece would be grounded until spring.

Again Reece looked at Lucas. The glare he received in response told Serena their friendship was already over. She hoped Reece saw the same thing. He looked again at his father before he turned his attention to Serena.

"It's just the group of us – me, Lucas, Brad, Stu," he explained.

Serena almost laughed at his decision to omit the girls from the story. "That's it?" she asked.

Reece's eyes grew wide, and everything in his manner revealed the lie. "Yeah, only us."

"And the condoms?" she asked.

Reece's head dropped and Serena was very pleased he was a far worse liar than Lucas or Andi.

"Yeah, I'm sorry. The girls too. Tracey and Marcy. Suzy's been up here with us lately."

Serena noticed he omitted Andi, but she had no interest in getting him in any more trouble than he already was. There was one more question that had to be asked, and she hated to do it.

"What about Lori-Ann?"

Reece looked up, clearly surprised she'd known enough to ask. "Tinsdale?"

Serena smiled. "Yeah. Did Brad bring her up here?"

Reece shook his head. "Andi and Tracey don't really like Lori-Ann."

"So that's a no?"

He looked to Lucas for a moment. "Brad wasn't allowed to bring her around," he said finally.

Serena considered the response. All in all, his story made sense. In the end, though, she had to wonder how important any of it was.

~ 26 ~

By the time Serena made it back to the station she was exhausted and frustrated. Other than the hangout in the woods, the search had been entirely pointless. No body. No sign of a body. No sign of much of anything.

Of course, it had been a long shot. She'd known that. But as far as she could tell it was the only shot she had.

She walked in with Riley, who kept looking at her as if he'd known all along that the search had been a bad idea. She was growing so tired of his smug look that she was considering punching him just to wipe it off his face.

That was the sleep deprivation talking. Or at least she hoped it was.

She was pleased to see Clay talking to Hayley when they arrived. Hopefully it meant he had something for her.

Seeing her, he held up a file. "I have some results I think we should discuss."

Serena nodded, trying to keep her hope in check. There had to be something in the forensic evidence. Didn't there?

"Hayley, who else is here?"

"Shane, Jake and Sheriff, um I mean, Mr. Marlowe, are in the conference room," Hayley replied.

Serena knew they all still thought of him as Sheriff Marlowe. Which inevitably left her without much of an identity, but she tried not to think too much about it.

"Doc, why don't you come with us? We need to have a big sit down and run through all we have."

Clay looked a little apprehensive at the prospect. His sidelong glance at Riley told her the reason for his concern.

Having had more than enough from him already today, Serena barked at Riley, "Tell the others to get the room ready. I'll be back in two minutes. I want everyone ready to go."

Serena ignored the slight eyebrow raise she received from Hayley, and she was pleased Riley complied without comment.

More gently, she turned to Hayley and said, "Do you think we could possibly get a fresh pot of coffee and some cups for the conference room?"

Hayley hurried off, leaving Serena and Clay alone at the front desk.

"Rough day?" he asked.

She only shook her head in disgust. "Please tell me you have some interesting stuff. Something helpful. Anything."

Clay offered her a tired smile. "I actually do have some interesting stuff. I don't know if it's helpful. But it's sure interesting."

Serena led Clay to the back conference room hoping like hell his interesting information might prove useful.

She found everyone milling about the room. It looked more like a murder room now. Crime scene photos were tacked to boards. The timeline on the heart was written on one white board. The timeline for Daisy Roman's abduction written on another. On a third was the beginnings of a timeline for the heart they'd just found.

William stood when she entered and grabbed his coat. Before she could say anything he slipped out of the conference room. She didn't catch up with him until he was halfway down the hall.

"Where are you going?" she asked.

William turned and laid a heavy hand on her shoulder. "This is your party, honey. I'm going on home. I'm probably going to read that piece of crap paper Norton writes and then I'll take Buster out for his afternoon walk."

She started to protest, but he stopped her. "You and me can talk things through. That's between you and me. Every man in that room was my deputy longer than they've been yours. I can't be in there with them. It'll screw the whole thing up for you."

"I think we can use all the help we can get," she replied.

William smiled. "You know my old man retired pretty late on. When his hip got bad, and he needed that cane, that was when he finally decided to hang it up."

Serena stared blankly at her father. She knew all this. He knew that.

"His mind was still sharp, though. So, he hung around a lot. Wanted to spend time with the deputies. Spend time with me. I was okay with it at first. Actually liked it a lot. It's a tough job making all the decisions. It was nice to share the load. But truth is, there's only one sheriff. Only one person can make the decisions. It's not a democracy. Can't be. And so long as my father stuck around, that one person was him. It didn't matter who had the badge. Didn't matter who'd been elected. I resented it until the day he died."

"Dad, I didn't know..." Serena began.

William shook his head. "No, you didn't need to until now. Serena, I'm going home. There's only one person who runs that room. You go do your job. Those boys need you."

She couldn't resist wrapping her father in a tight hug. He squeezed her back only briefly. Then he looked at her sternly. "You have work to do."

Serena watched her father walk away, almost overwhelmed with respect and fear. She'd read about how to run a homicide investigation. She'd watched when her father ran the investigation into a string of petty robberies a few years back. But this was another thing entirely.

She pushed the fear as far back as she could and went in to rejoin her men. There was no room for fear. She had to do this. There was no other choice.

~ 27 ~

Once everyone was settled with much needed coffee within reach, Serena yielded the floor to their coroner.

Clay addressed the group cautiously. It was obvious he would have far preferred to have submitted a written report and gone back to his office.

"I took tissue samples of the heart we found this morning and compared them to the samples of the heart we found originally. Between that and the various measurements we took of the heart itself, I'm confident this is the same heart."

Clay glanced around the table, looking for a response. Serena wanted to offer him one, but she was at a loss. This had always been a strange crime. It was only getting stranger.

When no one spoke, Clay continued, "The heart is back here at the station now. It can be transported to the state offices whenever you're ready."

Jake was quick to volunteer and Serena was even quicker to oblige. Getting out of town would do him good. Shane agreed to accompany him, leaving her and Riley to do the heavy lifting.

Once that was settled, Clay continued with his report. "I was able to look more closely at the blood you found on the floor of the room at the original crime scene. It came from two different people."

Riley spoke before Serena had the chance. "If there are two victims, then why the fuck is there just one heart?"

Clay shrugged. "I'm only saying there were two blood types."

"Can you tell if there was a lot of one type and only a little of another?" Serena asked, trying to decode the odd clue.

"Actually, yeah," he replied, seeming impressed with the question. "I'm still working on that, but it looks like there is far more of one type than the other."

"Which could mean the blood came from our killer or a second victim who suffered less serious injuries," Serena suggested.

Clay nodded. "Also the blood type I found more frequently in the pool matched the heart tissue."

"Well it makes sense that the person whose heart was cut out would bleed a bit more," Riley snarled.

Before Serena could glare at her deputy for jumping to conclusions, Clay continued, "The blood is probably from the same victim as the heart, but we won't be entirely sure without the DNA match. I just know the smaller quantity of blood was not from the same victim as the heart."

Serena knew the DNA would probably take more time than they had. Or, really, she hoped that by the time they got the results back from the state labs, they had long since caught their killer.

"Anything more on the animals?" she asked.

"The first animal was killed about six months ago and the others followed after. There's no pattern as to when each type of animal was killed. Missy and I suspect he merely used whatever he could gain access to."

Clay let the conclusion hang over them all for a minute before he said, "That's all we have at this point. And though I still have a couple things I'm looking at, I'd expect this is all I'm going to have for you unless you find me a body or something. With everything else, we'll have to wait for the state labs. Most significantly, I'm curious to hear if they agree with my belief that the heart isn't likely Daisy Roman's."

Serena considered dismissing Clay before she moved on with the meeting, but she decided against it. Maybe he'd see something the rest of them didn't.

She let Shane and Jake run through their pictures and notes of the second crime scene. As she'd expected, they'd found nothing at all. Just the heart. Placed neatly on the table.

It was about a half an hour later when Shane and Jake left for the state labs, leaving Riley, Serena and Clay at the conference table. She was trying to figure out exactly what to do next when there was a knock on the conference room door.

She looked up to see Coach Fletcher peering into the room. "I hope I'm not interrupting anything. Sheriff, I wanted to talk to you about the lights. One of the boys told me they weren't outside the hospital when he was there to help with the search. I was hoping maybe you were done with them."

Serena stood quickly, silently cursing Hayley's inability to understand that people from outside were not allowed in the conference room during an investigation. "Coach, I'm sorry, I'm going to need you to step out. Why don't we go across the hall to my office?"

Riley stood also and glared at her. "For Pete's sake, it's Coach. You let this guy sit in on the freakin' meeting," he added, jabbing a finger at Clay.

"He's the freakin' coroner," she snapped back, mocking his tone. She immediately regretted letting her exhaustion and bad temper get the better of the situation. She needed to focus on getting the coach out of her conference room.

She looked back at Coach Fletcher and realized she was already too late. He was focused on the crime scene photos, completely lost in them.

Without taking his eyes off the boards, he asked, "Is that a second heart?"

Riley started to respond, but Serena cut him off with a vicious look. Turning her attention back to Coach Fletcher, she answered honestly, "No, it's the same one."

Before he could ask anything else, she grabbed his arm. "Coach, I have a couple questions for you, actually. I'm glad you're here. Follow me over to my office."

Once she had him sitting in her office, she slipped back into the conference room. Locking eyes with Riley, she said, "I need you out on patrol, now. Check in on anyone who you can think of who is elderly or infirmed or maybe doesn't have anyone checking up on them."

Riley started to protest, but she cut him off. "You and I will discuss this later. And you better fucking hope I'm in a better mood than I am now."

Her deputy skulked off without a word, though he did manage to throw a look at Clay that telegraphed very clearly his opinion that this was all his fault.

"I'm sorry about that," she offered after Riley had left.

"You're sorry your deputy thinks I'm a killer?" he replied.

Serena shook her head with resigned humor. "This is as much about me as it is about you. Probably more about me, actually. I'm sorry you're getting caught in the crossfire."

As was so typical of Clay, he didn't seem bothered by the situation. "Do you need me for anything else?"

On impulse, Serena made a decision she hoped was a smart one and not just a way to punish Riley. "Would you have dinner with me tonight?"

"You don't have to squeeze me in to make up for him."

She laughed uneasily. "I was actually thinking of more of a working dinner."

Clay shook his head and smiled. "You still think I can discuss psych profiling with you? I am entirely unqualified to do that."

Serena smiled at that. "It's either you or Riley."

She was pleased to see him laugh. "I see your dilemma. What time? Six? Seven?"

"How about six-thirty at my place? We could eat here, but…"

"But Riley would accuse you of sharing secrets with the enemy," he finished for her.

"At a minimum."

With the plans set, Serena went to her office to deal with Coach Fletcher and try to find more stones to look under.

~ 28 ~

Coach Fletcher was sitting when Serena got back to her office. Though his legs were crossed casually, and his body language seemed to indicate he was fine, there was something in his eyes – a distance, a fear. Serena imagined the same could be said for most of them these days.

"Coach, I'm sorry to keep you waiting," she said in her best calm, cheerful, in-control voice, as she slipped behind her desk.

He smiled, again very casually, but the light didn't touch his eyes. "I imagine you've been pretty busy the last couple days. I'm sorry to have interrupted your meeting."

Hoping to repair a little of the damage done by her own short temper, Serena waved off the apology. "Coach, you are welcome here any time at all. How are you doing with all this?"

He sighed. "You worry, of course. Everybody worries."

Though she knew it was an honest answer, Serena didn't want to give it any more thought than she had to. The pressure was more than enough already. "Missed you at the meeting last night."

Coach shook his head. "Lauren wasn't feeling up to it, and with all that's going on, I couldn't leave her alone."

Serena wished she could tell him that he didn't need to worry, but it would have been a lie.

"Is she feeling better? I'm surprised you aren't home with her," Serena said.

The coach raised a graying eyebrow and chuckled. "Lauren never lets me stay under foot for too long. Even makes me teach summer school. I putter around too much, at least that's what she says. Says I take things apart just so I've got something to put back together."

Serena laughed. Though she and the coach had never been that close, she suspected that was about right. "I guess you didn't take the day off?"

He shook his head. "Nope, not allowed. I have a couple free periods today right around lunch time. Thought I'd come over here and ask about the lights. Guess Lauren's right, I can't stay still real long."

"Oh, right, the lights, we're still using them. We brought them back inside the hospital this morning so we could look the scene over again."

"What made you go back in there?"

Serena smiled. "Gotta keep checking the crime scene, Coach. It's where everything starts. Maybe it's how we find our way to the end."

Hoping to get him off the topic of her investigation, she asked, "How are the kids at the high school seeming?"

"You know high school kids. Not much bothers them."

Though she was a little worried that asking might lead to questions she didn't want to answer, Serena couldn't resist. "Did you have Lucas Denton and Reece Henderson in your history class last spring?"

The coach gave her a funny look, but he answered, "Of course. I have all the juniors. You know that."

"So, Brad and Stu, too?"

He nodded.

"How'd they do?"

Now it really looked like he wanted to ask her what was going on. Serena gave him credit for just answering. "Reece is a good student. Real good. He did very well in the class. No surprise there. Lucas did too, which was a bit more of a surprise."

"Guess he liked all those dramatic stories you tell, Coach," Serena suggested.

He smiled. "The boys tend to."

"Who were your best students last year?"

He stared at her for a moment before he answered. "The usual suspects were my standouts – Reece, Andi Sinclair, Lori-Ann Tinsdale. Lucas did well, for Lucas, but he was still only average. I'm not sure where you're going with all this, but I'll add that nobody else stood out – one way or the other. With the exception of Lucas, the kids did how you'd expect them to do."

Serena nodded, unsure what the hell she planned to do with the information.

"Since I'm guessing I'm not allowed to ask any questions about the case, you gotta give me one freebie," Coach Fletcher said.

Serena smiled at him. "You can ask whatever you want. I may not answer, but you can ask."

Fletcher laughed. "You're just like your father sometimes, you know that?"

She was certain she'd never received a better compliment.

His smile faded a little before he asked, "You and Riley back together?"

Serena wasn't sure what question she'd been ready for, but that wasn't it. She bit back a laugh. "No. I can assure you the answer to that question will always be no."

"Glad to hear it," he said, rising to his feet. "You're a good girl, Serena."

Serena knew the words that were left unsaid, that had been left unsaid by her father and her brother when she and Riley had been dating – *he is not a good boy*. She wished she'd seen the truth back then, but she thought she saw something the others didn't see. She'd been wrong about that. Really wrong.

"I was a little worried when I saw the way you two were fighting in there earlier. Looked familiar."

Almost five years later and it still felt familiar, but Serena didn't volunteer that information. Instead, she stood to walk him out. "You worried about me, Coach?" she asked with a smile.

He patted her shoulder kindly. "I suspect William and Liam are worrying about you plenty."

~ 29 ~

With Riley checking on any possible missing persons, Serena decided she needed to track the only other lead they had – the animals. Though Missy and Clay had determined how and when the animals had been killed, Serena was left to wonder where they came from in the first place. That meant a trip to Missy's office.

The office was crowded, probably because Missy had moved so many appointments over the past few days. In the large waiting area, there was an ancient beagle and a very enthusiastic-looking lab.

On the other side of the room was Madison Sinclair, with the family cat mewing in a carrier on her lap. Avery's wife had her head down, as if she was keeping a close watch on the cat, but Serena knew people well enough to know there was far more to it.

Serena was unable to resist the challenge. "Madison, good to see you," she said amiably, taking the seat next to her.

Madison looked up cautiously and smiled. Serena knew she was far too polite to avoid a conversation, no matter what Avery had told her. "How are you, Sheriff?"

Serena smiled. "I've been hoping to run into you actually. How is Andi doing? The trouble the other night must have been hard on her."

"Oh, she's been so brave. She wouldn't say a word to me about what she saw, but I overheard what she told Avery. It's so very awful. Who would do a thing like that? I mean, I just worry so much about her."

Serena nodded. "Of course. If there is anything at all I can do to help, I hope you'll be in touch."

Madison seemed to suddenly remember her orders. She stiffened a little and said, "I think it's really more of a family matter."

"Whatever you need," Serena agreed. Though she didn't make a move to leave, Serena didn't say another word. She didn't have any questions for Madison, but she was hoping she might volunteer something useful.

Unfortunately, only the cat filled the silence.

"He's just a kitten," Madison explained, as if she felt it was in poor taste for the cat to make such a ruckus.

It wasn't exactly the filler Serena had hoped for. "Really? How long have you had him?"

"About six months now. We got him after Buttons disappeared."

"Buttons?"

"I guess you wouldn't know. We had Buttons for five years. Every now and then he'd wander off for a few days. Last spring he wandered off and didn't come back. We put up signs, but we never found him. Naturally, Andi was devastated. Avery got her this little one to fill the void. He looks like Buttons – so we call him Buttons, too. He's much more of a talker than Buttons was."

"Can I see him?"

Madison smiled and turned the carrier in Serena's direction. "Of course."

Up at the front of the carrier was a tiny gray face with brilliant blue eyes.

"He really does look just like Buttons, right down to the white fur on his chest," Madison cooed.

Serena was peering into the carrier when she heard Missy's voice. "Hello, Sheriff, I hear you need a quick minute of my time."

She quickly wished Madison well and followed Missy back to her office. "Thanks for seeing me."

Missy smiled, closing the door behind them. "I'm guessing it's important."

"I was thinking about the animals this butcher cut up. Any thoughts on where they could have come from?"

Missy leaned back against her desk. "I've been wondering about that. Of course, there are missing animals – there always are – but I haven't noticed a steep rise in them."

"Could it be that people aren't reporting them?"

"We have patients who stop coming all the time. Never mind the people who don't bring their pets in to see me in the first place. It's more than possible that people's pets are going missing and they just aren't reporting them. You know people in this town. I bet you could make some pretty accurate guesses about who would notice their dog is missing and who wouldn't."

That had been the answer Serena had feared, but there was still one question she hoped might be answered. "In the bodies we gathered, was there a gray cat, five or more years old, with white fur on his chest? I think male, but I'm not certain."

Missy's brow wrinkled in confusion. "Where are you getting that from?"

"Was there?"

"It's hard to say for sure. You saw how bad the decomp was on the older bodies. But, yeah, one of the earlier bodies, there was a cat who could fit that description."

Serena shook her head. Interesting. But what did it mean? "The Sinclairs lost a cat fitting that description about six months ago."

Missy stared at her, seemingly trying to digest the information. "It's not necessarily their cat. I mean, that kind of general description, it's hard to say for sure."

Of course she was right, but it was an extraordinary coincidence.

~ 30 ~

When Serena made it back to the station, Norton Finwick was lurking in front, clearly waiting for her return.

"You know, you can go sit inside if you're waiting for me. Hayley might even get you a cup of coffee." It was all she could do not to add – *that way you won't be skulking outside like some kind of freak.*

Norton shoved his stringy hair out of his eyes. "I was waiting for you. I have no interest in coffee. I wanted to give you another chance to answer my question from this morning – what did you find in the old hospital?"

There was a glimmer in his eye. It was happening again. She didn't know how he knew, but he knew. Despite that, she couldn't give him the truth. There was still the smallest chance he actually didn't know.

"Like I said this morning, it's a crime scene. You know that. I had my father, Shane and Jake reviewing it."

"So there wasn't a new scene there this morning?"

Serena didn't answer. She simply stared. Where the hell was he getting this from?

"Isn't it true that there was a second heart placed where the original heart was?" Norton pressed.

The question almost made Serena laugh. He couldn't have phrased it any better for her. The truth was simple and entirely misleading. "No, there was not a second heart in the hospital this morning."

He glared at her. "The public needs to know the truth! You can't keep a lid on this just to save your job. Two hearts? That's a serial killer. Has to be. People deserve to know!"

Serena shrugged. "I've answered your questions, Norton. Is there anything else?"

"I'm going to print this quote, Sheriff. The truth will come out!"

"Then let me be very clear. There is not a second heart. There is only one. But as I said last night, we have reason to believe there is a second victim. People need to start keeping an eye out, and watching out for each other."

Norton initiated a very weak attempt to stare her down. "Do you really want this in print?"

She could feel her lips curl into a smile, despite her efforts to remain aloof. "If you have someone who's telling you otherwise, Norton, I would consider your own sources. If you start printing lies from anonymous sources, you'll be in some pretty hot water yourself."

And with that she left him standing alone on the sidewalk. The thing of it was, his source had given him some good information. Hopefully, she'd talked him out of using any of it. Which left her with one big question – who was his source?

~ 31 ~

Serena tried hard not to think of the day as a complete loss. Though they'd found their stolen evidence, they were no further along than they'd been the day before. In the search for answers, standing still was the same as moving backward. With time, the trail would only grow cold and harder to track. She was losing, and the fact that she was desperate enough to be discussing psych profiles with the town coroner revealed the truth of the situation.

Maybe she'd made a mistake not calling in the state police. They had more resources than she did, more manpower.

She spent the last hour of her workday doing the thing she'd dreaded most – drafting up a new shift schedule. They couldn't go all hands on deck indefinitely. She could see the wear on Shane and Jake already. And her fight with Riley made it clear that the two of them were also starting to show signs of exhaustion. She'd split the night shift between Shane and Riley – six hours each. Then they'd all go back on a somewhat normal schedule. They had to.

Unfortunately, knowing you had to do something didn't make it any easier to do it. Since Riley was certain he was superhuman, he was not going to like her decision, which meant she was going to start the day with a fight again. Just thinking about it was enough to remind her how exhausted she was.

She was rubbing a tired hand over her eyes when she walked into Liam's bar. Though she was careful not to make eye contact with the patrons, she could feel them watching her. The unspoken questions were an assault. Smiling and greeting them all would probably have been the smart thing to do, but she didn't have it in her.

Liam was at the bar pouring a beer when she walked up. "Give me a minute. I've got your food in the back."

She nodded and slipped onto a stool, a little away from the others. She felt more than saw Missy sit on the stool next to her. She spoke in hushed tones. "I figured if I was here talking to you, they'd leave you alone."

Serena smiled wearily. "Thanks. I need all the help I can get these days."

"Not getting better?" Missy asked.

She only shook her head in resignation. "It was a pretty crappy day."

After a moment, Serena looked more closely at her friend. "How about you?"

Missy shrugged. "Honestly, it was a busy day, which was nice. The worst thing I had to do was give a couple dogs their annual shots."

Serena had to smile. "I'm betting those dogs didn't think it was no big deal."

"I'm betting you're right about that." The smile Missy returned only accentuated the dark circles under her eyes.

"You sleeping okay?" Serena asked.

Missy shook her head. "I sleep fine. You're the one who barely gets five hours a night."

Serena largely ignored the response. "Nightmares?"

"You don't need to worry about me. You have more than enough on your plate right now."

"I'm sitting here talking to my friend. Not worrying. Just asking," Serena assured her.

Missy scowled at her. "That's a load of bull and you know it."

When it became clear Serena wasn't going to let it go, Missy answered reluctantly, "You Marlowes are a pain in the ass, you know?"

Serena only nodded.

"Yes, I've been having nightmares," she admitted. "Seriously, I have them anyway. This makes it worse, of course, but it's okay. I had a call with my therapist at lunch today. It helped."

"If you ever want to talk, you know..."

Missy interrupted her. "I know. Of course I know. Just like you know talking doesn't change it. It happened. It's over. It makes it worse that I'm glad he's dead. Makes it worse that a part of me doesn't hate how much he suffered."

Of course Jackson Skylar never cared about how much his daughter suffered. So Serena had no trouble accepting his brutal death as justice. But she understood why Missy might feel differently, or at least she tried to.

"It was damn bad luck you were there that night," Serena replied.

Missy nodded, and her eyes grew even more distant. Serena had always felt there was something they'd never known about the night he died, something Missy had never told them. Moments like this confirmed those instincts. But questions would only dig up a past they all wanted to forget.

Instead, Serena changed the subject, "Has Liam been taking good care of you this week?"

Serena was rewarded with a smile. "He always takes care of me. But, yeah, this week he's been particularly sweet. He's leaving early tonight so I won't have to spend the evening alone."

"He's a good guy," Serena agreed, as she watched him casually chat with his customers while he poured drinks.

"Liam said you were picking up dinner for two."

Serena could hear the smirk in her tone, and she couldn't help but smile. "I've got a lunatic cutting hearts out and you want to talk about my love life."

"He just cut the one heart out of the one person," Missy corrected. "And since when do you have a love life? I knew something was up with you two."

Serena rolled her eyes. "You are unbelievable."

Missy laid a soft hand over hers. "You're exhausted. You need to focus on something that's not work related at least for a couple of minutes. Otherwise, you'll be no good to anyone. Seriously, you need to clear your head."

"He kissed me," Serena admitted reluctantly.

Her old friend's eyes lit up. "Really?"

Serena glanced around the bar with some guilt. She was surprised to discover everyone had gone back to their meals. Missy had been right. The town was polite enough to leave her alone if she was sitting with someone.

"So, you're having dinner with him tonight?" Missy prodded.

"Yeah." Serena considered clarifying it was only work, but she had to admit to herself it wasn't, at least not entirely. They would certainly be working. But after last night, she was looking forward to having him alone.

Missy was sitting silently, staring at her intently.

"What?" Serena asked.

Missy laughed at the question. "Seriously, you are the most closed-off person I've ever met. I've known you my whole life. You know all about my crazy family, my crazy life. Give me something."

Serena smiled at the good-natured criticism. "You're right. Sorry, we Marlowes play it close to the vest."

Missy glanced at Liam. "I hadn't noticed."

Serena thought about Clay and his comment about wanting to ask her out since he'd arrived. "Can I tell you something?"

"Of course." Missy straightened up in the chair, turning her back fully on the object of her distraction.

"You thought Clay was interested in me, right?"

She smiled. "You really didn't notice? I figured you were just nervous about it."

Serena shook her head. "Honestly, I had no idea at all. I mean, I was interested in him from the start, but I kind of packed it away when I realized I was working with him. I had no idea he was interested in me."

Missy looked skeptical. "He crosses streets to say hi to you. He asks about your father's health. Hell, just the way he *looks* at you."

Serena shrugged. "I didn't notice, I swear."

"Seriously, Serena, you notice a drunk driver from a half mile away, you see fights coming ten minutes before they start."

It was all true, but it didn't change the facts. Serena realized Liam had already slipped back to the kitchen to get her dinner, so she leaned in closer to talk to her friend. "I'd bet a nickel Liam has no idea."

She didn't need to clarify what it was Liam had no idea about. Missy knew. Everybody knew.

Missy shook her head. "I'm fine with it. He'll get there eventually. I don't need a ring on my finger to know he loves me."

Serena continued, because the more she thought about it, the more certain she became. "With all you went through as a kid, with your mom leaving, your dad being, well, like he was, can you really tell me you never told Liam you thought marriage sucked?"

Missy frowned. "I don't think I'd say that. Why would I say that? I don't think marriage sucks."

"One time, you told me they give the marriage licenses out at city hall in the same place as the hunting licenses because one's a license to kill and the other's a license to torture."

Missy winced. "I said that?"

Serena laughed. "You did. Frankly, you think that. Liam knows that. He knows you."

Missy glanced at the kitchen doors, and then back at her friend. "Alright, sure, I think that. But not that way, you know. I love him. He loves me. He wouldn't torture a flea, license or not."

Serena put a hand on her shoulder. "You can see why he might not ask."

Missy shook her head slowly. "Even if this bothers me, and I'm not saying it does, what could I possibly do about it?"

Serena shrugged. "Getting relationship advice from me is like going to the Sahara for a glass of water. I'm just reporting the facts. Do with them what you will."

Even as she spoke, Serena heard the swish of the kitchen door. The conversation was over, at least for now.

Missy glared. "That is not a helpful response."

"You're the only one who really knows the answer to the question," Serena whispered back.

Before Missy could say anything else, Liam swept in and dropped two bags on the bar in front of Serena. "Dinner for two."

"Seriously, the two of you are unbelievable. He and I are working." Serena gave him a stern look and dared Missy to challenge her.

The statement had the effect she'd intended. Missy's smile hid most of the worry that had been written all over her face only minutes before. "It's not cool to lie to your brother, Serena," she teased.

Liam laughed and was completely oblivious to any hidden messages on Missy's face. "She's never been able to keep anything from me. You're an open book to me, little sis. And besides, I know Buster will kick his butt if he tries anything."

Serena leaned across the bar and gave her brother a kiss on the cheek. "Thanks for the food." She laid a gentle hand on Missy's shoulder and whispered in her ear. "Sorry. You deserve better than us."

Liam looked a little put out. "Secrets? Come on, girls, you're killing me."

"I was just telling her exactly what I was planning on doing tonight," Serena lied, raising her eyebrows dramatically.

Laughing, Liam slapped his hands over his ears. "Good God, I don't want to know about that."

Serena smiled at the successful distraction and headed out, optimistic that she'd actually solved one mystery today.

~ 32 ~

Serena wished she'd had enough time to do more than throw her damp hair into a ponytail, but Buster's excited barks told her someone had pulled into her driveway.

A glance at her watch told her it was six-thirty on the dot. She was going to have to explain to Clay that she was almost always running late. She did manage to put on some lipstick before there was a knock.

Buster was dancing happily when she got there, running from the front window to the door and then back again. She cracked the door before she opened it completely.

She ignored the happy skip in her heart when she saw Clay standing out front. "You should be warned, he's a jumper and he may lick you to death."

Clay grinned at the little snout trying desperately to squeeze outside. "I think I'll risk it."

Predictably, Buster raced onto the front porch and was bathing Clay in love before he could even get inside. For a moment everything faded away and it was just the three of them. A perfect safe reprieve from a day that had been anything but.

Buster led Clay into the living room where he practically pushed him onto the couch.

Before Serena could slip past them, Clay pulled her onto the now overcrowded couch. He deftly held Buster at bay as he placed a gentle hand on her cheek. "How are you doing?"

She realized she was better now. Much better. "I'm glad to see you."

Clay smiled and kissed her. Again, she felt the world almost gray out around her. It wasn't Clay who broke the contact, but Buster. He jumped between the two of them, with a big goofy expression.

Clay stopped Serena before she could apologize. "He's right. I'm supposed to be here working, aren't I?"

Clay took the stuffed dog Buster dropped in his lap. Picking up on the obvious signals, he threw the toy to the other side of the room.

"That's one of his favorites," she found herself explaining.

Buster already had the toy back and it was now laying at Clay's feet. "If you tell him to go deep, he'll run out and then you can throw it so he can jump and catch it."

Clay did as instructed and Buster obeyed perfectly. "Cool trick," he said as much to Buster as to her.

Clearly having decided he'd found a new friend, Buster raced back to drop the toy. "Do you want to work out here?" Clay asked between throws.

"If we stay out here, Buster's going to think this fun will last all night. We can sit at the table in the kitchen if you'd prefer. He usually respects that space."

Clay tossed the toy again and smiled. "I'm happy to do this as long as he wants. The distraction of playing fetch won't make me any less competent to discuss psych theories with you. Seriously, Serena, I'm entirely unqualified for this."

She rolled her eyes and grabbed her files off the kitchen table. "Did you have time to read up at all on any basic profiling?"

Laughing, Clay said, "Since I get the impression you actually have studied profiling, I'm going to have to guess you already know that me brushing up on my Psych 101 knowledge is going to be vastly insufficient."

"I've taken a couple courses, most of them online, read some books. I know enough to know how little I really know."

Clay waved Buster's toy at him and then threw it. "Well, now I'm sure you know more than I do on the topic. But hell, I'm willing to brainstorm. What are you thinking?"

"So, we have two blood types and at least one unknown victim," Serena began. "I can tell you, we've been all through town. Other than Daisy Roman, everyone's accounted for."

"Daisy could be the source of the smaller amount of blood," Clay suggested.

Serena leaned back on the couch. "The heart matched the blood type that appeared more often in the pool. It's the other type that doesn't match, right?"

Clay nodded. "Still, it could be her."

"I'd been assuming it was the killer's blood."

Clay shrugged. "It probably is. I'm just saying. It could be Daisy's."

Serena sat up. "We never checked Daisy's medical records. Do you have her blood type in your files?"

"I checked this morning. The blood type wasn't in there."

One of these days, they'd stop hitting dead end after dead end. At least that's what Serena told herself. "Even if the second blood type is hers, we're still looking for another victim and, of course, the killer. Unless you think Daisy is actually the killer."

Clay offered a half-smile. "If I say she fits the profile will it prove how incompetent I really am on these topics?"

Serena laughed. "There's no chance you're getting out of this."

"Well, then, I have to admit, I think we have two victims. I don't know if the extra blood is Daisy's or the killer's. Until we get the DNA back, we won't be able to figure it out."

Buster was slowing down a little with the game. This time he left his toy on the other side of the room and jumped up on the couch to settle in between the two of them. Serena couldn't help but think of Liam's joke that Buster would make an excellent chaperone.

"So, in a relatively short period of time we have two people abducted and at least one of them murdered. Why would that happen?" she asked.

Clay looked at her with a shade of confusion. "What do you mean why?"

"I mean, we live in a tiny little town where everyone knows everyone's business. There's no chance this guy was killing people in town before this. Why wake up one day and take two people?"

"What if the first victim wasn't abducted recently? The decomp on the heart only tells us that they died recently."

Buster laid his head up against Serena's leg, clearly asserting his desire to have his ears scratched. "You think someone had the victim chained up in their basement or something?"

Clay shrugged. "I find it hard to imagine someone would be like that, but hell, the guy sliced the heart right out of this person. I guess anything is possible."

And that was the disturbing truth. Anything was possible. "Either way, why would somebody start doing this all of a sudden? I mean, this is pretty intense stuff. You don't go through life without a parking ticket and wake up one morning and decide to cut someone's heart out."

Clay considered the question. "I guess that means you don't have anyone who's been living on the edge who might have jumped into the deep end?"

Serena sighed. "The town isn't perfect by any means. I have some domestics who are what you might call regular customers. I have a couple drunks. A few people who don't understand that 'don't drink and drive' is more than just a slogan. I have a couple fighters. Some kids who cause some trouble, but generally it's minor stuff."

"I guess the fighters could be a problem," Clay replied.

Serena considered the regular brawlers in the town – John Francetti, Toby Yinkel, and of course her best deputy. She found it hard to believe that any of them could be a serial killer.

"They're all hotheads. Nothing else. Something stupid happens, it sets them off and that's it. I don't think any of them could hold their focus long enough to do something like this," she replied.

Clay searched her face for a moment before he spoke. "I know how this is going to sound, but what about Riley?"

She let out a deep frustrated breath. "Oh good, you figure if he can accuse you of murder then you should return the favor? Come on, Clay, I expect better from you."

He held up his hands in surrender. "You asked me to come here and talk this out. That's all I'm doing. Riley seems like an okay guy. I don't mean him any harm. I'm just saying – you said none of your hotheads had the focus to do something like this. I don't know if you weren't counting Riley on the list of hotheads, or if you are seriously going to try to tell me that you don't think he's focused enough to do something like this."

Serena held his eyes without answering. She understood his point, but it still seemed crazy. Riley was never focused with his anger. He was a perfectly fine guy most of the time. He just blew up occasionally.

Clay continued, "You'll remember, I had a front row seat for a fight of his about a month ago. It took three guys to pull him off Norton."

"Come on, you know Norton, he probably had it coming." But the truth was, he barely said four words before Riley hauled off and started beating his ass. At least that's what the witnesses said.

Clay only shrugged. "Look, whatever, I'm saying it's a possibility. Just like the long-term abduction idea. To be fair, I think I have to point out it's a possibility that the killer used to live somewhere else, and he moved here. So this wasn't actually his first kill, it was his first kill in your jurisdiction."

Serena stretched across the dog and placed a hand on Clay's leg. "You aren't a killer. I'm sure of that."

They sat a few moments in silence, and as they did, the wheels started to turn in Serena's head. Remembering Reece's confession, she said, "A serial killer might wake up one morning and start killing because he's finally old enough to pull it off."

Clay's brow furrowed. "What do you mean?"

"I mean, a lot of psychological disturbances manifest in the late teens, early twenties, don't they?" Even as she asked the question, part of Serena's mind rejected the idea. There was no way this could be true.

"Around there, but I think serial killers are usually a little older," Clay replied.

"Should we be looking more closely at younger men?"

Clay shook his head, but even as he rejected the idea, he admitted the truth of it. "That actually makes more sense than the other theories."

"Is it really a coincidence that the heart was found by Lucas Denton?"

"You don't think Lucas is involved." His tone told her that he didn't want to believe it either, but his eyes said he saw her point.

"I didn't think he was involved." She paused and corrected herself. "Actually, I don't want to think he's involved. He's a petty troublemaker, or at least that's all I've ever seen."

They were silent a few moments before Clay said, "What about that? Do you have anyone who's been accused of things, anyone who maybe got away with other crimes and is now escalating the behavior?"

The question was a sword through the heart. "If they got away with something, how would I know?"

Clay sat forward, clearly seeing the truth on her face. "I'm betting you know a lot of things the big wide world doesn't know. Not being able to prove something doesn't mean it didn't happen."

Serena sat back, closing her eyes, as if it might hide her from the truth. "My dad was good at his job. If he thought someone was up to something, he wouldn't stop until he proved it."

Though she didn't open her eyes, she could feel the weight of Clay's stare. "So, no open cases?" he prodded.

Serena shook her head and sank deeper into the couch. The problem with working with another person in an investigation was you couldn't stop them when you didn't like the direction they headed. Especially not when you thought the direction made sense, at least in theory.

It was another moment before she heard a muttered curse and felt Clay's hand run soothingly down her arm. "I'm sorry," he said. "I don't think she did this. I swear, I don't. Of course I don't. How could anyone think that?"

Serena finally opened her eyes. Placing her hand over his, she asked, "You know what happened?"

Clay shook his head. "You hear things. I don't know much, obviously. Otherwise I would have thought twice before I accused your best friend of murder."

~ 33 ~

Serena sighed. "It's a good theory."

Clay shook his head. "No. It's not a good theory. There is no way Missy Skylar is a killer. None. She cried when she saw those animals. Cried!"

Serena's heart clenched. "She cried?"

Clay stood and began pacing the room. "She left the room. Said something about the smell and she needed a moment. But I saw her eyes when she came back in. There's no way she did that to those animals. No way she could have."

Frustrated, Serena wasn't sure if she wanted to cry or scream. She chose neither, but her voice sounded cold and strange when she spoke. "It's a good theory. Someone gets away with a crime. It escalates. It could escalate because they lose a sense of morality. It could escalate because part of them wants to get caught. You leave a fucking heart in a public place, it's a pretty clear sign you're hoping someone will find it."

Clay sat back on the couch with her, placing his hand over hers. "Serena, don't."

She shook him off. "It's my job," she growled.

She couldn't tell if the look she received was awe or fear.

Not wanting to see either, Serena looked away. "She was accused of murder," she began.

Clay's voice mirrored her own steady professional tone. "Her father, right."

Serena nodded. "She was away at school. Her senior year of college. I was working for my dad at that point. It was a Wednesday night. Late March. I was patrolling. Riley was back at the station. My dad was at the bar, getting dinner with some friends. I was about three blocks away when I saw the smoke. I could see the flames before I'd even finished calling it in. By the time I made it to the house, it was completely engulfed."

She focused on Buster. Rubbing the fur on the back of his neck, urging herself to ignore the flood of emotions that always came when she thought about that night. "Missy was sitting on the curb on the other side of the street when I got there. She had a bloody lip, a nasty gash on the side of her head, and she was covered in soot."

Since even her dog was looking at her cautiously, Serena finally met Clay's eyes. "We brought the state police in. They were far better equipped to handle an arson investigation. And I think my father was worried about his objectivity. He pulled me off the case completely. I guess he was even more concerned about my objectivity."

Clay laid a hand on her cheek, his eyes holding hers. There was something so calm in them. This was a man who knew pain, too. A man who'd found a way to be happy, even knowing all the world inevitably had in store.

His voice was quiet when he spoke, "Based on everything you've told me about Missy's father, I would have been tempted to call it an accident and move on. Whatever happened in that house, he deserved it. Probably deserved worse."

Serena almost smiled at the response. "That pretty much summed up how I felt about things."

"Did they determine it was arson?" Clay asked.

Serena nodded. "They found traces of accelerants. And indications that the rooms on the first floor were trashed to make them catch fire faster. That's why the place went up so quickly."

"I guess they cleared Missy?" Clay asked.

Serena rolled her eyes. "Nothing's that simple. The investigation dragged on about a month. Everybody in town had Missy tried and convicted. The only thing people disagreed on was whether her bastard father deserved it."

"How was she?"

Serena was certain she'd never seen anyone as psychologically damaged as Missy had been that night, in the weeks that followed. It was like she was just gone. There was no emotion at all. Except at night, when she'd thrash in her sleep, screaming, crying, and making Serena long for the version of her friend who walked like a ghost through her days. But there was no need to bring all that up now.

She said simply, "It was bad. Really bad. She was a mess."

"I guess our fathers are our fathers, no matter how badly they treated us," Clay suggested.

"In the end, the state police cleared her. Couldn't find anything at all to connect her to the crime scene. She'd been at school that afternoon and had driven to the house that night. There'd been receipts, witnesses, the whole bit. They decided she wouldn't have had enough time to set things up."

Clay searched her face and finally said, "You're worried she did it?"

It was a question Serena had been asked before. She had a well-practiced denial. But those weren't the words that came out.

"Missy shouldn't have been there that night. She was away at school. She never came home without calling me. She lived with us, not her father. That was something the state police never seemed to understand."

Serena paused a moment, wondering if she really could say it. If she could give voice to her gnawing worries.

Her voice was softer, but clear when she continued, "She never told me why she was here. Never really explained what happened. Her story didn't make sense. She said the fire had already started when she got there. That she tried to get in and save him but she couldn't."

"Sometimes these things just happen really fast, don't they? Maybe that explains some of the discrepancies?" Clay suggested.

Serena wished she could believe it. But the physical evidence didn't match up any better than Missy's story. Her friend had a split lip and a gash on her head. The state police had dismissed them as injuries from a fire. She'd seen too many examples not to know a punch in the face when she saw it.

They sat in silence for a few minutes, the full gravity of the suggestions weighing heavily on both of them. Sensing the tension, and clearly wanting no part of it, Buster sighed deeply and slipped off the couch. He curled up on his favorite chair, plainly exhausted from his long day.

Serena turned to look at Clay, really look at him. That peace was still there. That calm. How could he stay that calm?

Out of desperation, she voiced the worry that had been plaguing her all day. "I should have called the state police in at the beginning. I can't do this. Someone else is going to die and it's going to be my fault."

"I think the town would have panicked if you brought in outside help."

She saw sympathy on Clay's face, but she suspected it was probably pity. "A little panic would be a small price to pay if we could stop all this."

"Tell me one thing they could have done that you didn't do."

Of course, he was right. She'd spent the whole day blaming their dead ends on a lack of manpower, but the state police would only have meant extra bodies milling around her station. There was nothing to do. No leads to follow. They had confusing forensic evidence, no motive, and no suspects.

"How can there be someone this crazy in my town and I don't know who they are?"

"Unfortunately, some crazy people appear perfectly sane." Clay pulled her close. "Have you slept since this all started?"

"I'm fine," she replied. The truth was, she hadn't done much more than stare at her bedroom ceiling running the crime scene over and over in her mind. The last time she'd gotten any real sleep had been the four hours she'd grabbed Sunday afternoon before her overnight shift.

Tilting her chin so he could get a better look at her, Clay said, "I understand your frustration, but you need to give yourself a break. You can't work 24-7 until this is over."

Serena knew he was right, but it was easier said than done. With all that was going on, she was wound up too tight to think about sleep.

It wasn't until he started kissing her that she realized there was something that would take her mind off the job at hand. For a minute, she wanted to stop. There was so much to do, she couldn't possibly do this now.

Clay placed his hand on her cheek, locking his eyes on hers. That ridiculous calm was still there.

"We have to figure this out," she insisted. "Something this weird, it's going to happen again."

He ran his thumb along her cheekbone, barely touching the skin. "You will," he said.

It felt like he was almost dropping her into a trance; she could feel her muscles start to relax, the tightness that had been in her chest began to ease. She felt almost helpless to resist.

The helplessness was what set her back straighter, what caused her muscles to tighten up. She couldn't do this. How could she have thought she could do this?

Clay tilted his head slightly. "Tell me what you're thinking."

She tried to speak the words, tried to explain, but they wouldn't come.

Tugging gently on her ponytail, he asked, "Do you always wear your hair up when you're working?"

"Yeah. I mean, I wear it up most of the time."

Clay smiled slightly. "In my experience, you're working most of the time."

Serena started to sputter some explanation or excuse, but Clay stopped her. "Your job requires you to work most of the time. I understand that. Your job is a big part of who you are. I understand that too. But, I'm a bit more interested in the rest of you right this second. And I'm wondering about something…"

Clay slid his hand back over her ponytail and before she realized what he was doing, he'd slipped the band off her hair. He grinned at her. "Now, I think we can safely say, you're off-duty, Serena."

He feathered his thumb across her cheek again and ran his fingers through her hair. Again, it felt like she was melting. She wasn't sure if it was frightening or thrilling. Before she could stop herself, she leaned in closer and kissed him.

She could feel his fingers tangle in her still damp hair as he pulled her closer.

His lips weren't demanding, but warm, gentle; it was like a wave washing over her. Washing away her fears, her insecurities. As he trailed his fingers down her spine, she felt her muscles relax, and the tightness ease. Her mind was suddenly so foggy that it was entirely clear.

Through the haze, she felt compelled to open her eyes. To look at him, really look at him and try to understand what she was seeing, what she was feeling.

He pulled back the tiniest fraction and one side of his mouth turned up slightly in a smile.

"You're thinking again," he teased.

She ran her hand over his rough cheek, down his neck, over his shoulders, never letting her eyes leave his, just watching him watch her. There was something amazing in the look. He made her feel special, beautiful, and it swept her insecurities away.

He kissed her deeply and, again, the world blurred around the edges. Her body melted into his as he lowered her to the couch. She slid her hands under his shirt, gripping his strong back as she almost fell.

She didn't understand how she was here. How he was here. How any of this was really possible. But Clay's gentle, intelligent eyes were staring into her own. She allowed herself to be here. Just here. In this moment. With this man, who she'd been attracted to the first time she saw him.

As she laid there, feeling the weight of his body on hers, the warmth of his breath on her cheek, she realized there was no way she could allow this chance to pass.

He seemed to see the choice on her face. "You're off-duty, Serena," he said. "It's okay."

She was amazed to realize she agreed with him. She needed this more than she needed sleep, more than she needed to think. She needed to go somewhere else, just for the night. She needed it as much as she needed to keep breathing.

~ 34 ~

Serena woke up when the day's first sunbeam slipped through her window. She felt rested and cloudy-headed. So much so that it took her a minute to realize why she couldn't move. Clay's strong arm was draped over her, and Buster was laying across both of their feet. Her two men, protecting her from the world.

For a person who spent all her time looking out for others, it was a strange moment. Clay was sound asleep on his stomach, his arm wrapped around her own. Broad muscles intertwined with her own lean lines, dark hair against her pale skin. She ran her finger over his shoulders, enjoying the strength.

She was perfectly capable of living alone. The past few years had taught her that. But now, in this moment of peace, she saw how wonderful it was to share the load with someone, if only for a minute.

Clay rolled toward her, without opening his eyes. He pulled her closer and whispered. "It's early, Serena, go back to sleep."

She smiled and settled back in for a few minutes, enjoying the warmth. At the foot of the bed, Buster opened a sleepy eye, and seemed to tell her that she should listen to the smart man.

It was about a half hour later when she extricated herself quietly, kissing Clay lightly on the head. Buster peered at her and seemed to consider getting up, but decided to stick with the new guy.

"Traitor," she whispered, slipping into her robe and padding downstairs to put on the coffee.

While the coffee brewed, she sat down at the kitchen table, where a file of crime scene info sat. As she leafed through the reports, she realized she did feel more clear-headed. More able to spot the truth when it chose to reveal itself.

Clay's voice brought her out of her deep thoughts. "You left," he said.

He was standing in the doorway, leaning against the frame. He was only wearing his jeans and a sleepy smile.

"I didn't mean to wake you."

"Back to work, already?" he asked, noticing the file in front of her.

She smiled sheepishly. "Sorry, I was waiting for the coffee and it was here."

If he was bothered by her decision to get up, he didn't show it.

She stood and joined him. He wrapped an arm around her waist, lifting her toes almost off the ground as he kissed her.

"Good morning," he said, in a voice that made her want to take him back to bed. "I guess you're one of those people who doesn't really sleep?"

"I'm guessing that's a difference between us," she chuckled, leaning her head against his shoulder.

Clay smoothed her hair and pulled her close. "So long as you're making the coffee, I can live with it."

Buster's wet nose butted Serena's hand. He was holding his leash with a look of hopeful optimism. She scratched his head and took the leash. "Why don't you take care of business out back, buddy. I'm afraid it's not a morning for a long walk."

The look she received as she walked to the back door told her that Buster felt he'd been tricked into getting out of bed early for no good reason. She let him into the fenced-in backyard before she rejoined Clay in the kitchen.

He'd taken her seat and was leafing through her file, so she poured them both coffee before she rejoined him. He looked up when she handed him the cup.

He ran his free hand gently over her hip. "You're going to figure this out. You were right not to call in the state police. You know these people better than they do. That'll be an advantage eventually. You don't have enough pieces yet. You will though."

She was much more able to hear the encouragement that morning than she would have been the night before. She sat in the chair next to him and considered how odd it was to feel this close to him.

"I really do want to take you out," he said, as if he was reading her mind. "I feel a little strange that we're here and we haven't done that, you know?"

She did know. She also knew that was going to be harder to fix than it sounded.

Again, Clay seemed to read her mind. "Do me a favor, okay? Solve this thing quickly, so I can take you out without you thinking people are judging you for having a life."

Serena laughed. "Judging me for having a life? What about you?"

Clay smiled. "Who could judge me for wanting to be with you?"

A few people sprung immediately to mind. Though she had the right to have a life, no one was going to appreciate her moving on with it until she figured out what the hell was going on in their town.

~ 35 ~

Serena didn't even make it to the station before the day began to unravel. She was driving in when Hayley called to give her the day's first bad news.

"We got a call from Vice Principal Marx up at the high school," she began. "She's a wreck. It seems Claudia Daly didn't show up at school this morning. She insists Claudia's always early. School started about fifteen minutes ago and she wasn't around. Shane's just about to go off shift, should I send him?"

They both knew normally a call like this would wait until the next shift, which started in ten minutes. But they also knew things were no longer normal.

"I'll stop at Claudia's house. Shane should go home. Jake's on in about ten minutes, right? Don't send him unless I call you. Hopefully, I won't need to."

Even as she said it, Serena knew she'd need to. Claudia wouldn't miss a day of work without calling in.

Claudia's street was one of the nicer ones in town. At one time, her family had owned an interest in the factory. After her father had retired, he'd sold the interest to the group of investors who owned it now.

Serena passed the Sinclair house and Norton Finwick's home on her way to Claudia's at the end of the cul-de-sac. It was a little like wandering into the lion's den. All of her fans in one place.

From the moment Serena pulled into the driveway, she knew there was a problem. Claudia's front door stood wide open. Serena stepped out into the cool morning air with her hand on her weapon. As she approached, she felt a sort of resignation. She could already sense that there was no one in the house who would do her harm. In fact, she was pretty sure there was no one there at all.

When she saw the glass on the front door had been broken, Serena drew her gun. She pushed the door open carefully with her toe, revealing a large entryway. There was a small coat rack to her right. To the left looked like a living room. And a staircase led to a second floor. Nothing looked disturbed.

She called out to Claudia, but received no response. With her nine-millimeter leading the way, Serena checked the rooms on the lower level. She ascended the stairs, wishing she didn't already know how the search was going to end. The first door was a bathroom. The second, a small bedroom that had been made into an office. The door at the end of the hall was open wide, bright sunlight streamed through the windows.

From the hallway, there was nothing obviously wrong, but once she stepped inside, Serena saw the truth. The bed was wrecked. One lamp was on its side. Another was on the floor, shattered. Most disturbing was the corner of one nightstand that was stained a deep red. Similar spots on the rug told Serena that she was looking at another crime scene.

Claudia Daly had been taken. It looked like she'd managed to put up more of a fight than Daisy Roman, but it hadn't mattered.

Before she could call Hayley to tell her to send Jake, Serena's cell phone was ringing.

Clay's voice told her immediately that Whitefield had had a bad night. "Serena, I have a problem."

"You aren't the only one," she said, already calculating how long Riley had been off shift and how long Shane had already been on. She suspected somebody was going to have to work extra time.

"My office was ransacked last night. The file cabinets were emptied all over my floor."

Serena cursed to herself. "How'd they get in?"

"Broke a window."

Sounded familiar. "Can you tell if they took anything?"

"I checked all the samples I still had from the investigation. Those are all still there. It doesn't look like anything was touched other than my patient files."

"Clay, I'm going to need you to stay there, and please don't touch anything. I'll be there as soon as I can."

Plainly hearing the tension in her voice, he asked, "What is it? What's going on?"

Serena didn't even consider trying to explain the situation. She said the only thing she could. "I wish I knew. I really wish I knew."

~ 36 ~

Serena sent Jake to Clay's office to secure the crime scene. She decided that scene was going to have to wait until she was able to figure out what had happened at Claudia Daly's house.

Shane stayed on for a couple extra hours to help her process the scene at Claudia's. She'd give Riley the morning off, as planned. She needed somebody who'd be sharp that afternoon.

Serena was pulling fingerprints from the nightstand when she heard Avery Sinclair's voice booming from downstairs. Since Sinclair was the last person she wanted crashing her crime scene, she left Shane to finish the room.

She ran into Avery in the hallway, though the low murmur of voices from downstairs told her that he wasn't the only one in the house.

Serena placed a firm hand in the middle of his chest and turned him back toward the stairs. "What part of the yellow police tape across the front door did you not understand?"

She ignored his protests as she pushed him back toward the stairs. At the top of the steps, Sinclair finally caught his balance and turned to face her.

"My wife called me home from work because she was worried about Claudia. Who the hell do you think you are keeping us in the dark?"

From the top of the steps, Serena could see the small crowd that was gathered just inside the door. "I need you all out of the house. Now!" she said, in a voice that sounded a lot like her father's.

The people milling about at the foot of the stairs quickly scurried out, with the exception of Norton Finwick, who stood perched in the doorway, technically complying with her order without really giving much ground.

Serena pulled out her handcuffs and locked her eyes on Sinclair, much in the same way she'd stared down innumerable belligerent husbands over the years. "Avery, you have two choices – you can either step outside or I will be taking you down to the station."

Avery looked between her and the cuffs and, like all cowardly bullies, he retreated.

"You don't have to make such a big deal out of nothing," he declared. "We just want to know what's happening."

Serena didn't answer. She followed close behind, causing him to quicken his step. From the corner of her eye, she watched Norton. Surprisingly, he didn't challenge her. He actually looked like he might have been a little impressed.

Outside, Serena reattached the crime scene tape and surveyed the crowd standing on Claudia Daly's front lawn. The front step was crowded with most of Claudia's neighbors.

Serena didn't blame them for their curiosity. Actually, she realized it may have been her mistake not to figure out a way to watch the scene out here more closely. With all that had been going on, the police car must have scared them. She wished she had better news.

She raised her voice so she could be heard by everyone. "Thank you for stepping out. I'm going to need you all to stay out of Claudia's place for the time being. I'm sorry to say, Claudia's been reported missing and we have reason to believe someone took her from the house last night."

The murmurs in the crowd were frantic, and their faces told Serena everything she needed to know. They all believed this was the second of two kidnappings and most likely the second murder as well. She wished she could tell them they were wrong.

"At this point, we don't know that much, but…"

Before Serena could finish, Avery Sinclair cut her off. "Of course you don't know much, you never know much. There's a psycho killer running around our town and you aren't doing shit."

Predictably, the crowd seemed to agree.

"Look, everybody, I share your frustration. Standing out here fighting about things is not going to help anyone. I would, however, like to talk to each of you individually about last night. I think it would be easiest if you'd go back to your homes. I'll talk to you there. Please, the little details are often the most important, so think carefully about the night."

She turned back to the house once the group began to break up, but before she could slip inside, Norton grabbed her arm. "Do you want to give me a formal statement, Sheriff?"

Serena saw the ever present notepad in his hand – scrawled at the top was what she suspected would be the headline later that day – SECOND WOMAN MISSING. SECOND MURDER? For the first time in her career, Serena cursed her father's bad heart.

"Norton, look, I really told you guys all I know. Claudia's missing. We have reason to believe someone took her from her home."

"That reason being the broken glass in the front door?"

"I am not going to discuss the crime scene with you. You know I can't do that."

Norton seemed to consider leaving, before he thought better of it. "I do have one other question, Sheriff. Do you have reason to know that Clay Drayton had nothing to do with this?"

At first she heard the question as an accusation against Clay, but the smirk on Norton's face immediately told her otherwise. The little shit wasn't accusing Clay of being a murderer. He was accusing her of having a sex life.

She glared at him. "What is that supposed to mean?"

Norton chewed on his pencil thoughtfully, his smile broadening. "I was out for a bike ride early this morning. Couldn't sleep. I went by your house. There were two cars in your driveway."

"The number of cars in my driveway is newsworthy?" she replied, her teeth clenching.

"Look, you know, whatever, I'm just saying that a lot of people in town think Dr. Drayton is probably the guy who is doing all this. So, I thought you might be happy to tell people that you know for sure he's not involved. Though, I guess they might be a little angry you were so unconcerned about it in the first place."

Serena thought of a thousand names she wanted to call the muck-raking weasel who was leering at her, but she stood her ground. "I am sure you have better things to do than print gossip. And I know I have better things to do than stand here discussing it."

Cheeks flushed with frustration and anger, she turned on her heel to make sure Shane had control of the scene before she did the neighborhood interviews.

~ 37 ~

Serena went to the Sinclair house last. She knew she'd be accused of personally harassing them with the delay, but the truth was far less sinister. Since the Sinclairs' house was closest to Claudia's, they were in the best position to have seen something useful. She hoped to have as many pieces as possible in place before she talked to them.

Serena already knew Claudia typically left the house at six-thirty every morning and arrived home around five o'clock.

The Taylor family could see into Claudia's kitchen and knew she made gourmet dinners most nights. She ate alone most of the time and usually ate around "the time Wheel of Fortune came on" – which Serena knew meant around seven.

Last night was no exception. She turned off the kitchen lights "probably right before the last puzzle."

Not a Wheel-watcher, Serena could only guess that meant about seven-twenty.

The only person who thought Claudia had frequent visitors was Ella Parker, whose glasses were so thick her frail nose could barely hold them up. In her better days, Ella could have written the town gossip column. These days her stories were a little suspect. Serena thought she might be in the early stages of dementia.

Ella thought it was "awfully nice Claudia was helping that boy out." After several follow-up questions, Serena discovered the boy who Ella thought Claudia was "tutoring" was Lucas Denton. And these "tutoring" sessions typically happened around eleven or twelve at night. Ella had noticed this on several nights because that was about the time her little dog – Tutu – liked to "take care of his business."

If Ella's story was true, it told Serena two things: this was the second crime scene Lucas was at, and Lucas might have been the last person to see Claudia before she was taken. So, the Lucas thing was going to require more investigation.

These were the facts Serena was armed with when she knocked on the Sinclairs' front door.

As she expected, Avery greeted her with an expression of complete exasperation. "It's about fucking time."

Serena considered explaining her reasons for the delay, but thought better of it. He was lucky she hadn't arrested him earlier.

"I'd like to talk to you all about anything you might have seen last night or early this morning," she said simply.

Sinclair grunted at her, and led her into his living room where his wife and daughter were sitting.

Madison was clutching Andi's hand desperately, her eyes red-rimmed from crying. Andi looked bored. Serena was beginning to think it was her only expression.

Madison looked at Serena desperately. "Please tell us you know who did this to Claudia."

Before Serena could answer, Andi snapped, "Of course she knows. It's the same guy who carved out Daisy's heart."

Serena considered correcting her, since they were still pretty sure it wasn't Daisy's heart, but she thought better of it. "We're looking into everything," she said. "It would help me if I could ask you a few questions."

Serena took a seat opposite the women. Avery stood next to the fireplace, eyeing her skeptically.

Through their living room window, Serena could see Claudia's house, though not as clearly as you could see her kitchen from the Taylors' home. "Did any of you see Claudia yesterday?"

Madison nodded. "I see Claudia every morning. She's usually going to work when I go out to get the paper for Avery."

"Did you see her this morning?"

Madison choked back a dramatic sob. "No, I didn't see her this morning. She'd told the kids they could stay home from school for a couple days. I thought maybe, maybe she'd done the same."

"Did any of you see her later in the day yesterday?"

Madison shook her head. Andi continued to examine the nails on the hand her mother wasn't clutching.

"Avery? Andi?" Serena asked.

"I get home at eight o'clock most nights, Sheriff. I don't have occasion to see her much."

"Andi?" Serena repeated.

Andi looked annoyed to have been distracted from her important nail assessment. "The last time I saw Ms. Daly was at school, a couple days ago."

Serena glanced out the window. "Did any of you notice any lights on at her house?"

Madison seemed to think this was the most brilliant question she'd ever heard. "Of course, the lights! Yes, yes, I was here watching my shows last night. And the lights went out a little early. I think about ten. Wouldn't you say, sweetheart?" she asked Avery.

Her husband looked as bored as his daughter. "I didn't notice."

Serena considered pressing the point, but she decided Avery probably hadn't noticed. As far as she could tell, Avery didn't notice much unless it affected him personally.

"I'm sure," Madison insisted. "You wanted your ice cream, you know like you usually do right around ten. When I came back in with the bowl, her lights were out. I remember thinking she turned in early."

Serena focused on Andi when she asked, "Is Claudia friendly with Lucas Denton?"

The question got the reaction Serena had hoped for. Andi's eyes snapped up. She knew what Serena was suggesting, which told Serena that Andi had already suspected something.

More surprising, however, was Avery's reaction. "What the hell is that supposed to mean? Claudia Daly is the principal of the high school. How dare you!"

From the nervous glance Andi shot her father's way, Serena thought it looked like Andi had been concerned enough about Lucas and Claudia that she'd talked to Daddy about it.

"Avery, I'm not accusing anyone of anything. I'm asking if they were friends. Lucas has a rough family situation. There's nothing wrong with Claudia taking an interest in him. I heard she had, that's all."

Avery glared at her as if she'd tricked him into some sort of confession. In what Serena assumed was an attempt to convince her there was nothing wrong, he explained, "Lucas mows her lawn in the summer. He's a good boy. Like you said, he's got a rough family."

Serena tried not to think about Claudia having a fling with the lawn boy. Instead, she considered the situation. She had a psycho killer who had appeared out of nowhere. She had a kid from an abusive background. Maybe he'd snapped. Maybe he was finally old enough to act on his violent tendencies. She thought again about Coach Fletcher's class. The timeline worked.

As much as she hated it, Lucas was looking more and more like a plausible suspect.

~ 38 ~

Serena made it to Clay's office three hours after he had originally called. She found him chatting with Jake on the front porch. As she came up the front walk, Jake jumped to his feet, as if he was embarrassed to have been caught not standing at attention.

"Sheriff, Hayley said there was a scene at Claudia Daly's house?" Jake's face never hid his emotions. This moment was no exception.

Serena sat in the chair next to Clay and gestured to Jake that he should do the same.

She explained as calmly as she could, "It looks like somebody grabbed her last night, probably sometime after ten. Her bedroom's a mess and we found some blood at the scene."

She turned to Clay, and said, "Any chance you know Claudia Daly's blood type?"

Clay's eyes lit up. "She organizes a blood drive at the high school a couple times a year. I help them out.

There should be notes about the blood types of the donors in my files."

"The files that are all over the floor of your office?" Serena asked.

Jake stood. "Sheriff, you should have a look in there. It's an awful mess."

"It's just the office? Just the files?" she asked.

Clay nodded. "That was my first worry. I checked everything. All the samples in the lab, everything else, looks completely untouched. It looks like they broke into the office, nothing else."

"It looks like vandalism," Jake replied.

Serena wondered about that, but she didn't say anything more. Following Jake inside, she asked Clay to stay on the porch.

Inside, things looked just as Jake had described. The burglar smashed the glass in the window, unlocked it, and climbed in. The locks on the filing cabinets were broken, probably with a crow bar.

The office was a wreck. It looked to Serena like someone had purposely made the mess – maybe to cause trouble, maybe to obscure what was missing.

The timing of the break-in left her with a troubling question – were Claudia's records in this mess?

The problem, as it always seemed to be, was time. These were people's private medical records. She was pretty sure the only one who should be organizing them was Clay, and from the looks of things, organizing was going to take a while.

She left Jake with instructions to dust the window and the filing cabinet and see if they could find any prints. It seemed pointless, but it had to be done. Once again, she was going to get the camera out of her car to photograph the scene.

Outside she found Clay exactly where she'd left him. He looked up when he heard her coming.

"Sorry to make you deal with this nonsense today. I'm sure you have better things to do," he said.

Serena slid into a chair next to him. "I'm not sure things are entirely unrelated."

Clay raised an eyebrow. "It looks like somebody just vandalized my office, don't you think? They're probably trying to give me a hard time because they think I'm involved in Daisy's disappearance."

It could be, but Serena doubted it. If this had really been an attack on Clay personally, she'd expect some spray paint or something stupid like that to go along with the mess.

"Let's not assume anything, okay?"

She explained that Jake was going to dust for fingerprints and asked if Clay would be willing to sort through the files as quickly as he could.

"In particular," she added, "could you try to confirm Claudia Daly's file is still in there?"

Clay stared at her in astonishment.

She threw up her hands. "I know I'm jumping to conclusions, but I'd like to rule it out."

"Actually, no, I was thinking it made sense, in a weird way."

Serena shook her head. "I hope to hell I'm wrong."

They sat quietly for a moment, before Serena remembered her stupid conversation with Norton earlier in the day. She didn't know what he was really planning to print, but she figured Clay deserved the heads up.

The pink in Clay's cheeks told her that he was as embarrassed as she was. Serena had no idea what was between them yet, but she was certain this was no way to start it.

"Clay, I'm really sorry to drag you into all this."

He interrupted her immediately. "There's no reason for you to be sorry."

Serena started to protest, but Clay stopped her. "We talked about this already. I don't care who knows about us. I want everybody to know. But this will probably create trouble for you. I'm really sorry about that."

Serena rarely found herself speechless, but she could only stare in amazement at the response.

The moment was shattered by the squeal of breaks and the sound of a car door slamming. Serena turned to see Riley marching toward her with a ferocity that had her on her feet in self-defense.

"What the hell is your problem?" he bellowed as he stomped up the sidewalk.

Serena was getting a little sick of the question, but she answered as calmly as she could. "I could ask you the same thing."

"Claudia Daly's gone missing and you don't even call me in?"

Serena was glad she was on the steps of Clay's porch. From her perch, she was almost as tall as Riley. Normally, if he was this close he'd be glowering down at her, a position of superiority he enjoyed using.

"Your shift doesn't start until three. You've been on pretty much full time for days now. You needed sleep," she replied. The calm was fading from her voice now, her own temper rising.

"I don't need sleep. I need you not to cut me out of the fucking loop. You'd rather go with the B-team than me? You'd really risk the whole investigation to protect your little boyfriend here?"

Serena gave up her position on the step to shove her ex-boyfriend out of her face. "Step back, now, *Deputy*," she ordered.

"Don't fucking pull that," he shouted back at her. "You got no business being sheriff and you know it."

And there it was. Years of tension and this was how it was finally going to go down.

"You think I'm so fucking incompetent, how come you didn't run?" she shouted back.

"Have to be an idiot to run against a Marlowe."

"You'd have to be an idiot to run against *me*. It's got nothing to do with the rest of it. I've got more state police training than you, more FBI training than you, more commendations. I've spent my whole life training for this job. You know it and everyone in this damn town knows it. You didn't run against me because you knew you'd lose."

Riley glared at her. "Stupid classes. Stupid awards. Don't mean nothing."

Serena met his eyes with steel. "Then how about this, Riley – nobody was going to elect a hothead with an ego problem. Everybody knows all the times I've peeled you off somebody after you forgot how to control your temper. All the times my father had to do the same. Now, you need to step away. Go home. Rest some. And you need to stop thinking of me as your girlfriend, and start thinking of me as your boss, because I'm not going anywhere."

Riley turned on his heel and stormed off. It wasn't until he'd pulled away from the curb that Serena allowed herself to exhale.

For the second time that day, she'd managed to control a situation that was precariously close to turning violent. She was trying to catch a psycho. She didn't have time to be fighting with people about petty grievances.

Remembering Clay was still sitting on the porch, she turned slowly to face him, bracing for the worst. Much to her surprise, he was smiling.

"You've got to be kidding," she said. "What are you smiling at?"

"You dated him?"

Serena felt the day's tension evaporate as she melted into an exhausted laugh. "I almost got into a fistfight with one of my deputies and you're wondering about my dating history?"

Clay's smile only broadened. "I'm new here. I'm just trying to catch up."

Serena sank into a chair. "Yes, I dated him. We dated on and off for years actually. It looked a lot like what you just saw, but I typically lost most of our fights."

"Is that why you broke up?"

Serena sighed, wishing it was. "He hit me. I mean, it wasn't out of the blue. We were fighting, kind of like that. And he slapped me. Hard. I've spent a good chunk of my career pulling abusive spouses off each other. When he hit me I realized how close I was to being one of those people. I didn't want that."

Clay's eyes grew dark with anger. They shifted away from her and in the direction of the man who'd just sped off.

Serena placed her hand on his leg to get his attention. "It's over. It's been over a long time. I'm fine. In fact, I'm glad it happened. If not for that slap I might have married that jackass. Look, he is a good deputy. He's sleep-deprived. It'll be fine. He'll get it under control. That fight was a long time coming."

Clay looked skeptical.

"I promise," Serena assured him.

His eyes narrowed. "I know you're the sheriff, but seriously if he ever touches you...."

She cut him off. "He won't. It's fine."

Clay stared after Riley. Serena gave him a minute before she said, "What is it?"

"I was thinking about our little list of possible suspects from last night."

He didn't say anything more. He didn't need to. Of course he was right, the hothead was showing his true colors. Could Riley be a killer?

They'd been looking for the why. Suddenly, the possibility seemed obvious – was Riley creating a forensic disaster and public panic to get rid of her?

~ 39 ~

Leaving Clay with the mess in his office, Serena took Jake with her to interview Lucas about his relationship with Claudia. She'd been hoping to have Riley along for the interview, but she couldn't trust him right now. Not until they could talk about things rationally.

Jake was quiet for most of the ride, but eventually he said, "He doesn't mean it, you know?"

Serena didn't have to ask who he was. "I know, Jake, it's fine. Riley and I will work it out. We always do."

"He really cares about you. A lot. He was all busted up when you broke up with him. I don't think he ever really got over it."

It was an interesting take on their breakup. Serena longed to correct the version of events, but knew better. This was Riley's kid brother. It wasn't fair to bring him into things. And besides, it was bound to make an already tense situation worse.

"Honestly, Jake, I don't want to talk about this."

From the corner of her eye, she could see Jake's puppy face, so she kept her eyes on the road.

"Doc Drayton's a good guy, too. I guess I understand why you like him better."

Serena felt her temper spike. Damn small towns and their gossip. She'd been a vestal virgin since her breakup with Riley. She had every right to date somebody. It was nobody's business.

"It wasn't an either-or situation. It's not that I like Clay better than Riley. I'm never going to date Riley again. That's done."

Though Serena had tried to keep the anger out of her voice, she knew she'd failed for the most part.

Hoping to smooth out her tone she added, "Look, Jake, it's difficult having Norton and his stupid paper printing tabloid crap while I'm in the middle of a murder investigation."

It only took a second for Serena to realize how uncomfortably quiet Jake became. She glanced over at him. "What? It was in the paper, wasn't it?"

Jake's silence spoke volumes, as did the embarrassment that was so clearly written on his face.

"Jake Scott," she said in her best sheriff's voice. "What the hell aren't you telling me?"

He lowered his head and said, "Hayley told me. She called to tell me your status. She said Shane overheard what Norton was saying to you and he told her. She was just keeping me in the loop. Please don't get mad with her."

"And you called Riley and told him." With all the pieces in place, the timing of Riley's blow-up made more sense.

"I didn't know he'd get so mad. I just thought somebody should warn him, you know?"

Serena thought back to Shane and Hayley's flirtation, which had seemed so unimportant days earlier. What else was he telling her that she shouldn't know? And who was she telling?

~ 40 ~

When they arrived at the Denton house, Serena took a moment to focus Jake.

Meeting his eyes, she said, "I'm not mad with you. I'm not mad with Hayley. I'm not mad with Riley. It's fine. It's all going to be fine. Right now, we need to go in there and talk to Lucas. Can you do that with me?"

Jake's eyes were big and helpless and she wished desperately that he was a tougher cop. What a motley crew she had. It was a miracle they got anything done.

"Are you ready?" she asked again.

Jake nodded.

Serena had hoped for a better answer, but she knew one was not forthcoming. She climbed out of the car and waited for Jake to follow behind.

When he didn't let his nerves get the better of him, Jake was a pretty good officer. She hoped he could do that today. She wasn't terribly optimistic.

Lucas answered the door wearing only boxers. He squinted as the sun hit him in the face.

"Look, I don't know anything about the hospital. I don't have any idea what Reece was talking about yesterday. I swear," he grumbled.

"Can we come in, Lucas? Jake and I have a couple questions for you."

Lucas shrugged and retreated inside the house. Serena thought it was as close to an invitation as she was going to get.

She found Lucas in the living room, pulling on a pair of jeans. She pushed a food carton off a chair and made herself comfortable. Following her lead, Jake did the same. Lucas slumped on the couch, his expression still groggy.

"Out late, Lucas?" she asked.

"What's it to you?" he snapped.

She took a chance and dove right in. "What time did you leave Claudia Daly's house last night?"

The boy's expression told her all she needed to know. So, Serena pressed ahead, exploiting his surprise.

"I need the truth, Lucas. Claudia's missing. I need to know when she was last seen."

"What the fuck? Claudia's missing? When did that happen? What are you talking about? Are you jerking me around? You are, aren't you? She didn't do anything wrong! I'm eighteen, you know. I can make my own decisions."

Serena sat back and let him gather himself. It was an interesting outburst. If it was a cover-up, it was a very good one. He looked genuinely worried about the relationship. He really looked like he thought she was lying about the abduction. And for a moment, he looked like a kid. A very young, very upset kid.

Of course, sociopaths are generally pretty good liars. Was she looking at a sociopath, or a horny teenager? A couple days ago she wouldn't have hesitated, but someone was lying to her and whoever it was, he was very good at it. And frankly, with Lucas, lying was nothing new.

It was time to push things. See where they went. "You done with the stories, Lucas?" she mocked. "Are you gonna tell me what you did to her?"

His eyes grew wide. "Did to her?"

"I have two crime scenes. You're the only person I can place at both of them."

"What? What?" he stuttered, as he flailed to his feet. "Are you serious that Claudia's missing? That fucking psycho took Claudia?"

Part of her was elated. He looked so sincere. But she boxed away the feelings. She knew nothing. She gave him a couple minutes to pace and mutter his way through his anger.

He finally stopped pacing and faced her directly. "He took Claudia?"

The despair in his eyes was real. Serena was certain. Or at least she wanted to be.

"Lucas, please, sit. We're going to figure this out, but we need your help."

The boy slumped back onto the couch, looking every inch the victim.

"Were you with her last night?" Serena asked, keeping her voice even and calm.

Wariness crept into Lucas's eyes. "You aren't trying to tie her up are you? She said you two didn't get along in high school."

"The last thing I care about right now is Claudia's sex life. What I need to do is narrow my timeline as best I can. I need you to be honest with me so we can find her quickly."

Lucas seemed to believe her. He settled back on the couch. "I went over to her place last night around ten. I left there around three. My mom was off last night. She gives me all kinds of grief if I don't come home."

Serena was a little surprised anyone noticed. "And Claudia was okay when you left?"

"She was asleep. I'm not sure she even woke up when I left."

"Did you leave the house through the front door?"

"You crazy? Andi lives right next door. If her dad ever found out about this, he'd kill me for cheating on his daughter. And she'd tell him, spoiled bitch."

So much for young love, Serena thought. "How did you leave?"

"Same way I always do – out the back. She's got a door off the laundry room in the basement. I cut through the woods, park my car over by the playground on Pine Street."

It made sense. If Serena was sneaking in and out of that house, she figured that was the way she'd do it.

"Did you notice anyone? Anything weird? Anything at all?"

Lucas shook his head. "I was pretty tired. Wanted to get to the car and get home. I didn't notice anything."

A day that had started with some good leads was starting to fade back into the same litany of dead ends. Serena left Lucas to worry about the well-being of his secret lover, while she went back to the office. Maybe if she started writing up a report, she'd know what to do next.

~ 41 ~

Serena was clumsily typing up her report when she was interrupted by a knock on her office door. She called for them to enter without looking up. She pecked her way through her thought before she saw it was Riley standing in the entryway.

His face bore a familiar expression. It was a look she'd grown all too used to during their relationship. This was the part when he'd say he was sorry; it used to be the part where he told her he loved her and he didn't know what he'd do without her. She wondered if he really thought she believed the speech. More, she wondered if he believed it.

She motioned for him to sit and waited to hear his story.

"I overreacted," he began. "I, well, I don't like to hear about you with other guys."

Serena took a deep breath; losing her temper was not going to help this. "Riley, I'm not saying this to be mean. I'm saying it because it's the truth. There is no you and me anymore. There hasn't been for a long time. If you think there's a chance we're getting back together, then you need to reevaluate. That has nothing to do with Clay Drayton."

Riley wouldn't meet her eyes. She didn't know if it was resignation, or just an attempt to persuade her.

"I like working with you, Riley. You're a good cop. We both know that. But there is no you and me," she repeated.

"I understand," he said without looking up.

Serena considered stopping there, but thought better of it. "If you have a problem with the way I'm doing my job, you are welcome to come in here and talk to me. But I need to make one thing very clear – if you ever come at me in public again, I'm going to take you down – hard. And then I'm going to take your badge. You got it? I'm not messing around, Riley. That will never happen again. Ever."

He finally met her eyes. "I know. I'm sorry. I was out of line. I won't do it again."

Serena wished she hadn't heard those words from him so many times before.

Switching subjects, she asked, "Did you have a chance to look at the Daly crime scene?"

Riley seemed to relax, clearly more comfortable talking about work. "Not a real helpful scene. It was totally clean. This guy is not big on prints, huh?"

"And no prints at Drayton's either."

"You think that's connected?"

Serena still had no direct evidence to back that up, but she couldn't shake her gut feeling on it.

"I guess we could have two people who are breaking and entering through windows. It's not the most original technique in the world, but it's an awfully big coincidence. And both scenes were wiped clean. We aren't just dealing with someone who's wearing gloves. He keeps wiping everything down. When he's done there are no prints anywhere. It strikes me as connected."

Riley shifted in his seat and began to slowly crack his knuckles as he pondered the scene. He finally met her eyes and asked, "He was really with you last night?"

"Riley! What did we just talk about?"

He held up his arms in surrender. "No, I don't mean it that way. I swear. I think it's a little convenient, though. We had the whole heart thing, I was suspicious of Drayton and he gets knocked on the head. Then Claudia's abducted and Drayton is a victim of another crime. It seems like someone is trying to make it seem like it's not the doc."

Serena rolled her eyes. "Or maybe it doesn't just *seem* like it's not Clay. Maybe it isn't him."

"Maybe," Riley replied skeptically.

"You seriously want to interview me like a witness? Fine. Go ahead. Clay showed up at my house at six-thirty last night."

Riley straightened in the chair, a little uncomfortable with the situation, but willing to power through. Serena had to admit part of her admired his tenacity.

"What did you do?"

"Seriously?" she snapped.

"You said interview you. Let me interview you."

"We talked a bit. We had dinner. We ended up upstairs."

Riley seemed to consider asking more details about that part, but blessedly he didn't. "When did you fall asleep?"

Serena knew that was relevant, so she did consider it for a minute. "Around one-thirty."

"He could have left and then came back before you woke up."

As much as she hated to say it, Serena knew she had to. "You've been in my house. You've been in my bed. Can you think of any time that you getting out of bed didn't wake me?"

"Could he have slipped something in your drink?"

Serena snorted at the prospect. "It was hours between dinner and when we went to sleep and I felt rested this morning. He didn't drug me. You got anything else?"

She knew Riley well enough to know he wished he did, but he knew the "interview" was over.

Serena sat back in her chair and asked, "Can we officially rule Drayton out?"

Riley reluctantly nodded.

She thought of her conversation with Clay the night before, the profiling. All they'd come up with were hotheads and young men. Since her most intelligent hothead was sitting in her office, she was a fool not to ask. She knew Riley well enough not to ask directly.

"Okay then, my turn," she began. "I know how you feel about Dr. Drayton. And I know somebody broke into his office. You want to give me a sense of what you were doing last night?"

His eyes narrowed. "What are you asking me? You think I'm responsible for what's going on in town? You have a lot of fucking nerve!"

Serena smiled easily, hiding her racing pulse. "Of course I don't think you have anything to do with Claudia or Daisy. Somebody broke into Drayton's office and basically trashed the place. For all we know at this point, it was vandalism, plain and simple."

"You said you think it's connected!"

"I do think it's connected, but I wouldn't be doing my job if I didn't check the other possibilities. So, Riley, where were you last night?"

The rage radiated off him. His hands gripped the chair so tightly she was waiting for the arm to snap off.

"I was in bed. I was asleep. I was off-duty for the first time in a while. I was tired. Really tired."

Serena locked her eyes on his. "Bullshit. You don't sleep. You never sleep when a case gets intense. You don't sleep when the Stanley Cup playoffs get intense. Come on, Riley, give me a little credit."

Though her own tone and demeanor remained calm, it was not having the desired effect. Riley's temper was in the red zone and showing no signs of abating.

"Shane came on at three. I left around three-thirty, quarter to four. I drove home. Turned on the television."

"What did you watch?" Serena asked.

"Jesus, it was crap. It was four in the morning. I don't remember."

"How about you try to remember?" Serena sharpened her tone a little. He knew why she was asking – it was probably the only part of his story she could confirm. He knew it was a question he would have asked. He was either lying or being a dick if he stuck with the "I don't remember" answer.

"There was some ultimate fighting thing on cable. I watched that a while. Then I flipped on Cinemax."

Serena didn't need to ask what he was watching on the premium network. At that hour of the morning the shows had very little to do with plot and story. She suspected Riley would honestly have no idea what bit of smut he'd been watching.

"When I went to bed the sun was coming up," he explained. "I slept a little. That enough info for you?"

It was all pretty vague, which was awfully convenient, but it also sounded like an accurate description of a night in the life of Riley Scott. So much for getting confirmation of his story.

She merely nodded. "I guess if we're done with interrogations, we can run through the day."

Serena gave him the full rundown, typing much of it into her report as she went. She finished by telling him about Lucas and Claudia.

Riley whistled through his teeth. "That's crazy. I would never have thought she'd do something like that. Wow."

"You should do a follow-up with Lucas. I think he was telling the truth, but I think a second interview is important to confirm he's not involved in the abduction."

"You're still thinking Lucas could be our psycho?"

Serena wished she knew. "I don't want to think anyone in the town could do this, but somebody we know is completely nuts and we have no idea who. Lucas is eighteen, comes from an abusive home, was at both crime scenes. It's worth a look, don't you think?"

She watched as Riley considered the information and nodded. "Eighteen's a bad age for psych stuff?" he asked.

"It can be a reasonable window for things like schizophrenia." Serena was tempted to point out she'd learned that in one of the classes he'd called stupid earlier in the day.

"I'll talk to him. Maybe if I make it seem like I think he scored big with Claudia he'll tell me more."

Riley stood to leave.

Serena stopped him before he got to the door. "I need you on the team, Riley. I don't want our personal baggage getting in the way of that."

"I am sorry about what happened. I'm glad for you, really, I am."

Serena believed the first part of the sentence, and wished she believed the second part. She again considered Clay's accusation. She couldn't believe Riley was a killer. But she came back to the same troubling truth – somebody was.

~ 42 ~

The state labs were even less helpful than Serena had expected. She was transferred from one supervisor to the next, and treated to every excuse from staffing problems to budget cuts to the governor's personal vendetta against law enforcement. Serena would have kept pushing, but the lab supervisor had suggested she should ask for help from the state police if she wanted her case prioritized. Since that suggestion could only lead to attention Serena didn't want, she knew it was time to end the call.

She'd just hung up when there was a knock on her door. She looked up to see her brother holding a brown paper bag from his bar.

"It's too late for lunch and too early for dinner. If I know you, that means you haven't eaten since breakfast. So the turkey sandwich in here is just what the doctor ordered," he said.

"You ever get tired of being right all the time?" she asked.

Liam took the question as an agreement and pulled a chair up to her desk and handed her the sandwich. He pulled a can of soda out for himself.

"I was actually stopping by to talk to you about that," he said once she'd dug into the sandwich.

Serena raised an eyebrow. "About you being right? Come on, Liam, it's been a rough week already."

He smiled uncomfortably. "I talked with Missy last night."

After a moment, it became clear he wasn't going to say anything more. Serena put down her sandwich. "Is she okay?"

He shook his head. "No, it's not that. She's fine." He paused again, and said, "She told me what you two talked about."

It had been a long day. A long week. She was still digging through her brain, trying to remember the last time she talked with Missy, when Liam said, "About getting married."

It came back in a flash and, suddenly, Serena felt incredibly uncomfortable. She held up her hands.

"I have spent most of my adult life trying to stay out of your relationship. But she's my best friend. I was just trying to help her."

Liam laughed. "You're an idiot, you know that?"

Serena smiled cautiously. "You aren't mad?"

Liam's grin only broadened. "I'm the opposite of mad. We had a great talk. I'm going to go look at rings tomorrow."

"You didn't know?"

"I didn't have a clue. I've been gearing up to ask her to move in with me for a year, but with all she's been through…" his voice trailed off. "I didn't think she'd ever consider marriage. I knew she loved me. I figured that was going to have to be enough."

Serena could feel the tears burning in her eyes. Reminding herself that she was at work and had to keep up appearances, she pushed the emotions back. "Liam, I think this is great."

Her brother seemed to see the tears. "Sorry to do this to you at work. Honestly, I wanted to thank you. And these days, you're here all the time."

Serena shook her head. "No, I'm glad you came by. I needed some good news today."

Sliding out from behind her desk, she gave Liam a hug. "You guys are going to be very happy together," she said.

Liam embraced her tightly. "I sure hope so."

Serena allowed herself a moment before she returned to her desk and her sandwich.

"You tell Pop yet?" she asked.

"I'm heading there next. I thought you deserved the first stop, though. Since you made all this possible."

Serena laughed. "You would've figured it out eventually."

Liam shrugged. "Maybe. I'm glad we don't have to wait that long."

Once she settled back into eating, Liam said, "Word around the bar is Claudia Daly's been abducted."

Serena nodded. "Last night."

"That's not good," he said.

Serena marveled at her brother's ability for understatement. "Wasn't the best part of my day. I expect it wasn't the best part of Claudia's either. What's the general feeling around town?"

Liam leaned back in the chair. "People are upset, nervous. I think when folks heard it was Daisy who'd been taken they relaxed. I mean, she was so helpless in so many ways. But Claudia, if somebody can take Claudia you have to worry, you know?"

Serena did know. "We're pretty sure Claudia's the third victim," she said.

Liam smiled. "I know that, but people don't believe you. Or they didn't. They figure you don't have Daisy's body. So how can you know it's not her heart?"

"There's science behind it," Serena insisted. "I'm not making this up."

"You're preaching to the choir," he said. "I'm passing along what people are saying. That's all."

"Do they believe me now?"

Liam almost laughed. "Maybe. Sort of. I guess it depends on who you ask. Don't take it personally, Serena. They wouldn't have believed Pop, either."

Serena wished she was sure of that, but there were certain battles that would never be won. Her father had been a great sheriff. It was going to take a lot before they trusted her the same way. If they ever did.

"There any rumors I should know? Any suspects from the popular opinion polls?"

"By popular opinion polls, you mean the drunks at the bar? Oh, yeah, they have a suspect, but it's not what anyone would mistake for a helpful tip."

"Clay?"

"Of course. They're simple people looking for a simple answer."

Serena wondered what it was like to live in such a black-and-white world. She suspected it was a whole lot easier than the world she lived in.

"Anybody behaving oddly? Anything seem off?" she asked.

Liam laughed. "Everybody's behaving oddly. We've got somebody snatching people from their homes."

Serena rolled her eyes. "I thought you were here to make me feel better."

He stood. "A big brother's job is to distract you in the middle of your work day and then rush off, leaving you with only a sandwich."

Serena raised the sandwich. "And a good one at that. You go talk to Pop. He's going to be thrilled you've finally decided marriage is a viable life choice."

He laughed. "You aren't ever going to let me live this down, are you?"

Serena winked at him. "I don't expect that I will."

~ 43 ~

A distant corner of Serena's mind noticed the sun had set. A smaller part of her brain noticed Hayley had gone home and the night girl who she disliked so much was on. The happy buzz from Liam's visit had worn off, and it was just her and the investigation.

She noticed Shane was back on duty and he'd walked by her office four or five times, clearly worried he was going to get in trouble for telling Hayley what he'd heard. She fully planned on talking to him about the situation, but for now, she needed to let him stew and worry. It'd be good for him.

Ultimately, it was the knock on her door that finally got her attention. She looked up from the reports and papers to see Clay leaning against her doorframe, smiling at her.

"What's that look for?" she asked.

He stepped into the office, closing the door behind him, and slipped around to her side of the desk. He was standing very close when he said, "I missed you today. I was almost hoping for a catastrophe so I might get a chance to see you."

"These days you have to be very careful what you wish for," she replied, tugging gently on his shirt to pull him down to her level. "But I missed you too."

He gave her one of his fabulous kisses she was growing so fond of, and Serena realized she really had missed him. With all the work and all the chaos she hadn't really noticed it, but now, with him this close, she saw there'd been something missing from her day. Actually, something had been missing for a long time.

When she finally disentangled herself she said, "You are not allowed in my office. You're far too distracting."

Clay laughed and settled into a chair on the other side of her desk. "I'm actually here to talk to you about the case. I figured you'd still be working."

Serena straightened up and pushed non-work thoughts from her mind. "What do you have?"

"It took all day, but I searched the mess in my office. It's a long way from organized, but I can tell you with confidence – Claudia Daly's file is not there."

"You're sure?" She asked the stupid question even though she knew the answer. She just wished that he was wrong.

Clay didn't reply, seeming to realize that she wasn't really asking.

She ran a hand over the tension that was creeping into her neck. "Is hers the only file missing?"

Clay shook his head. "I have no idea. You saw the mess in there. I spent the whole day putting people's files back together. Nothing's sorted yet. I knew you thought there might be a connection between Claudia's file and her disappearance. So I watched specifically for her file. It's not there. As for everyone else, it's impossible to say. By the end of the day tomorrow, I'll have things sorted and re-filed."

"So someone took Claudia's medical records, and then took Claudia?"

"Or someone took Claudia and then took her records."

Serena thought of Lucas. "Had Claudia been in to see you recently?"

"Serena, I can't answer that."

She glared at him. "Don't give me that patient-doctor privilege crap. If what's in that file helps us find Claudia, then I bet she'd like us to know."

"How can anything in the file be helpful?"

"Claudia was having an affair with one of her students. I was thinking maybe she was pregnant, or she had some type of sexually transmitted disease?"

Clay's eyes grew wide at the news. "Well, I'm not sure if doctor-patient confidentiality is still protected when there's a kidnapping like this, but I'm sure Claudia would want me to tell you that she didn't come in recently for a pregnancy test and I have never diagnosed her with an STD."

Serena was about to ask another question when her intercom crackled to life. The voice of the annoying night girl informed her that Shane had called in from the old hospital.

He'd found Daisy Roman.

~ 44 ~

When Serena and Clay arrived at the scene, Shane was standing over a body. Both were bathed in the full glare of Coach Fletcher's spotlights. The sight was more than Serena could take at the end of a very long day.

She turned to Clay before he could move. Anger barely contained, she said, "You stay here."

Without waiting for an answer, she was out of the car. "Deputy Gilbert! You left this body here in the middle of the fucking parking lot to get the lights? What were you thinking? You never leave the scene. Never. You wait for back-up!"

Shane stared at her dumbfounded. It took a moment before he found his voice. "Sheriff, you don't understand. The lights were up when I got here. This is the scene, just the way I found it."

Serena looked from Shane to the lights and then back again. This wasn't a body dump. This was a scene. A designed scene. This was getting so much worse.

She laid a hand on Shane's shoulder. "I'm sorry, Shane. I shouldn't have assumed."

He shook his head. "I imagine you've been dying to shout at me all day, Sheriff. I deserve it."

Serena offered him a tired smile. "I'm pretty sure I'm not done shouting at you, but we'll save that for tomorrow, okay?"

She motioned to Clay to come join them and then took a position to better examine her scene. Daisy Roman was lying near the old emergency entrance to the hospital. A closer look at the body only confirmed Serena's initial instinct. The body looked dumped. Like it had been thrown out of a car. That was why she hadn't considered that the lights had been used for staging.

When Clay was close enough to see, she explained, "The killer placed the lights when he placed the body."

His expression told her that he was seeing the same thing she was.

"Can you tell anything from a distance?" Serena asked.

"Not a lot really. You're seeing what I'm seeing. There's the bloody nose, but no other obvious injuries. I'm going to need to do the autopsy before I'll be able to say much. I really can't tell with that sweater on her, but now that we have a body we'll be able to see if it was her heart we found."

"Boss, I'll get the camera and the kit. We can get started," Shane offered.

Once she was alone with Clay she asked, "The body looks like it was thrown out of a car and left very haphazardly, don't you think?"

"But then the killer took the time to place the lights," Clay finished.

Serena tore her eyes away from the body and looked at Clay, "Why would you do that?"

"Maybe the body placement is more significant than it looks at first glance?"

Serena looked again at Daisy. She was mostly on her back, with one leg bent under her, the other twisted awkwardly at the ankle, her arms were splayed out, and her head lolled to one side. She looked like a rag doll tossed to the curb.

"Why the lights at all?" Clay asked.

The question struck a cord for Serena. What was the purpose of the lights? "Could it be that he placed the lights to make sure we found her?"

"Maybe. Why the rush?"

"Do you think he's trying to tell us something? Maybe we aren't understanding something and he's annoyed we're missing it? He wants us to catch up."

Clay seemed to agree. He stood in silence for a moment and then said, "The heart? He wants us to know the truth about the heart?"

It actually made sense. The heart was plainly important to him. The ritualistic way he kept placing it inside the hospital told them that. Was he mad there were reports that the heart had belonged to Daisy, or mad they were saying it might not be hers?

Careful of the scene, Serena picked her way over to the body. With gloved hands, she stretched the neckline of the sweater. As she'd expected, underneath there was no evidence of injury to the chest. No incision meant they'd been right. Daisy Roman was not the only person missing. That meant three victims, not two.

Now it really was official. They had a serial attacker.

Shane returned and handed her the camera, taking the kit for himself. "I'm not sure how much I'll be able to gather at night."

Serena knew he was right. "Once we get the photos of the scene, we can reposition the lights and get a broader area."

"Is Riley on his way?" Shane asked.

"He's out doing a second interview with Lucas," she explained. "When he finishes up, he'll meet us here."

The strobe of the camera flash was quickly making the already disturbing scene worse. It was probably the lack of sleep, but Serena felt almost unsteady on her feet as she was barraged by the bursts of light.

She cleared Clay to look more closely at the body, and then shifted one of the spotlights to illuminate the rest of the scene. As she'd expected, there was nothing helpful. No tire tracks on the pavement. No obvious fibers left behind. They did have a body now, which might prove useful, but she knew her resources well enough to know that if this came down to a CSI-style investigation, she was screwed. They didn't have the manpower or the expertise.

~ 45 ~

Morning came brutally early. Or at least it felt that way. Another late night processing a crime scene was more than Serena had been up for. What was worse, she had a meeting with the mayor at nine.

Mario Smith's respect for sleeping late was well known in town. So an early morning meeting was not likely to be anything but unpleasant, even under the best of circumstances. And this was not the best of circumstances.

Grumbling to herself, Serena shuffled downstairs for coffee. She was about halfway to the living room when she realized she could already smell some brewing.

That meant only one thing.

Smiling, despite her bad mood and exhaustion, she snuck up behind her guest, who was sitting at her kitchen table reading the paper, and gave him a hug. "Morning, Pop."

William smiled at her. "Late night?"

Serena poured herself coffee and joined her father at the table. "Buster is still in bed. I'm so glad I have him to protect me from intruders."

"Buster is the worst guard dog ever. Fortunately for him, he's got a great nose for hunting." William gave her a good once over and said, "You look like hell, honey."

Serena took a long drink of her coffee. "You already hear about Daisy?"

William raised an eyebrow. "What about Daisy?"

Serena glanced up at the clock. "Looks like the town gossip mill's a little slow this morning. Seriously, you didn't hear?"

"You found her?" William guessed.

"She was dumped at the hospital. A weird scene, Dad. I'd like you to look at the pictures later. Tell me what you see."

William only nodded, waiting to hear the rest of it.

"Clay has the body. There weren't any obvious signs of trauma."

"The heart?" William asked.

"Not hers."

William cursed to himself. "I'd really hoped the doc was wrong about that."

"Yeah, me too."

"So you got two murders and another missing person?"

Serena pushed her sleep-tossed hair out of her eyes. "It's looking like that."

"Well, hell, that's just about the worst damn thing that's ever happened around here."

She shook her head and stared vaguely into her cup of coffee. After a moment, she said, "If you aren't here about Daisy, then what brought you out this early in the morning?"

William met her eyes with a very paternal look, which told her immediately that she was now talking to her dad, and not the man who was their former sheriff.

"Clay?" she asked, though she already knew the answer.

"I believe the last time we talked about him you were trying to convince me there was nothing to talk about. You keeping secrets from your old man?"

Serena's heart pounded a little at the accusation, much like it always had when she was a kid and she'd been caught doing something wrong. "It's kind of complicated."

William shook his head. "You kids make everything complicated. You know that? Things used to be easy. You like someone you ask them out on a date. And *you introduce yourself to their father*, like a proper gentleman."

Serena laughed at the suggestion. "You want him to introduce himself? Pop, he's your doctor. I suspect he feels you've already met."

"You know what I mean," he grumbled.

"I would love to go out on a regular date with him, but I can't do anything at all in this town without a hundred people talking about it. And right now, I can't have people thinking I'm starting up some kind of romance. They'll flip. I'll get fired. Hell, half of them are damn sure Clay's the one doing all of this."

"Are you sure he's not?"

To her father's credit, it wasn't a prejudiced question. It was just a query and a smart one. The only thing worse than starting a romance in the middle of a town crisis would be starting a romance with a murderer.

She thought of Riley's interrogation the day before. "I'm certain he's been cleared of suspicion."

"Is that just based on him getting hit over the head? I respect Missy's skills, but I don't feel certain he couldn't have done that to himself."

Serena knew she should come clean, but she couldn't do it. When they were kids, Liam always told her it's better to confess, but she always held out a ridiculous hope she could keep secrets from her father.

She went to get more coffee. "There's more than the head thing."

When she turned back around, steaming mug in hand, Sheriff Marlowe's eyes locked on hers. Of course, he knew, but he was going to make her say it.

"Hell, Pop, come on. He was here when Claudia was taken. He was here when his office was broken into. And if you saw the knot he has on the back of his head you wouldn't think for even a second he could have done it himself."

William's face was unreadable. Serena suspected it might be for the best. "That why you and Riley had a big blow-up in front of the doc's office yesterday?" he asked.

Sighing, she took a long drink of her coffee. "He flipped out about Clay and me."

"Did you tell him about it?"

"It's a long story, but Norton Finwick threatened to put it in the paper. One of the deputies heard him, it got back to Riley."

The anger on William's face was so obvious that Serena immediately regretted her admission.

"Norton threatened you?" William asked.

"Not really. I mean, he did, but he was just being a little weasel. You know how he is."

It was a complete lie. Norton was threatening her. That's why she'd assumed her secret had gotten out because he'd printed the story. It was probably only a matter of time before he actually printed the "news."

After taking a long moment to consider the situation, William said, "You have a meeting this morning with the mayor, right?"

"We've got a killer on the loose. Since no one can remember the last time someone could say a thing like that, yeah, I have a meeting with the mayor this morning."

"Would you be terribly offended if I joined you?"

The look on her father's face told Serena that she shouldn't be offended. It looked like William knew something she didn't and she'd be well served to have him on her team for the meeting.

"I'd be happy to have an ally."

William took a sip of his coffee and then stared at it for a long time. When he spoke again, his tone had changed completely. "You like him? The doc?"

Serena was normally cagey with questions like that, but she thought better of it. "I actually do. More than I would have thought."

"Has he been nice to you?"

Serena almost scoffed at the question. They had barely spent any time together yet. It was far too early to answer that. But then she saw the look in his eyes. Riley. This was about Riley.

"Riley wasn't that bad, Pop. I'm fine. I took care of myself fine."

William shook his head. "I wish I'd have stopped it before it started, but I like Riley, always have. I'd hoped he'd be different with. But he wasn't. He was manipulative. When he had a bad day, he'd take it out on you. Critique your work on the job, belittle your clothes or your hair or something stupid. I rejoiced the day you dumped him. I knew you had to do it yourself; I couldn't make it happen. But it was hard not to protect you from it. Really hard."

Serena didn't remember the relationship being as bad as everyone seemed to think it was, but she was starting to think maybe her decision not to date after Riley had had less to do with not being interested in the other guys and more to do with not being willing to put herself in a position of weakness again.

"Clay's nothing like Riley. He's sweet, supportive." With Clay it didn't feel like she was putting herself in a position of weakness. Somehow he made her feel stronger, more confident.

Before William could say anything more, Buster shuffled into the room, stretching. He nudged his buddy's hand to get his attention. William scratched his ears, but his eyes never left his daughter. "What did the mutt here think of him?"

Serena smiled. "Buster thought he was the best thing since you, Pop."

~ 46 ~

Serena was freshly showered and as bright-eyed as possible when she and William walked into the mayor's office at five minutes before nine. Serena had expected that an early meeting would ensure the mayor's late arrival, but she was surprised when they were sent immediately back to the conference room. Serena wasn't sure if the swift action was a good sign or a bad one.

The sight of Norton Finwick sitting comfortably across from the mayor answered that question. He'd been there a while already. His coffee cup was mostly empty.

Serena glanced up at her father. She couldn't help but notice he didn't look anywhere near as surprised as she felt.

The mayor stood when he saw them in the doorway. "It's both the Sheriffs Marlowe." Like a true politician, he thought his joke was very funny. "Good to see you,

William. I'm surprised you're out this early in the morning."

Though Mayor Smith extended his hand, William only glared at it. Suddenly, it was clear her father had reason to believe this was going to be a brutal meeting, and he was playing bad cop – most likely to make her look like good cop. She wished he'd let her in on the little game before they'd arrived.

William took a seat at the conference table. "I didn't know the press was going to be here this morning."

His rudeness clearly made Smith uneasy. He scurried back to his seat, across from Norton. Serena slid into the seat at the head of the table, between Norton and the mayor.

She turned to Norton, politely wished him a good morning. Then, turning her attention to the mayor, she said, "You asked to talk to me about the case this morning. I guess we're doing an interview instead." Serena tried to keep her tone authoritative, but pleasant. No need to be aggressive. Her father was clearly taking care of that.

The mayor glanced between her and William and said, "I was hoping you could update me on what's going on."

Serena smiled. "I'd be happy to, Mayor Smith, but it's an ongoing investigation. We can only give certain information to the press."

"Norton here was telling me a couple of things I didn't know," Smith began. He glanced at William, clearly wary of his reaction. "He said the heart was stolen from police custody."

Serena wished she didn't already know where this was going. How had her father known this was going to happen?

"Clay Drayton was going to transfer the heart to the state police…."

Before Serena could finish, Norton cut in, "But he lost it."

Smiling her sweetest smile at Norton, Serena said, "He was attacked from behind. Hit over the back of the head with a two-by-four. When he came to, the heart was gone."

"So he says," Norton insisted.

Serena looked at the mayor. "So the lump on the back of his head says. I'm sure he'd be happy to let you see it if you'd like. Someone attacked him and stole the heart. We're pretty lucky he didn't quit on the spot. Nobody takes a job as a small town coroner expecting to be attacked like that."

Before Norton could say anything else, Serena added, "You should know we have the heart back. Also, and I suspect this is why we're really here, you should know Clay Drayton and I are involved in a relationship."

The only person in the room who didn't seem shocked by her voluntary admission was her father. He just looked pleased with her ability to handle the situation thus far. Serena wished she had his confidence. Her pulse was pounding so hard she feared she was close to having a massive heart attack that would land her in early retirement, like her father.

The mayor stuttered and then said, "You're admitting to having a relationship with a primary suspect?"

"No, sir. I have a relationship with Clay Drayton. I assume Norton already told you Dr. Drayton has been completely eliminated as a suspect." She, of course, knew he hadn't. The way that Norton squirmed in his seat confirmed her suspicion. "He has an alibi for the time Claudia Daly was abducted."

"You can't actually know exactly what time Claudia was taken," Norton insisted.

Serena didn't even try to suppress her smile. "Claudia was seen making dinner earlier in the evening. Her living room light was turned off around ten. She was last seen in her home at three in the morning."

Norton straightened up. "Who saw her then?"

Serena looked between the mayor and the reporter. As sweetly as she could, she said, "I know I'd hate it if people were discussing my sex life unnecessarily. I suspect Claudia would feel the same way. The who isn't important. She was last seen at three. She was left alone in the house."

Mayor Smith shot Norton a cold look. He was embarrassed by this whole encounter and blamed Norton entirely. Serena was thrilled. It looked like she might have won this odd little skirmish.

Smith looked at Serena far more kindly than he had all morning and asked, "Do you have any leads?"

It was a good question. The first one that had been asked so far. "We have a couple. And now that we have Daisy Roman's body, I'm hoping there will be some forensic evidence to assist us. Also, the state lab has several blood samples and the heart itself. But we're hoping this investigation doesn't take as long as that. You know how the state can be."

The mayor nodded as if he had a clue what she was talking about, which, of course, he didn't.

It was, unfortunately, time to relay the bad news. "We now are certain there is a third victim. The heart we found that started the whole investigation does not belong to Daisy Roman. There's still another body out there. Sir, we are doing all we can and moving as fast as we can. We uncovered several very interesting things yesterday. Hopefully, today goes as well."

Smith continued to nod appropriately and tried to look like he was in control of the situation. Serena had to wonder if he was this bad at all aspects of his job or just the crime-related ones.

"Do you have a suspect?" he asked, looking more optimistic than she would have liked.

"No, sir. We don't. Like I said, we have some leads. But no suspects."

"People are frightened," he declared, as if he thought she might be surprised by this news. "They need you to figure this out as quickly as you can. Things like this don't happen in Whitefield. People come to Whitefield to get away from things like this."

Serena knew that all too well. That was the only thing that was keeping her going on almost no sleep – she was on a steady diet of adrenaline, caffeine, and fear.

"I know, sir. I promise you we are doing all we can to figure this out." Serena hoped she sounded earnest and not desperate.

The mayor smiled his campaign smile and said, "I'm going to hold you to that, Sheriff." Then he stood. "I don't want to take up any more of your time."

Serena maintained a calm façade as she followed her father out of the conference room. It wasn't until they were outside, standing in the morning sun, that she took a deep breath and tried to release the anxiety. She almost felt compelled to drop her hands to her knees, as she might after a long run.

Her father seemed to see the look on her face, and he gave a gentle disapproving headshake. They were in the center of town. She needed to keep her game face on. Instead, he led her to the coffee shop and his favorite booth in the back. He motioned for them to send two coffees.

"You were fantastic in there," he said, once they were alone.

Serena shook her head. "I can't tell you how completely freaked out I was. He was going to fire me, wasn't he?"

William laid a hand on hers. He waited for the waitress to drop their coffees before he spoke. "He was going to threaten to fire you. I'm not sure he would have had the courage to do it."

"How did you know? I was told it was a status meeting."

"Norton started working with his dad his freshman year in high school. That was the same year your mother got sick. We'd decided to keep it quiet for a while. We knew it was bad, and didn't want you kids to realize how bad. You were so little. So, we made that decision."

William poured some sugar in his coffee and stirred it absently as he spoke. "I was a deputy at the time, but your grandfather was starting to have trouble with his hip. People were already talking about me taking over. When your mother got sick, I cut back on my hours so I could help out. Norton caught wind of it. He approached me about it. He acted like it was the biggest story since Watergate. I blew him off. About a week later, I found myself in a meeting with the mayor, like the one you just had. It was both me and your grandfather. It caught me completely off-guard. It was ugly. The only good thing I accomplished was I didn't end the meeting by beating Norton half to death. In the end, we had to tell you kids more details about your mom, and we had a town meeting about whether or not I was capable of working my job in the middle of my personal troubles."

"Norton did that to you?" Serena was stunned. How had she never heard this story?

"A *fourteen-year-old* version of Norton did that to me. When you told me about Clay this morning, I realized you were in trouble."

"You could have told me."

William shook his head. "I could have been wrong. You have enough to worry about right now. I didn't want you to worry about Norton, too."

Serena drank her coffee. She was starting to feel like herself again. "A warning might have given me a chance to get prepared."

Her father smiled. "Let me do what I can to help, honey. Even though it's pretty clear to me that you don't need it."

It was a high compliment, but a fairly ridiculous notion. She had a bunch of strange, unrelated clues and no idea what to do with them. She needed help all right. She was beginning to think all the help in the world wasn't going to be enough.

~ 47 ~

Serena finally made it to the station a little after ten. She hadn't previously thought it was possible to be this tired so early in the morning.

Hayley greeted her with a cautious smile. "How did the meeting go?"

It was obvious Hayley didn't care about the meeting. She was trying to gauge how mad Serena still was about the prior day. Feeling she'd let her dangle long enough, Serena sat on the edge of the large reception desk.

"Do you understand why things that happen within the station have to stay within?" It seemed like the best place to start.

Hayley's eyes grew wide. "I would never tell anyone outside of the station about what goes on here. Never. My little brother, he's always bugging me to tell him about working here and I won't tell him a thing."

Well, at least that was something. Remembering the morning's events, she asked, "How about Norton Finwick?"

"That worm? He's always trying to get me to talk to him. Bought me some drinks one night, and he was totally trying to get me to spill, but I wouldn't say a word."

"Does he pester you often?"

Hayley rolled her eyes dramatically. "Any time we're out at the bar, I swear, he's right there."

Again, Serena cursed small towns. Hayley must be gossiping when she drinks. Otherwise, Norton would have given up by now. It was probably nothing huge – frankly, there was rarely anything huge going on – but at times like this every piece needed to be protected.

"Hayley," she began gently, still trying to figure out what to say. "I appreciate all you do here and I appreciate how hard you try to keep our confidence."

And that was when Hayley started to cry.

Serena wouldn't have been more surprised if she'd run out of the room screaming. She quickly snatched two tissues and handed them to the girl. "What is it?"

Hayley waved off the tissues and looked away. "I'm sorry. You're right. I'll just go. I'm so sorry."

What the hell? "Go? Go where?"

"Go home. I understand. I'll pack up my things. I can be out in a few minutes."

Serena grabbed Hayley's arm before she could get up. "Why would you go home? I don't want you to go home. Do you think I'm firing you? I'm not firing you."

Hayley's weepy eyes met her with pure adoration. "You aren't? You really aren't?"

"Hell, no. Of course not." Serena extended the tissues, again. "It's fine. I mean, it's not *fine*. I really need the gossiping to cease. I talked to Shane about it, too. Even in-house, it's not okay. If people need to know things, they'll be told. Besides, I think it was fairly clear this was gossip. It wasn't a work thing."

Hayley nodded contritely, taking the tissues. "Of course, Sheriff. It'll never happen again."

Serena was pretty sure it wouldn't. She patted Hayley on the arm and stood.

Before she could go, Hayley stopped her. "I almost forgot. There's a message for you. Dr. Drayton called. He wants you to meet him in his office when you get a chance. He said he has something you'll need to see."

On another day, Serena might have pointed out that was exactly the sort of information that should have been conveyed the moment she walked in the door, but there'd been enough conflict for one morning already. Instead, she thanked Hayley and headed back out.

Before she could reach the door, Hayley called after her. "Sheriff?"

Serena turned, trying hard not to look impatient.

Hayley's expression was that of a teenager swooning over a pop star. "He's absolutely adorable. You're so lucky."

The comment was so absurd Serena almost asked who she was talking about.

Hayley took her silence as agreement. "I mean he's not movie-star handsome or anything, but he's kind of hot. And you can just tell he's super smart. I bet he's a great kisser. Is he a great kisser?"

Serena shook her head and slipped out. Plainly the lecture about not gossiping at work had really made an impression. She dreaded to think what conversations

Norton might be listening in on the next time he was eavesdropping at the bar.

~ 48 ~

For another day, the "in surgery" sign was up at Clay's office. It was a sign of the times – autopsies were becoming more of a full-time job than general medical care.

Though she received an intimate smile from the good doctor when he opened the door, it wasn't until they were safely alone in his waiting room that Clay pulled her close and gave her a toe-curling kiss. Hayley was right. He was a fantastic kisser.

"How's your day going?" he asked.

Serena considered filling him in, but thought better of it. "It's better now."

She gave him credit for not pressing her any further. Instead, he said, "I'm not sure if I'm about to make your day better or worse. I haven't started the autopsy yet, but I did have a chance to examine the body more closely."

They both sat on his waiting room couch and Clay handed her a folder. "There are pictures in there and a quick write-up. You'll get the formal report after I do the full autopsy. Unfortunately, it's going to have to wait until this evening. I have some patients who I have to see this afternoon. They can't wait any longer."

Clay's primary job had to be caring for the living in the town. They all understood that. "So, what's the preliminary?" she asked, opening the file.

"Daisy was bound for a period – there are markings on her wrists and ankles that indicate restraint. Also, there's cracking and blood around her mouth, which indicates a gag was used. The ligature marks are showing some signs that they'd begun healing."

Serena looked up. "Meaning?"

"She was bound initially, but more recently was not."

"Like maybe she was locked in a room or cell or something like that so they didn't need the restraints any longer."

Clay shrugged. "There's more. There was a substance smoothed over the cuts – I've collected samples to go up to the state lab, but I'm confident the cream is Neosporin or a similar product."

"He was treating her wounds?"

"Sure looks like it. And there's one more thing – I found several long brown hairs on the victim's body."

Serena paged through the file to the pictures. Sure enough, there were several photos. All long hairs with a slight curl at the tip.

Clay explained, "The hairs are very long – about eighteen inches. Definitely brown. I'm sending them up to the state lab. I have to say – I haven't lived here too long, but I don't think I've ever seen a man in Whitefield who had long hair."

It was exactly what Serena was thinking. Long hair on men was simply unheard of here in town. There were a couple teenagers with shaggy hair, but nothing long enough to account for this kind of length.

"You think the hairs belong to a woman?" Serena knew he did, but she needed a minute to get used to the idea.

"I think I'm glad my job is reporting the evidence, not interpreting it."

Serena considered all the other possible sources of the hair. There weren't many. Daisy was a shut-in, which meant her world was very limited. She knew there were five women who checked in on her daily, but none had long brown hair – including Claudia.

"I have long brown hair," she suggested.

"When was the last time you saw Daisy?"

Serena thought back. "About three weeks ago maybe."

Clay looked skeptical. "I'd expect her clothes would have been washed in that period of time. And you always wear your hair up, so you're less likely to leave stray hairs."

"Any thoughts on cause of death?" Serena asked.

"There's still nothing obvious. It could be a poison of some kind. I see some indications of hemorrhage – the bloody nose we saw last night, and there's blood in her ear canal. Her skin is jaundiced. I need to get inside to see more. To warn you, I expect we won't get a very satisfying answer until we get results back from the state labs."

More delays. No matter where she turned and what she did, more delays. But she did have some new things to think about. Riley was scheduled to come in soon. It was time for a brainstorming session. They needed to focus on suspects.

~ 49 ~

Riley's shift started at one. Knowing he would be early, Serena had her lunch in the conference room. As she expected, he arrived a little after twelve, just as she sat down to eat.

He joined her immediately, clearly anxious to get yesterday's embarrassment out of the way. "We have anything on the body yet?" he asked.

Serena slid the file across the table to him. "Drayton has no thoughts yet on cause. We're waiting on tox results, that sort of thing."

Riley turned his attention back to the file. "He found a woman's hair on the body?"

"Several, actually. He's not sure of gender."

Her deputy gave her a look.

"I know, but maybe the guy isn't local? Maybe he's from a couple towns over?"

"Why the hell would all the crimes happen here and why the hell would he stage his weird ass heart display in our abandoned hospital?"

Of course he was right, even though Serena wished he wasn't. "So, I was running through in my head the people who have been in contact with Daisy. It's a pretty short list and really no one obvious with long brown hair. Lauren Fletcher, of course, but I never got the impression she visited Daisy all that often."

Riley nodded. "She is her neighbor. So, she may have been around her."

"There's also me, but honestly I haven't been to her house in a while."

"So, if we exclude you two, then that leaves us with a long-haired killer?" Riley asked.

"Well, I was thinking maybe there's a woman in the killer's house and that's where the hair came from."

Riley laughed. "I'd think you of all people would have given a woman credit enough to be our killer. I mean, are you suggesting a woman couldn't do this?"

A woman *could* do something like this, certainly. "Classically, violent serial attackers are men."

Riley leaned back in his chair. "You know, these crimes don't really seem all that violent if you think about it."

"Two people are dead, Riley."

"Yeah, but not violently. So far, Daisy's death sounds like poison or something passive."

Serena stared at him in amazement, not sure if he was making a brilliant observation or a ridiculous one. "How about the heart that was ripped out of the other victim's body? How about the blood all over the room?"

"I don't know about the blood, but that heart wasn't ripped out. Didn't the doc say it was cut out carefully? Don't we think the person was practicing for months on animals? This heart guy is more of a surgeon than a butcher. Maybe he's not a he."

It was troubling how much sense the explanation made. Now they had to consider both men and women as they figured this out. Their list of possibles just doubled.

"That would make these the killer's hairs?" she wasn't really asking, more considering.

Riley turned his attention to the file. "I mean, it could be, you know?"

Serena knew. She just wished she didn't.

"Drayton also said the killer treated Daisy's wounds."

Riley gave her a look that screamed – *that sounds like a woman* – but he didn't say anything. Instead he closed the file and slid it back across the table to her.

"Do you have any idea who could be doing this?" he asked.

"What did you think of Lucas during your interview last night?"

Riley shook his head. "He's a kid. It sounds like he was pretty hot for Claudia Daly. I can't think of any reason he'd hurt her."

"What if she dumped him?"

"That could do it. You think maybe he came over that night, she dumped him, and he flipped his top?"

Serena sighed. "No, I don't think that, not really. If he flipped out, we'd have a body, or blood, or something more than we have. We have a relatively quiet-looking scene. Someone snuck into her house. I don't think she really even knew what hit her."

"Maybe the kid convinced her to give him one for the road? Maybe he did it after she'd fallen asleep?"

"Did what? Kidnapped her? And then did what with her? He lives in a small house with his parents. They aren't the greatest, but I think they would notice the high school principal tied up in his room."

"And his mom has short black hair – not long brown. So where would the hairs come from?" Riley asked. "Is it possible Claudia's disappearance is not related to the other crimes?"

Serena considered the question. It was possible, but it didn't seem likely. "I won't pretend to know what happened here, but it sort of feels like our man took Daisy and then that didn't work out for him – so he killed her. Then he needed to fill her spot with a new person – Claudia."

Riley sat up straighter in his chair. "You think that's why he broke into the doc's office? Was there something wrong with Daisy? Something medical? Some reason she died?"

Serena considered it. Was that the link between the break-in and the abductions?

"That could be why he broke into the office," she agreed. "But what could have been in that file to make him focus on Claudia?"

"You should ask the doc about that. Maybe that'll help him with cause of death. Even if he can't give us anything definitive without the labs, it'd help to have a couple theories to work on."

Serena scribbled in her notebook. This felt like a lead. "So, for now, we have to focus on the hair samples."

Riley nodded. "You think we can get samples from anyone in town who has long hair?"

"I can call around, see if we can convince somebody to get us a warrant."

"In the meantime, I can make up a list of people with long brown hair. The more I think about it, the more I think there aren't that many. I mean, running through town off the top of my head, I'm coming up with only fifteen. I'm thinking twenty, max. I bet most of them will provide hair samples willingly."

The town was in a panic. Serena suspected Riley was right; people would be happy to help narrow the suspect pool. At least most of them would.

"Both Andi and Madison Sinclair have long brown hair. There's no way Avery lets them hand over their hair. He's still steamed we talked to Andi without him," Serena pointed out.

"You think it'd help get us a warrant if there were only a couple of people in town who declined?"

Serena had no idea if it would help. It seemed like it wouldn't hurt.

~ 50 ~

By mid-afternoon, Riley was out picking up hair samples. His final list contained twenty-three people. He began the process of asking people if they'd help, starting with the most likely to volunteer without question.

In the meantime, Serena had a painfully long conversation with the D.A.'s Office about the likelihood of getting warrants. The discussion ended with her promising to send over the paperwork and the D.A. telling her he'd think about it. It was a relief when she was finally able to rejoin Riley and the investigation.

"You cannot believe how cooperative people are being. Everybody I asked was practically falling all over themselves to volunteer. I only have seven left," Riley explained. "I decided to leave Missy Skylar for you. I doubt she'd refuse to give a hair sample because I'm the one who asked her, but just in case, it seemed better for you to ask."

Serena couldn't have agreed more. "Who's left?"

"I tried the coach's house first. They weren't home. I'll swing by later tonight."

Serena nodded. "How about you catch up with Lauren and I'll take care of Missy."

"You got a deal. That leaves a couple more for us to take care of first – Yvonne Beech, Lori-Ann Tinsdale, Veronica Martin and the Sinclairs."

Yvonne was unpredictable. She was a retiree, and more than a little paranoid, but, generally, she considered the police to be helpful. Serena hoped this would not be an exception.

But Lori-Ann and Veronica were high school students, which was probably going to be trouble. Hopefully her friendship with Lori-Ann's grandmother would help.

Riley waited while Serena considered the information. Then he added, "I left off kids for the most part. I know it may be a problem later. I mean, if the killer was using a basement room or something and the long hair was his kid's and it was on the blanket or something…"

Serena cut him off. "It's not even worth pursuing. We run around town asking people to volunteer hair samples from their kindergartener, we're going to get a lot of doors slammed in our faces. The high school girls are bad enough. Did you just pursue the seniors?"

"I cut the age off at seventeen. I can't believe anyone younger than that could be capable of this."

Serena was a little concerned they were being too conservative, but she told herself it was the first step. "That age cut-off keeps Andi Sinclair on the list. I really doubt she's involved, but I've got her boyfriend sleeping with one of the victims and her house right next door. We need to check the Sinclairs. We'll worry about the rest of the loose ends later. And hopefully, by then, I'll have a better sense of how likely a warrant is."

They approached Yvonne Beech's house together. Riley hung back enough to let Serena do the talking. She couldn't help but notice how tired he looked. She really hoped she didn't look as bad, but unfortunately, she knew the truth.

It took a while for Yvonne to get to the door, which was not unexpected. Serena had no idea how old she was, but she knew Yvonne had been retired for as long as Serena could remember. Though the doctors had tried for years to convince her to get a knee replacement, she insisted she would do fine with the one God gave her. Unfortunately, that one seemed long past its useful life.

Serena was pleased to hear the woman ask who was at the door before she opened it. The sound of locks sliding followed after Serena identified herself and she was greeted by the ageless Ms. Beech.

"What are you two doing out here?" she asked, showing them in. "Can I get you some tea?"

Serena smiled. "We'd like to talk to you for a minute, if we could."

Yvonne led them into the living room where she settled into a stiff-looking recliner. There was a romance novel open on the table next to her, and a china cup which seemed to contain tepid tea.

Once Serena and Riley sat down on the couch, Yvonne volunteered, "I've been hoping you'd come out. Remember I was telling you about them boys on the block? I think they might be trouble."

Serena stared blankly for a moment, before she remembered Yvonne's comment during the town meeting about the boys on her block who she thought were Satanists. Though she knew it was a ridiculous theory, Serena went with the flow. "I was hoping you could tell me more specifically who caught your eye. Every bit of information is helpful."

She was pleased to see Yvonne eating up the prospect of being helpful. "Well, there's Timmy Green and Leon Rent. They're neighbors – live two houses down."

Serena knew where they lived. She also knew Timmy and Leon were in their last year in the middle school and didn't cause enough trouble to have even appeared on her radar before. She had seen them skateboarding with vigor, which she suspected was the bigger problem here.

She took out her notebook and wrote the names down. Riley, following her lead, asked, "Was it just them?"

"Well, no, I mean, I think they're the ringleaders, but there are two other boys who are over there all the time. I don't know their names." She paused long enough that Serena was about to jump in, but then she added, "I'm sure Lucas knows. I'll ask him when he comes by later in the week."

Serena almost fell out of her chair. "Lucas Denton?"

Yvonne smiled. "Oh yes, Lucas is such a good boy. He does my yard work you know. Comes by once a week. We've got leaves falling. He'll be over to rake them up soon."

"What day do you expect him?" Serena wasn't sure how it was relevant, but she needed to keep the conversation going while she figured out why she kept running into Lucas Denton.

"Oh, you just never know with him. It's always later in the week. He comes by whenever it suits him. He has a key to the house. He's such a nice boy. He has dinner with me some nights."

Serena didn't hear much after – *he has a key to the house.* Yvonne was a sweet lady, but Serena was sure a boy with a key to this house could get away with all sorts of things without anyone noticing.

"He is a nice boy," Serena found herself saying. "He must help you a lot around the house."

"Oh, so much. I can't really get up and down those cellar stairs anymore. That lovely boy helps me with that now. In the summer he carries all my winter clothes down there. In the winter, he switches them. You know, with those nice plastic boxes with the lids. What do they call them – RubberMate?"

"Rubbermaid," Serena corrected her absently. Deciding on a strategy, she went ahead with her original purpose. She'd get to the rest at the end. It might work better that way. "Well, I would sure like those other boys' names. If you can get those from Lucas, that'd be wonderful."

Yvonne nodded helpfully. "I will call you the moment I know."

Serena smiled back. "Thanks. While we're here, though, there's one other thing. We found some hairs at one of the crime scenes, and we'd really appreciate it if you'd be willing to give us a sample of your hair, just to exclude it."

Yvonne cackled with laughter. "Sheriff, I'm hurt you don't think I could be a suspect. Is it because I'm old?"

Serena laughed, relieved at the response. "I would never call you old, Ms. Beech. My daddy taught me better than that."

Without another word, Yvonne plucked a hair right out of her head and extended it to Riley. "You take that and exclude me, like the lady promised."

Riley quickly pulled out an evidence bag and packaged the hair properly. Serena suspected this was the first time all day he'd watched a hair get plucked on sight.

Yvonne looked back at her. "It's not dyed either. Believe it, Sheriff. After all these years, not a gray hair on my head. It's clean living. You'd better believe it. It's the drinking and the shenanigans that give a person gray hair. And that's the truth."

Serena suspected days like this were going to give her gray hair, but she thought it better not to express that opinion. "Thank you so much, Ms. Beech. Is there anything we can do for you while we're here? Riley's got a strong back. I'm sure he'd be happy to move anything downstairs you might need."

"Oh no. Thank you, though. Lucas takes care of all that for me. I'm just fine. Besides, you two have other things you need to do, I'm sure."

Though Serena tried several different angles on small talk that might lead to either she or Riley getting access to the basement, she eventually had to give up. It was pointless and Yvonne was eventually going to get suspicious. Without more, they couldn't act. And without more, they wouldn't convince Yvonne not to trust the "good boy" who looked out for her. Better not to aggravate her; she might try to take the hair sample back.

Serena really wondered about the relationship. There were a couple ways to look at Lucas. He had a terrible home life. Was he turning to Yvonne and Claudia to provide support and love in a way he didn't find at home? Maybe he was a good kid who was trying to get by. Or maybe he was manipulating all of them.

~ 51 ~

Serena cringed a little as she knocked on the Tinsdales' door. It felt utterly absurd to be standing here, waiting to hassle Lori-Ann Tinsdale yet again. Even knowing her reasons, knowing she had no other choice, Serena felt like a jerk.

Betty Tinsdale opened the door to greet them. Her smile was genuine, but there was an ounce of caution in her eyes that hadn't been there two days earlier.

"This is a surprise," she said.

The absence of an invitation into the house was telling.

Serena smiled, hoping her face conveyed her regret. "Mrs. Tinsdale, I'm really sorry to bother you again. Can we come in?"

She hesitated a moment before she led them back to the kitchen. "I took the week off of work. Lori-Ann, too. Jack was adamant, and honestly, I can't blame him," she explained.

Serena nodded. "Hopefully we'll get this all figured out real soon."

Mrs. Tinsdale looked skeptical, but she offered a smile. "Well, you'd better. Lori-Ann's about to pull her hair right out. She's going stir crazy missing a week's worth of classes."

Serena tried to appear capable and confident. "We're pursuing several leads. I think we're starting to make some progress."

Through tiny wire-rimmed glasses, Mrs. Tinsdale gave her a close look. After a moment she said, "You look awfully tired, Serena."

Serena laughed. "I'm feeling fine. Don't you worry about me."

Then Mrs. Tinsdale turned her attention to Riley, and added, "Don't look so smug, you look even worse."

Riley grinned. "Sure. She was always your favorite."

"Why are you two showing up on our doorstep? I can't imagine you're here to talk about how tired you are. Jack's in his cave working. My daughter-in-law is out grocery shopping. Are you looking for them?"

Serena got down to business. "I was hoping to talk to Lori-Ann, actually. We're collecting hair samples from the women in town with long brown hair. I know Lori-Ann has nothing to do with any of this. We need a sample to exclude her."

Since Betty Tinsdale was no fool, questions were inevitable. "You think the person doing this is a woman?"

Serena tried to play it off. "I'm not jumping to any conclusions. We found some hairs at a crime scene. We're hoping to match them up."

"Which crime scene?"

Smiling as respectfully as she could, Serena said, "I really can't say anything else about it. I'm sorry. Like I said, we're trying to work the leads as quickly as we can."

Mrs. Tinsdale gave her a hard look, but didn't say anything as she seemed to consider the request.

"Did Lori-Ann tell you why I was here the other day?" At least that might be a way to provide more information without affecting the investigation.

"It was about Brad," she said. She paused, again seeming a bit uncertain, but then added, "I was suspicious of that situation actually. I'm glad she decided to tell us what really happened. Poor thing. You know how vicious Andi and her friends can be."

"I really don't think Lori-Ann has anything to do with this," Serena assured her.

Mrs. Tinsdale patted Serena on the arm and slipped out to find her granddaughter. A few minutes later she returned with the girl, a brush in hand.

"I talked with Jack," she explained. "He's fine with this."

Riley held up the evidence bag and Lori-Ann helpfully placed some hair inside.

"So, your killer has pin-straight mousy brown hair, too, huh? Guess that explains his anger," Lori-Ann joked.

Serena smiled. "I had to provide some of my hair, too. So, that means unruly brown hair is also on the list."

Lori-Ann laughed and she and her grandmother joined them at the table.

"Do you know what's going on yet?" Lori-Ann asked.

Serena looked between the girl's hopeful eyes and Mrs. Tinsdale's concerned frown. She wanted to give them optimism, but she couldn't lie. "Not really, no, but we'll figure it out."

Lori-Ann looked at her grandmother. And in answer to some silent query, Mrs. Tinsdale simply nodded.

"I was talking to my grandmother about our conversation," Lori-Ann explained. "I was thinking more about the hospital. I'm really pretty sure they spent most of their time in the woods. I think it was just the one party that they had right around the hospital. I sit behind Andi in English class. So I get to hear all about her weekends. And it really sounded like that night when Deputy Gilbert busted them was the first time they were up there. I remember her talking about it because they were going on and on about how hot he was and how much they were hoping he'd join in the party."

Serena shuddered at the thought. "Isn't Andi dating Lucas?"

Lori-Ann shook her head. "Andi dates Lucas, but that doesn't mean she's not more than willing to give somebody else a happy ending."

Mrs. Tinsdale perked up at that innuendo. She swatted her granddaughter on the hand. "You know better."

The girl shrugged. "I'm only telling you what I know. She and her friends had competitions about who could be with the most guys."

The librarian looked aghast, and Serena couldn't help but notice the eyebrow raise the revelation got from Riley. She suspected he was thinking the same thing she was – things had certainly changed since she was in high school.

"Did Lucas know?"

"Probably. After things went so badly last summer, I kinda doubt Lucas would do anything to challenge Andi."

"Any rumors about Lucas that I need to know?"

Lori-Ann shook her head. "He's kind of a deadhead. Always getting into trouble. Stupid stuff. Drinking in the bathroom, picking fights. I'm pretty sure you probably know about all that."

Unfortunately, the girl was right, these were all things she already knew. "He spends a lot of time in Principal Daly's office?"

"Sometimes it's half the day. I swear he acts up just to get out of class."

Serena suspected that might actually be true, but she wasn't about to volunteer that piece of information.

All in all, it seemed like Andi Sinclair had no reason to be jealous of Lucas's relationship with Claudia Daly. In fact, she might have been happy for the free time to pursue other boys.

But if Serena were to believe Lori-Ann's previous statements then Andi was certainly upset enough about Lucas and Kylie Fulton to take drastic action. Serena knew that Andi knew about Claudia and Lucas, or at least suspected. Did it really make sense that she would just let that go?

~ 52 ~

Serena had been feeling confident and almost cocky when she reached Veronica Martin's house, but that was where their luck took a turn. Veronica's mother was suspicious. It seemed she was concerned this was all some farce to test the high school kids for drugs.

Veronica's mother was Riley's age, and it was immediately clear she had used drugs in high school and was rather annoyed Riley would be a part of this sort of Orwellian police work. No amount of persuading would convince her.

Which left them with one final destination before they parted ways for the evening. The Sinclairs. Serena thought it was almost pointless to proceed, but she found herself standing on the Sinclairs' cozy front porch, knocking on the door and exchanging resigned looks with Riley.

When Avery Sinclair opened the door, she knew it was over.

She put on her best smile. "Hi, Avery, can we come in?"

Sinclair shifted so he blocked the entire doorway. He sneered at her and said, "Not a chance in hell."

Serena dropped the smile. "Avery, I am trying to conduct a murder investigation and I'm trying to find out who kidnapped your neighbor before I have another murder to investigate. I am sick and tired of wasting my time with you and your ridiculous antics."

"You waste plenty of time without my help. How's the doc doing?"

Riley grabbed Avery by the collar and lifted him off the ground, before the words had even a moment to hang in the air. "You remember who you're talking to, you son of a bitch," he growled.

Trying to pretend she wasn't even more surprised than Avery at Riley's reaction, Serena put a hand on Riley's shoulder and eased him aside.

Avery gulped air, more for effect than out of need. Rubbing his neck dramatically, he said, "What the hell is wrong with you? I'm friends with Norton Finwick. We'll talk to the mayor."

Serena smiled at the threat. "Norton and I both met with the mayor this morning. Based on your ridiculous little remark, you already knew that. Mayor Smith told me the only thing he's worried about is finding this killer." Avery stared at her with disbelief, so she added, "You want to call Norton and ask him?"

Avery glared at her and ultimately stepped aside, allowing her and Riley into his house.

"Are the ladies of the house around?" she asked when he led them into the empty living room.

"You talk to me, first. They've already been through enough."

Serena considered fighting, but decided to put it off for now. She settled onto the couch and carefully examined the man who sat in the recliner across from her. Noticing the window, she said, "You have a pretty good view of Claudia's house from here."

Avery nodded, and gave her a look that said he wanted to know what the hell she was up to.

Serena barely noticed it. Now that she knew about Claudia's affair, seeing the view they had of Claudia's house, she was certain she knew why Avery and Andi had been exchanging nervous glances the last time they'd talked.

"You knew about Lucas." It was a statement, not a question.

The surprise shone on Avery's face before he could conceal it.

Though no one in the room could possibly have believed he didn't know exactly what she was talking about, Avery protested, "What about Lucas?"

Serena ignored the question. She rose and walked over to the window. She could see the basement door Lucas had told her about. It was a good distance away. Most nights you wouldn't be able to see a thing. But if it was clear, and the moon was bright, you would see. And Serena had no doubt Avery would have recognized his daughter's boyfriend immediately.

"Did you confront Claudia about it?" Serena asked without looking his way.

The pause was long enough that Serena was wondering if she'd misjudged the situation, but Avery caved as she'd hoped.

He snorted and said, "Honestly, I don't know why you care about this. Yeah, I talked to her. That woman was a lost cause. She wasn't worth my time."

"What about Andi?"

"My conversations with my daughter are none of your business."

Serena turned to face him. "I'm going to level with you, Avery. I have some evidence we're looking into. At one of the crime scenes we found some hair – long brown hair."

She let the last part hang in the air for a moment, and then continued, "I can see you calculating how many people in town have long brown hair. There are as few as you think there are. How many was it exactly, Riley?"

"Twenty-three, counting you."

Serena suppressed a smile. Including her was a nice touch. "Twenty-three, counting me. Riley and I have been all over town talking to people with long brown hair today. And so far, only one of them has declined to volunteer a sample. We have four left – two of them live in your house."

"Now if you think…" Avery began.

Serena stopped him. "Oh, I don't think. I know. And here's what I know. I know there is a woman in this town who has long brown hair who has somehow come in contact with the crime scene. Now, Riley here, women's rights activist that he is, thinks it means the killer is a woman. I'm not really convinced a woman is likely to be hard-wired that way. I think it's more likely the scene was just connected to her. Like a woman lives in the house where the victim was kept, or a woman visited her boyfriend's house and that was where the victim was kept."

Avery jumped to his feet. "You think it's Lucas?"

"I think it would be a damn shame if Andi made herself look more guilty by not cooperating at this point."

Avery looked desperately between her and Riley.

Playing things perfectly, Riley shrugged, "I like the idea it's a woman. The evidence kind of fits with that. But she's the boss."

"What do you want from me?" Avery asked.

"We need hair samples from Andi and your wife. That's it. They'll be sent up to the state lab and compared to the samples we have from the crime scene. While we wait for those results, we're going to have to assume anyone who was willing to hand over their DNA has nothing to hide. And if anyone decides they want to hold back, then we will have to work under Riley's theory until those tests come back."

When Avery turned and called for his daughter and his wife, Serena knew she had him. She barely believed it was possible, but it really had worked.

~ 53 ~

Serena was still smiling about the way she'd managed to turn what had looked like one of the worst days of her life into a pretty decent one when she arrived at Liam's bar. She'd called Clay on the way. He was finishing up some work, but he wanted to give her the update on what he had so far on the body. She'd suggested they discuss the findings over dinner, because it seemed far more pleasant. And besides, she was pretty sure she'd earned a nice dinner. They agreed on take out from Liam's and dinner at Clay's place.

On route, she'd called Missy to see if she'd meet her at the bar. Serena felt fairly confident her life-long friend wouldn't need personal cajoling to convince her to hand over a hair sample, but it seemed better to kill two birds with one stone.

Serena staked out a booth in the back corner so she and Missy could have a little privacy.

Missy wiggled out of her coat and tossed it on the seat before sliding into the booth. "You sounded all sheriff-y on the phone. Please don't tell me you need my help in a professional capacity again. Seriously, Serena, I don't know if I've got another round in me."

Serena shook her head. "Happily, I have no need for your professional services. Though, now that you mention it, I'm thinking Buster's due for his annual check-up pretty soon."

"He's already got an appointment in two weeks. Your dad called to set it up."

Serena was certain Buster wouldn't last a day without her father's supplemental care giving. "Thank God for that man."

Missy leaned in. "Before we get into the rest of this, I want to thank you."

Serena smiled. "Liam stopped by. I guess the conversation went well."

Missy grinned back. "I'm glad you talked me into having a conversation."

The sparkle in her friend's eyes was the brightest spot in Serena's day. "You've always been a sister to me. I'm happy to hear that my idiot brother's finally going to make it official."

Missy's smile only broadened. "I couldn't have said it better myself."

After a moment, Missy tapped her hand on the table. "Okay, enough about me. What's going on? You did sound serious on the phone."

"We found some evidence at one of the crime scenes – several long brown hairs. We're collecting samples from anyone who fits the basic description."

Missy sat back in surprise. "A woman? How could a woman do a thing like this?"

Serena ran a hand over her tired eyes. "I don't really think it's a woman. It could be a woman was just around the crime scene. We can't really tell."

The answer didn't seem to make Missy feel any better.

"So," Serena coaxed, "I was hoping you'd be willing to volunteer a hair sample."

Missy's eyes widened. "You think I could be involved in this?"

Serena laughed. "We're getting everyone with long brown hair. That includes me, and I'm certain I'm not involved."

Before Serena could say anything more, Flo arrived to take their order. Flo had been a waitress at the bar since before Liam owned it. She was efficient and nice, and looked ten years older than she actually was, probably because of her heavy cigarette habit.

"You girls ready to order?" she asked.

Serena smiled at one of the few people in town who still thought of her as a "girl." "I'm actually getting takeout, but I could use an iced tea while we're sitting here."

Once they were alone again, Serena picked up where she left off. "Please don't take this as an insult. It's not that I think you have anything to do with it, but we're getting samples from everyone. It's voluntary, if you'd rather wait for me to get a warrant…"

Missy cut her off before she could say anything else. "Of course not. I'm sorry. I didn't mean to seem unreasonable. I was just surprised. Tell me what you need."

Serena was placing Missy's hair in an evidence bag when Flo came back with their drinks. Seeing the bag, and the hair, she paused. For a moment, it looked like she was going to walk away, but then she said, "Sheriff, I heard you were gathering hairs. Long brown ones?"

Serena was reluctant to confirm the details of an ongoing investigation, but she'd have to be a fool not to think that very fact was going to end up on the front page of the paper tomorrow morning. And more importantly, Flo clearly had something she thought might be important.

Choosing her words carefully, Serena said, "I can't comment on that officially. I will say Missy just volunteered a sample of her long brown hair."

Flo seemed to understand. She leaned in close and said, "I wanted to make sure you got a sample from the lady who's been hanging out here on and off the past few months."

Serena stared in shock. "What lady is that?"

"I don't know who she is. Never seen her before in my life until recently. She's been showing up every now and then. Sometimes she's here a couple times a week. Then sometimes it's a week or more between visits."

"Someone from out of town has been hanging out in the bar?" Serena was trying to grasp the words. Whitefield didn't get random visitors. It didn't have accommodations for random visitors. There was no good reason for a woman to be showing up occasionally. And there was one very bad reason for her appearances.

"When was the last time she was here?" Serena asked.

Flo smiled. "Why don't you ask her yourself? She came in a little bit after you. She's sitting right over there."

Serena's heart stopped. "Where?"

Flo pointed to a table on the other side of the bar. Serena's eyes scanned over people she'd known her whole life. Just past a table where Hayley sat with some friends was a booth with one lone occupant. A woman. Tall, very tall, probably close to six feet. And thin, sort of lanky. Her head was bowed slightly and a dense mane of brown hair concealed her face.

Serena eased out of the booth without a word. With one hand on the butt of her weapon, she eased past the other occupants of the bar. When the mystery woman cast a furtive glance in her direction, Serena quickened her pace. She was laying money on the table and starting to stand up when Serena arrived. She laid a heavy hand on the woman's boney shoulder, sitting her back in the booth.

Positioning herself in front of the woman, while still blocking her exit, Serena said, "I don't think we've met. I'm the sheriff here, Serena Marlowe."

Without looking up, the woman muttered an unintelligible response in a squeaky voice.

The false voice was enough to convince Serena she was dealing with a situation.

In a firmer tone, she said, "What's your name?"

The odd voice broke a little, and she said, "Jill Smith."

"Really, Jill, you have some identification?"

"I really have to be going," she said, starting to stand.

Serena had expected the evasion. She pushed her back into the seat with more force this time.

"You can't keep me here," the woman insisted, her voice cracking and squeaking awkwardly.

"Actually, I can. Your behavior, combined with that long brown hair of yours. Yeah, I have plenty to keep you here talking to me."

The woman merely lowered her head further.

Tired of the woman's attempts to conceal her face, Serena said, "Why don't you look at me, Jill? That would be a fabulous start."

When she didn't respond, Serena used a firmer tone. "Or I can arrest you. Your call."

With some hesitation, the woman raised her head slowly. Nothing in the world could have prepared Serena for what she saw.

Despite the hair, despite the clothes, Serena was looking at Norton Finwick.

It took her a second to gather herself, and as she did, several pieces fell into place. He was sitting in the booth right next to Hayley. Serena suspected that spot allowed Norton to hear everything Hayley said.

Though she wasn't entirely sure why she was arresting him, Serena was certain she had no other choice. Without a moment's hesitation, she told Norton to stand up so she could read him his rights.

~ 54 ~

Riley was still on duty when she reached the station, which saved her the trouble of calling him in. After a call to Clay, she found herself sitting in the conference room with her best deputy and their coroner, wishing they'd stop looking at each other with such hostility.

She tossed Norton's wig over to Clay. "Could this be the source of the hair?"

Clay turned the wig over a few times. "It's a little hard to say without my equipment, but this looks like natural hair. My preliminary thought is, yes, it could be. I'll need to look at the follicles more closely to see if these match-up. Frankly, to see if there even are follicles."

Seeming to notice the blank stares from both her and Riley, Clay explained, "Where the hair attaches to the scalp has a distinct appearance, and important qualities. I'll need to look at samples from the wig and then look at the samples we found at the scene and see if they are consistent."

Serena nodded and turned her attention to Riley. "Do you think this is possible?"

Riley rocked on his chair a moment before he answered. "That little shit is a malicious son of a bitch. Always has been. Possible he'd flip out and do something crazy, I guess. Why the wig? Some sort of weird gay thing?"

Serena was pretty sure gay men had nothing at all to do with wigs, but she let it go. "I think the wig was a disguise, or at least it was tonight. He was sitting at a table near Hayley. I think he was eavesdropping. I suspect it's how he's managed to get various tidbits of information about our office over the past few months."

Riley gave her a strange look she couldn't quite place.

"Maybe he used the wig as a disguise when he grabbed the victims?" Clay suggested.

Serna hated the idea that this killer was one of their own. The fact that it was Norton didn't make that any easier.

"Riley, I need you to get us a search warrant for his home and office. Immediately. Claudia could be in there."

Clay raised an eyebrow. "Don't you want to wait until I look at the follicles?"

Serena stood. "It doesn't matter. He could have fifteen other wigs at his house we don't know about. Even if this one didn't match, I'd want to get the warrant. Please check what we have though. I'm going to go talk to Norton while Riley gets the warrant."

Clay and Riley both headed out, and Serena slowly descended into the basement where they had their holding cells. Norton was the only one there that night. He was stretched out on a cot looking perfectly ridiculous in heavy makeup and women's clothes. At the sound of Serena's shoes on the linoleum, he sat up and glared at her.

"What exactly are you holding me on?" he snarled.

Serena pulled a chair over so she could sit a couple feet from the bars. She didn't say a word, instead waiting to see what Norton would do.

"This isn't some prison camp. You can't hold me here. I have rights. I have the right to know why I'm here."

In a calm easy voice, Serena said, "You do have rights. I enumerated them earlier. Would you like me to repeat them? I don't want you to feel you don't have rights."

"I don't need you to read me the stupid warnings again. I want to know what the hell you're holding me on."

"Suspicion of murder, actually."

Norton jumped to his feet. "What? Murder? Are you insane? Whose murder? The crazy serial killer thing? That's ridiculous. Ridiculous! Is this about this morning? Because even for a Marlowe that's outrageous."

Serena almost laughed at the suggestion. The events of that morning felt so far away she could barely even remember them.

"I have you skulking around town in a wig. And not just any wig. A wig of long brown hair. If you are half the reporter I think you are then you already know why that's important."

His eyes grew wide. "You can't think I…."

"Oh, but I do. I'm not going to lie, Norton, I'm surprised as all hell, but I am very interested to see what we find when we execute the search warrants of your home and office."

The threat had the intended effect. Norton raced toward the bars, grabbing and shaking them. "You cannot do that! You can't go into my home. You can't invade my privacy like that. There's no way."

Serena smiled. She'd gotten what she'd wanted. They'd start at his home, not work; he seemed a bit more protective of that.

"I wanted to let you know we can hold you for a day, and we will. At a minimum, I'm sure you were eavesdropping and being a general asshole. And after we search your place, I'll know if there's something more sinister I need to deal with."

~ 55 ~

The search warrant came through quickly. It was less than an hour after her interview with Norton that Serena and Riley entered his home.

Though he shared a neighborhood with the Averys and Claudia Daly, Norton's house was substantially smaller. The décor was spartan, which made the initial sweep of his living room, dining room and kitchen a fairly quick process. Similarly, their run through the upstairs revealed nothing more sinister than one bedroom, a small office, and a bathroom. It wasn't until they entered the basement that things got interesting.

At first glance, the basement also seemed perfectly normal. There was only one problem – it was small, too small. Basements should be about the same size as the footprint of the house. This one was not. Serena would have estimated it was about half the size it should have been.

She could see Riley scanning the walls, clearly thinking the same thing she was. She scanned the floor, looking for unusual wear. That was how they caught their break. In a back corner, the paint that covered the cement floor was scratched.

Her heart rate spiked. Was Claudia hidden behind this wall?

It was Riley who noticed the doorknob, concealed behind an old lawn chair and a garden hose that had seen better days.

A light switch inside the door illuminated a bare bulb, revealing a large work room. Five whiteboards had been permanently fixed to one wall. They were entirely blank. The bookshelves next to the boards held thick binders. Handwritten on the binding of each was a name. There had to be at least a hundred different names. All residents of Whitefield.

Serena's eyes locked on four binders – Marlowe, Liam; Marlowe, Serena; Marlowe, Wendy; Marlowe, William. Seeing her mother's name among theirs was surprising. She'd been dead for decades – what purpose could there be to a binder with her name too?

Serena slid the binder with her own name off the shelf first. The first page was a large photo. A shot that had been clearly taken with a distance lens without her knowledge. Next to the photo was a list. Vital statistics – date of birth, parents, address, phone number, Buster's name and basic information – most specifically that he was not aggressive.

If it was possible, that was not the worst of it. There had to have been close to two hundred pages in the book, broken into several tabbed sections – schedule, background, and weaknesses.

The "schedule" section was horrifying. It listed her patterns – what time she typically went to bed, what time Buster got his walks, what time she typically woke up, her shift schedule, what days of the week she went to the store, when and where she ate dinner, what she typically ate for dinner – the list went on and on.

Serena turned to face Riley, who'd been reading over her shoulder. "This is exactly what I'd want to know if I was planning on abducting someone."

Riley shook his head in amazement. "How the fuck would anyone gather that kind of information?"

Leafing ahead in the section, Serena quickly realized how. Sheet after sheet detailed specific days in her life. Minute by minute schedules with everything from what food she ate to when she went to the bathroom. He'd been watching her. And based on the dates on the sheets, it looked like he'd been watching her since the day she graduated from high school.

"You think he figured you weren't fair game until you graduated?" Riley asked.

"Well that's awful nice of him," Serena sneered.

The rest of the book was no better. The background section listed every boy she'd ever dated, noted her friendship with Missy Skylar, her close relationship with her brother, and a litany of other things, most of which were true.

Serena took issue with the contents of the "weaknesses" section. "I am not wilting in my father's shadow," she insisted.

Before Riley could reply, they both noticed the line below – *Plainly has self-esteem issues, since she failed to end an emotionally abusive relationship with her co-worker.*

"What is all of this?" Riley asked, sidestepping the elephant in the room.

"Are these the ravings of a lunatic?"

"In case the writings aren't bad enough, the pictures in there are creepy as hell. Those were taken with a telephoto lens."

In the back of the binder was an envelope, which contained pictures of her in any number of different places over the years. Most recently, there was a picture of her standing in the doorway of her home. Clay was standing on her front porch. Based on the date on the picture, it was the night he came over for dinner. Norton hadn't "ridden by on his bicycle" as he'd suggested. He'd been watching her – watching them. Knowing Clay was at her house, Norton could easily have broken into Clay's office without worrying he might be heard.

Serena placed her binder on Norton's desk. With dread, she reached up to the top shelf and removed Claudia Daly's binder.

~ 56 ~

Serena and Riley sat in the interrogation room with Norton sitting across from them, looking more than a little belligerent.

He held up his cuffed hands. "Are these entirely necessary?"

"You're lucky I didn't get out the shackles for your legs," Riley snapped back.

Serena silently begged Riley to calm down. Though she was seething with an unstable cocktail of rage, fear and disgust, she knew she had to hold it back. This was going to require calm.

Her whole life she thought she'd known Norton Finwick, but it was suddenly very clear that the man she knew was an illusion. She was face to face with a sociopath. A man who'd lived through his camera for years – spying, watching and, when that was no longer enough, taking people. He removed them from their lives because he couldn't stand that they had what he didn't. Or at least that's what it was starting to look like.

"Norton," she began, her voice even, "we found the binders. We'd like to talk to you about them."

He looked at her with confusion that appeared feigned. "What binders? What are you talking about?"

From a bag on the floor, Serena pulled out Claudia Daly's binder and placed it on the table in front of her. And she waited.

Norton lowered his head into his cuffed hands.

Serena started out with what they had. She'd build to the rest. "I'll have to talk to the D.A., but this is pretty bad. I think we've got over a hundred counts of stalking. Add in all the related offenses and you're looking at a lot of time. And I'm not going to lie to you, Norton, the whole thing looks creepy, you know? A judge is not going to like the creepy factor. Why don't you tell me what this is all about?"

Norton peered at her over his folded hands. "What do you think it's all about?"

She leaned forward. "I've never liked you. I don't think that's a surprise to you. But I don't like that this was happening on my watch and I had no idea. You look bad here, and so do I. So, let's not fuck around. Tell me what this is about. Tell me the truth. Make me feel better."

Serena was certain there was nothing he could say that would make her feel better and there was nothing she could do that was going to make her look better. But she didn't care about any of it. Frankly, after this investigation, she was thinking a nice career bagging groceries might be the way to go.

Norton seemed to buy into her pitch. "This isn't stalking," he explained. "It's investigating. Don't you see? I'm doing my job. I wasn't hiding it. Well, not really, at least. It's just that I knew people wouldn't understand."

The pieces were beginning to fall into place. "You knew my mother was sick because you were watching her. You noticed the change in her schedule?" Serena hadn't read the binder, but she'd never been so certain of something in her life.

Norton's face lit up. "See? That's what I do. I watch. I wait. You have to know the patterns to see the changes. If you see the changes, then you'll be at the edge of the story. I have a job. An important job. Somebody needs to tell the truth. Somebody needs to tell people what's really going on."

Serena thought of Norton's ambush from earlier. She thought of her father's story. The same thing so many years earlier. It wasn't about truth. It was about power.

"I bet that's how it started, right?" Serena asked. "But you don't report everything you see, do you?"

Norton shook his head. "I'm not a gossip columnist."

"You didn't report on Claudia's affair with a student. Actually, based on what's in this book, it looks like Lucas wasn't the first one. You knew about a principal who was sleeping with high school students, and you thought it was just gossip?"

Norton shrugged.

"I noticed this morning how well you use that type of gossip when you get your hands on it. Was it like that with Claudia?"

He sat straighter in his seat. "What's that supposed to mean?"

Serena leveled her voice. "Some things are just wrong. Maybe they aren't news in the classic sense. Maybe they don't go in the paper. But sometimes you have to do something, right?"

Norton looked at her skeptically.

Serena looked to Riley. "He agrees with you, you know? He's furious about me and Clay. Thinks it's effecting the investigation. Just like you. Once you knew the truth, you did what you had to do."

Riley's eyes were filled with confusion, but he played along. To Norton it would appear that Riley knew what had happened with the mayor that morning.

Leaning in, Riley said, "There's no place for her personal feelings in an investigation. I've been watching over things extra closely from the start. She's always been a little too cozy with the doc."

Serena turned her attention back to Norton. "Riley was happy to hear you sold me out to the mayor."

From the corner of her eye she saw Riley seem to understand. He leaned forward. "You were right not to put that in the paper. Like you said, it's just gossip. But when you know stuff, don't you have an obligation to take action?"

"Did you talk to Claudia?" Serena asked, feeling more and more certain he'd done more than talk.

Norton lowered his head. "Not at first. I mean, I would have loved to have had a lady like her teach me a thing or two when I was that age. But when I saw Lucas…."

"Andi's boyfriend," Serena coaxed.

"Avery's my friend, my neighbor. She's his sweet little girl. I couldn't let it go by without saying something."

"So you talked to Claudia?" Riley prodded.

Norton looked up. "No. Not Claudia. Claudia doesn't talk to me. Never has. Thinks she's better than me."

Serena was pretty sure Claudia felt that way about most of them. "Who'd you talk to, then?"

"Avery."

Serena sat back in her chair and considered the revelation. When he'd seen her doing something bad, he ran to an authority figure to get her into trouble. Now he was saying the same thing happened with Claudia and Avery. Would a tattletale be violent enough to commit this kind of crime?

Then she remembered the treating of the wounds, remembered the absence of violent trauma to the body. Their killer was gentle enough that he sounded more like a nurse than an abductor. A tattletale might do that.

"Come on, Norton," she insisted. "We know you talked to Claudia."

He shook his head.

His reaction told her it was time to push. "Maybe you talked to Avery first, but then she kept seeing the boy. He was sneaking in at night. Slipping out at all hours. All that sex. A couple hundred feet from where Avery's little girl was sleeping."

"I don't think Avery ever talked to her. I don't understand that," Norton replied absently.

"So you took matters into your own hands?"

He looked up, suddenly realizing where she was going with this. "No," he insisted.

"She was disrespecting your friend. She wasn't behaving appropriately."

"I didn't do anything to her!"

Serena sat forward. "You knew the truth. You knew what she was. You needed to expose her. If Avery wouldn't do it, then you had to do it yourself."

"No! I didn't touch her," he cried.

Riley spoke in a soft voice. Using soothing tones, he played good cop perfectly. "I understand, man. You did what you had to. But it's over now. Tell us the truth. We'll figure it out."

Norton turned his eyes to Riley. "You think I took her? I didn't take her. I didn't do anything."

"Where is she?" Serena prodded. "It's time to stop lying. Did you kill her? Tell us the truth. We just want the truth."

Norton shook his head. Tears rolled down his cheeks. "I didn't do anything. I swear. I didn't."

Serena shifted gears. "Then tell me about Daisy. You didn't have a book on her. Did you destroy it?"

He sniffled back a sob. "There's no book for Daisy because there was no point. She was homebound. Boring. No story there."

Riley leaned in. "Okay, buddy, it's alright. I want to understand. Tell me about the heart. Explain it to me."

Norton only looked at him blankly and then he looked back at Serena. "I didn't do it," he said with despair. "I know you don't believe me. But when the next person goes missing you'll see. I didn't do it. You've got the wrong guy."

~ 57 ~

Serena didn't leave the station until close to one a.m., but Clay's message on her voicemail asked her to stop by, no matter how late. It wasn't until she was standing there, waiting for him to answer her knock, that she realized how exhausted she was. It had been a long day. A long, awful day.

Clay greeted her with a smile and bleary eyes.

"You said stop by no matter how late," she said.

Clay took her hand and led her inside. "Did you arrest him?"

Serena sank onto the couch. "We found books in his house. Crazy stalker binders filled with details on peoples' lives. You wouldn't believe how many. He's been watching people for years. Watching, taking pictures, and I'm sure he's been using all of it as leverage against folks."

Clay didn't really seem to be listening to the details. Instead, he was looking at her with a strange expression on his face. "But you didn't arrest him?"

"How could you possibly know that?"

He smoothed a hand over her hair. "It's written all over your face."

"I arrested him for stalking. I haven't sorted out the specifics of what the hell we should be charging him with, but he's in on that. I just can't believe the rest."

Wisely, Clay replied, "Can't or won't?"

Serena leaned her head back against the couch and cursed under her breath. "I wish I knew."

"I guess he didn't confess?"

She turned her head slightly so she could see Clay's reaction. "He cried. He just cried."

"You pushed him and he cried?"

Serena nodded.

"Does that usually happen?"

She laughed ruefully. "Usually? There really isn't a usual situation to compare this to. This would be my first interview of a stalker, never mind a sociopath."

"You deal with aggravated assaults, robberies. You've done this."

The encouraging tone was appreciated, even though it didn't help. "They've never looked like this." Serena looked deeply into his eyes. "Is he a killer and I'm too afraid to admit it to myself?"

"I don't know."

Serena could feel the day's emotions crashing down on her. "Everything points to him. The wigs. The stalking. He knew about Lucas and Claudia. He admits he told Avery. He admits Avery didn't do anything. It makes sense he got angry. Took matters into his own hands."

"What about Daisy?"

And that was one of the many reasons Serena was balking. Appreciating Clay's effort to play devil's advocate, she pushed through. "He abducted Claudia because he was judging her. He must have seen something with Daisy."

"Did you find anything to suggest that in her house, in his house?"

"No, but that's going to be the problem with Daisy no matter what we do. There's no reason at all to hurt her. She's a dead end."

"And the heart?" he asked.

Serena sighed. "Is even more of a dead end. We don't even know whose it is."

Clay rubbed her arm gently. "I read once that true sociopaths don't need a reason."

"You read that in some psych textbook?"

Clay laughed. "No. I read it in some mystery novel. Good stuff in those mystery novels."

Serena squinted at him, trying to get a sense of where he was going with this. "Is that true?"

He shrugged. "I told you, I'm not the one to consult on psych stuff. I know nothing. But it does sort of sound right. Don't you think?"

Serena did think it sounded right. She just didn't know what to do with it. "So I should stop asking why and just look for someone who looks like a psycho?"

Clay wrapped an arm around her and pulled her close. "I guess the only trick is figuring out what a psycho looks like."

Serena sighed and leaned into his chest, enjoying the feel of his strong arm around her, enjoying the protection. "Maybe I'm just afraid to make the arrest."

"What do you mean?"

She closed her eyes, hating to even hear the words. "The simplest solution is the most likely one. I have a guy who looks like a psycho. He's acting like a psycho. He's crying during police interviews. He's the classic guy who keeps to himself, but always seemed like a good neighbor. How many times have people described crazy killers that way? It sure sounds like Norton. It's him. It has to be."

Clay pulled away and made her look him in the eye. "Serena, you said it yourself, you already have him on other charges. If you have questions, you don't need to rush it."

She shook her head. "It's him. It has to be. Otherwise, I have two psychos in my little town. What are the odds of that?"

But even as she made the joke, Serena considered the question. Was it possible? What were the odds of something like that occurring?

~ 58 ~

By the next morning, Serena didn't feel any better about the situation. Knowing she wasn't ready to face the station yet, she allowed herself a second cup of coffee and a romp in the backyard with Buster. They both needed the time together.

When she managed to leave the house, she headed to Clay's office. They'd never gotten a chance to discuss the autopsy or the hair samples last night. Both of those things needed far more attention than the nonsense that awaited her at the station.

Clay had mentioned he was going to be spending the morning with the body and blocking off the afternoon for patients, which meant this was her only chance to talk to him about the case until evening.

Though he usually talked to her about cases in his waiting room, Clay led her to the autopsy room. The smells of death and chemicals were almost more than she could take on so little sleep. A wave of nausea and dizziness swept over her with enough force that she grabbed the table for balance.

"You okay?" Clay asked. "You should sit."

Serena shook the cobwebs from her head and took several deep breaths. "I'm fine. Fine. I don't have a problem with bodies. It's fine."

He put a hand on her arm. "You're white as a ghost. I'm not calling you a wimp. I just don't want you passing out on me."

Serena took another slow, deep breath. Feeling her strength returning, she met his eyes. "I'm fine."

"How much sleep have you gotten in the last week?"

"I got as much as I needed," she replied.

"Your color's coming back." Clay started to turn away, but then stopped. "Seriously, Serena, I'm saying this as a doctor. You need sleep. People can't just decide not to sleep because they're too busy."

He was right, of course. But she was pretty sure that didn't change anything. She smiled vaguely, and asked, "So what did you want to show me?"

Clay led her over to the body on the table. Serena had seen autopsies before and, as far as she could tell, this one didn't look much different. The chest was cut open, as was the skull, and the organs were removed. "What am I looking at?"

Clay shook his head. "I'm really not sure. I wish I was. I can tell you she died from a stroke, but she was also in kidney failure. As far as I can tell there were no other significant injuries."

"So, poisoning?"

"It could be. I sent the blood samples to the state lab. We'll see what they say after the tox screen comes back."

Serena looked at Clay now. "But you don't think so?"

He avoided her eyes and continued staring at the body. "I did find one needle mark in her left arm."

"A needle mark doesn't suggest poison?"

Clay motioned for her to come closer to the table. "Tell me what you see."

He lifted Daisy's arm and pointed to her wrist. On her pale skin, there was obvious bruising, much like what occurs when a nurse has trouble finding a vein. In the center of the bruise was a darker mark, which was probably a needle prick. Serena was about to ask why Clay thought she might have any ability to assess this situation when she saw something else.

"Do you have pictures of this?" she asked without taking her eyes off it.

"Yeah, and samples. Don't worry about that."

On one side of the bruise was a dark substance. Serena was not surprised to find it slightly sticky to the touch. There wasn't much, just a trace. "It's adhesive?"

"As if there was medical tape on her arm," Clay agreed.

"Why would you need medical tape to inject someone with poison?"

"You wouldn't."

Serena looked to Clay, sensing he had a guess. "Why would you need tape?"

"If you were to hook someone up to an IV or a blood supply, you would insert the needle and then tape it in place."

"You could poison someone through an IV, couldn't you?" Serena asked, already knowing the answer.

Clay nodded, but his expression was clear – why the hell would you?

Serena thought of the other signs that the killer was acting as a caregiver. "She was abducted and then hooked up to an IV? Why might someone need an IV?"

"Any number of reasons. You think he was treating her with an IV?" Clay asked.

Serena thought of Norton. Sleeping on the situation hadn't made her any more comfortable with the idea of him as a killer. Norton the stalker actually made some sense, but killing just seemed off. And Norton taking the time to give someone an IV or tend to their wounds seemed even more off. He was a wimp, a tattletale. Maybe even a bully. He was not a caregiver.

Serena shook her head. "I don't know what I'm thinking. What are you thinking?"

Clay looked away and began pacing. "I wish I knew what to make of this."

That was when Serena realized she'd been so deep into her own head she wasn't really paying attention to what was right in front of her. "You have a theory."

Clay stopped and looked up. "No, no. It's nothing. It's stupid."

Serena leaned back against a cabinet. "You listened to my stupid theory that we have two psychos running around our bucolic little town. Now I want to listen to your theory. It's just brainstorming. There's nothing wrong with it."

"It's not really a theory. It's just, well, when I was an intern, there was a clerical mix-up at the hospital. Two patients' charts were switched and one of the patients was given the wrong blood type during an emergency transfusion. The patient was older, frail. The mistake wasn't caught in time and the patient died."

"That happens? They actually mix up blood types."

Clay raised an eyebrow. "Trust me, you don't want to know what actually happens. Anyway, I got permission to observe the autopsy."

"What does that have to do with Daisy Roman?"

He shook his head as he spoke, clearly not believing he was even going to say this out loud. "The whole time I was doing this autopsy, I just kept thinking how much this damage looked like the damage I observed during the autopsy all those years ago. When a person gets the wrong blood, the body attacks the foreign blood. It clumps, causes hemorrhage, organ failure, stroke."

"Just like we have here?"

"Just like we have here." Clay walked back over to the body. "And when you add in the needle mark in the arm and the signs of adhesive…."

Serena was suddenly following the connection. "It even looks like someone who's been given a transfusion."

Clay nodded. "But, as I said earlier, there are other reasons you might see something like this. Far more logical reasons. The tox results should tell us something."

She was barely listening, trying to process if a transfusion made any kind of sense. "If someone had done a transfusion on the first victim – the heart – you would have seen that, right?"

"There were no signs of this in the heart."

In her mind's eye, Serena visualized the boards in the conference room, the victims, the evidence. "Do you have all the blood types for the heart, Daisy and Claudia?"

Now it was Clay's turn to look confused. But without a word, he pulled the files off his shelf. "The heart was A positive, Daisy was O, and I don't know Claudia's because we lost the file."

"Weren't there two blood types at the original crime scene?"

"A positive and AB."

Serena wanted desperately to see a pattern in all those letters, but it meant nothing to her. In fact, it sounded fairly random. "Would someone do this on purpose? Would this be a way to intentionally kill someone?"

Clay stared back at her for a minute. "What do you mean – a way to kill someone?"

"I don't know. Like, a method of torture, or something?"

Clay shook his head. "Maybe. I guess. Well, it'd work every time. But it's sort of nuts, don't you think? I mean who'd do a thing like that?"

Serena shook her head. "Who'd cut someone's heart out and leave it on an operating table for us to find?"

"You really think someone used a transfusion as a murder weapon? I mean how would they even know the victim's blood type?"

And that was when it hit her. "The break-in. Hell, I keep forgetting about the break-in. Claudia's file would have had her blood type."

Clay sank back against the counter. "Son of a bitch."

Serena couldn't have said it better herself. "He's playing doctor. He practiced on those animals. Learned. Surgically removed that heart. Now he's capturing women and performing procedures on them. Do you think?"

Clay shook his head slowly. "This is beyond my expertise."

Of course, it was beyond all of their expertise. But there was one thing Serena was sure of; this was sounding less and less like Norton Finwick.

~ 59 ~

Serena found herself in the basement of Norton's house. She'd been wandering around town since she'd left Clay's, thinking, processing, going in circles, and getting nowhere. All she could think to do was to slow it down. Go back to where things had started falling into place and consider how well the pieces really fit.

She was standing in a basement. A basement with a secret room. Another search of the space confirmed what she already knew – there were no other rooms where Norton could be keeping Claudia.

Serena sat at Norton's desk, scanning the binders on the shelves. Claudia's binder was already in the evidence locker at the station, but the others remained on the shelves. She'd have to box all of them up.

She understood that the binders were going to have to be reviewed to evaluate the charges against Norton, but she wished she could make all this go away without ever reading the secrets that were kept on those pages. People had a right to their skeletons.

With a heavy heart, she pulled Liam's binder off the shelf and began to scan the contents. She pulled her father's file next, then her mother's. It was strange to see how Norton had improved his techniques over the years. The older files were sketchier, fewer pictures, less detailed summaries. Originally, the notes had been handwritten. More recently, the notes were typed. Serena suspected he must be using the tablet they found in the newspaper offices.

Having fully invaded the privacy of all her family members, Serena turned to the next closest thing – the Skylar family. Serena pulled the binder for Missy's father first. It didn't take long for her exhaustion and frustration to contort into full-blown rage. There were photos, dates, times. Evidence. Goddamned evidence.

Serena no longer cared about charges or guilt. She was going to kill Norton Finwick herself.

~ 60 ~

Inside the stationhouse, Serena was assaulted by the sounds of cheerful voices and laughter. Hayley was animatedly telling a story, and Jake was leaning against her desk hanging on her every word.

Hayley was waving her arms dramatically. "And then the sheriff is all like, look at me, bitch. And Norton looked up. Can you believe it?"

"I'm certain I did not call him a bitch." She'd intended the retort to be a joke, but her mood sharpened her tone.

Her dispatcher and her deputy both jumped at the sound of her voice.

Serena didn't even consider trying to work things out. Before either of them could say anything in response, she cut them off. "I'm going back to talk to Norton. If anybody needs me they're going to have to wait."

Serena marched past them and back to the holding cells. Norton was still alone in the cell. One advantage of having a killer on the loose, people were staying home and staying out of trouble.

She pulled a chair over to the bars. Norton ignored her completely. He was laying on his cot, continuing to stare at the ceiling.

Serena threw the binder against the bars to get his attention. "Look at me, you son of a bitch!"

Norton lifted his head, and then glanced down at the binder on the floor. The pictures had fallen out and were now sprawled on the floor for the world to see.

He raised an eyebrow. "Of course you read his binder first. I can't imagine there's anyone you'd find more interesting."

"You have pictures of him!" she practically shouted.

Norton sat up now, clearly enjoying the spotlight. "I have pictures of a lot of people."

"You have pictures of that evil bastard hitting his daughter!"

"Don't think I ever got one of him actually hitting her. I mean, it's pretty clear if you look at all the photos. But I never really got that money shot."

Serena stood, completely incapable of separating herself from the emotions of the conversation.

Norton smiled. "I wonder who will take the pictures of me after you've hit me? Won't look good, Sheriff. Won't look good."

Serena thanked God he was on the other side of the prison bars. "My father couldn't do anything to protect her because he couldn't prove it. You sat on the evidence. You have pictures that would have gotten her out of that house five years earlier and you didn't do shit!"

Norton shrugged. "William the Great had it covered. He was looking into every angle, following the guy around. I knew he'd get him eventually. No reason for me to blow my own cover."

"Blow your cover?"

"We already discussed this, Serena. I knew people wouldn't understand. I start using pictures I shot through my telephoto lens, people will freak out. They wouldn't understand that I'm discreet. They'd worry. It'd be bad for business."

Serena forced herself to sit back down. To breathe. She needed to breathe.

Norton continued on, clearly thrilled to have an audience. "William knew about the abuse. If he hadn't, I would have tipped him off. I would have come up with a way to give him a heads up. An anonymous tip if I'd had to. I mean, she was a kid. I wouldn't have let that go without a word."

Serena wished she believed that. And she wondered, again, if she was looking at a sociopath, a murderer. A person who could document child abuse and do absolutely nothing. Yeah, he was starting to sound more like her killer.

"What about the rest of it?" she asked.

Norton smiled at her. A slow evil smile. "I was there that night."

Serena's heart was pounding so hard it seemed to be forcing the air out of her lungs. She was glad she was sitting. She wasn't sure she was steady enough to stand.

"The file says you watched Missy pull up to the house. Saw her run in."

"You're skipping the good part," he insisted. "I'd been watching Jackson Skylar that whole week. He was acting strange. I'd noticed. Stopped monitoring everyone else, just focused on him. He was a wingnut, that one. Jail didn't help him any."

Serena wanted to interrupt, wanted to point out that he'd sat silent again. Didn't make any effort to help a blessed soul.

Norton rambled on, enjoying every minute, clearly not noticing the look of disgust on her face. "He'd rigged the house up. He was going to burn the whole place. I took my position a little ways away. Close enough to see, you know, but I'm no fool."

"Missy was there!" Serena snapped.

Norton shook his head. "Well, yeah, when she showed up, I was worried. I actually went over there to help her. I heard them shouting."

"That's not in the file."

He looked down at his hands. "I left my equipment. I just went myself. I was going to get her out. I wasn't taking notes anymore."

His reaction was puzzling. The look of shame seemed real. He was actually embarrassed he'd put the story aside. That he'd actually considered intervening.

He met Serena's eyes. "I'm curious about something. Maybe you can explain it. He tried to kill her. She managed to get out, managed to get away, but before she ran out she tried to save him. That's what I never understood. She tried to save him. Why?"

Serena shook off the question. "Wait. What are you saying? Jackson Skylar was trying to kill Missy?"

"Oh, right," Norton said. "Of course, it's not in the notes. I assumed Missy had told you."

Serena knew there was probably some appropriate response, but she had no idea what it was.

Norton seemed to consider her silence an indication he should continue. "It was a trap. He'd called her or something. I didn't quite get all that. But once she was in the house, he tried to get her to have some iced tea with him. I guess he'd drugged it. She didn't want any part of it, any part of him. They fought. He hit her, almost knocked her out. Came at her with a bat. She fought him off. Finally, he just lit the match and the place went up. He'd done a good job dousing the rooms with accelerants."

Serena's eyes grew wide and she gradually began to understand why Missy never talked about what happened that night. It finally made sense.

The exhaustion began to settle into her bones again and Serena put her head in her hands. She just needed a minute. She didn't care if she was sitting in front of her suspect. She didn't care about much anymore.

After a few minutes, Norton said, "You just going to sit there?"

"I might," Serena replied. "Town's pretty quiet now that you're in here."

Norton stood, coming right up to the bars of the cell. After another long pause, he said, "Town's going to fry you when they realize you've got the wrong man. The Marlowe name isn't going to be enough to save you."

Serena shook her head. Truth was, she couldn't have cared less about the politics, but if she lost another person because she was too stubborn to listen to what her instincts were telling her, she wouldn't be able to live with herself.

But she had no intention of letting Norton know that. She shook off the pain, the sadness, the exhaustion. She had to focus on the case.

"So, let me get this straight – you're just an investigator, a keeper of the town's secrets. You dress in drag, skulk in alleys, and seek out the truth in all the dark corners of the town."

Norton's obvious pride at the list of accomplishments told her that he'd missed her sarcasm. "There really aren't any alleys in our town, Sheriff. Lot of trees, though, lot of bushes."

"Tell me this: the night you saw Drayton show up at my house, who were you watching? Him or me?"

Like all classic villains, Norton seemed thrilled at the chance to explain his evil plan. Serena was struck that he was more a cartoon character than a murderer. "I was watching you actually. Had been since the investigation started. I needed to know what was going on with things. You seemed like the best person to track."

"You just followed me home, sat outside and waited?"

He shrugged. "I almost went home myself. Typically, you go home, you turn in, that's that. But you'd come home with a pretty big bag of takeout, and you didn't go out back to play with the dog. The deviation from the pattern made me stick around."

She suppressed a shudder. Maybe even cartoon villains could be creepy. "Come on, Norton, I'm betting there have been other times I did the same sort of thing. Did you stick around every time?"

His chest puffed with pride. "I always stick around if there's something off. I don't always hit pay dirt, but I always wait and see. You don't want to miss the big one."

"Like the one where you catch the sheriff with your favorite suspect and you decide to use the evidence to get her fired?"

Norton held up his hands. "Hey now, I was just doing my job. I'm still not convinced Drayton doesn't have something to do with all this. I didn't watch your house all night. And I can't imagine you didn't catch some sleep yourself. He could've slipped out."

Serena sighed. It was the same stupid conversation. This was getting her nowhere. Hell, maybe Norton had been watching her so he'd know when she'd be distracted enough that he could take his next victim.

"You're so smug," Norton scoffed. "You think you know everything. You don't."

It was a ridiculous taunt, the type a six-year-old would use, but Serena was so tired, she bit. "What don't I know, Norton?"

"You've got a leak in your station and you don't even know it."

"Would that be Hayley? I know you've been harassing her at the bar. That's not a leak, Norton. Again, that's just stalking."

He scowled at her. "Not her. Hayley's actually a really good little soldier. It's your boyfriend that's the trouble."

~ 61 ~

Serena's mind turned immediately to Clay and she considered the revelation in utter disbelief. There was no way he was leaking information to Norton. If the reporter had told her the sky was purple she would have considered that more credible than his accusation.

She was about to challenge him when she saw the laughter in his eyes. The leering, mean joke. This was the Norton she was more used to seeing.

He didn't mean Clay. He was referring to the co-worker with whom she had the "emotionally abusive relationship."

"You expect me to believe Riley is feeding you information?" she asked. Though she kept her voice sharp and skeptical, the accusation sounded disturbingly believable.

"He's been a source of mine for a while now. He came up to me one night at the bar, sat down and just started talking. I can't imagine you have any idea how much he hates you."

The statement hit with force because it sounded a lot like the man she knew. He resented her being his boss. He wanted her job. They both knew that as long as there was a competent alternative, he'd never get it. But if he got rid of her, it would change everything. It was a small town. They'd never look outside for help. Without Serena, there'd be no other choice.

Serena realized Norton was still talking, telling her about evidence Riley had leaked to him from other cases. Information that had ended up in the paper that had caused some trouble. It wasn't much. There wasn't much to know before this case. The problem was – it sounded like Riley. It sounded like the truth.

"He told me you found a second heart. And then you lied to me, told me there was only one heart. I was waiting to print that, waiting for the right time. That's just the type of false information that can kill a political career."

"When could he have told you that?" They'd rediscovered the heart just before the search of the woods. By that afternoon, Norton was already making wild accusations.

"He and I were on the same search team. Remember, Sheriff?"

Serena had thought she'd gotten to a point in her life when Riley couldn't hurt her anymore. She realized now that wasn't true.

When she stood to leave, Norton offered her a toothy grin. "Come on now. You can't leave just because I'm telling you the truth. I report the facts, Sheriff, I don't create the news."

She didn't even consider staying. This wasn't helping. Sitting here was actually less productive than walking in circles around her crime scenes. At least there she wasn't verbally abused. She was just too tired to withstand the assault.

Before she could reach the door, Norton called out. "Wait, there's more. I've got a good one for you, Sheriff. A really good one. Something you're going to want to know."

Serena turned, but she didn't return to the chair. In a voice that sounded wearier than she would have expected, she asked, "What other fabulous scoop do you have for me?"

Norton was visibly disappointed that she didn't return to her seat, but he continued anyway. "Lauren Fletcher is sick."

Serena rolled her eyes. "I know that. Coach told us."

Norton wagged his finger at her disapprovingly. "Again, you think you know more than you actually do. When was the last time you saw her?"

She wouldn't have admitted it, but Serena didn't like the direction this was going. "I don't know. A month, maybe more."

"This is a little town. That doesn't strike you as odd?"

"It's not that little. There's plenty of people I don't see for weeks at a time." But the denial was a lie. The town was that small. She rarely went a week without seeing a person.

Norton ignored her protest. "She hasn't been out of the house in a few weeks. I have the exact date in my book if you need it. And she and the coach have been going to some place outside of town once a month for about a year now."

"You can't possibly know she hasn't left her house in weeks. You aren't watching the house every minute of every day." But again, Serena didn't believe her own words. This bastard was good enough that he would know the truth.

"I'm guessing the cancer's back. I'm guessing it's bad. She'd been losing weight for a while and she's gotten awfully pale. Before all this broke with the heart, I was planning on really zeroing in on them, finding out the truth."

It was awful news. So very sad. She'd never been that close with Lauren or Coach, but they were nice people. This must be so difficult for both of them.

But of course, none of that mattered. This was gossip at best, and stalking at worst. She had far better ways to be spending her time.

"Look, Norton, I know you expect I'm going to fall at your feet in awe of your journalistic prowess, but again, I have to say – this isn't news, it's stalking. And it's not only wrong, it's illegal. I don't have time for the town gossip. I have a killer to catch. You might want to let me do that before I decide I already have him in custody."

Norton shook his head and returned to his cot. "I'll be here when you need me, Sheriff."

Serena left him alone with his gossip and his conceit, knowing she had no time for either. The town was going to want her head when they found out she hadn't arrested Norton for murder. And she couldn't even begin to articulate why she couldn't bring herself to do it.

~ 62 ~

Serena stood alone in the conference room reviewing the evidence. For the first time, she forced herself to seriously consider Riley as a suspect.

The motive was there. She'd been aware of it for days.

This investigation was going to be the end of her career. That was becoming more and more of a reality. She now had evidence Riley had been sabotaging her for months.

The scenario almost made sense.

Riley was more competitive than anyone she'd ever known. With the new information she had it was possible to see all of this as a twisted type of head-to-head battle. His own version of catch me if you can.

But this wasn't a game. This was cold, calculated murder. Did she really believe Riley was capable of that?

She'd told Clay that she only really knew a few people in town; that most people had secrets. But she counted Riley among those she really knew. There were days she wished she didn't know him as well as she did, but she did know him. He couldn't do any of this.

Or at least she thought he couldn't. She'd been wrong about him before. Was she wrong again?

She was staring at crime scene photos and seeing nothing when Hayley buzzed her on the intercom.

"Sheriff, I have Doc Drayton on the line. He wants to know if he should send the hair samples to the state lab."

Instead of attempting a message through Hayley, Serena picked up the call. "You don't have to invent reasons to call me. You can just call," she said.

Clay laughed. "Look who has the enormous ego. I was seriously calling about these samples. Do you want me to send them?"

"Of course I want you to send them," she replied. Then, catching a hesitation on his end she asked, "Why wouldn't I want you to send them?"

"You're still missing a sample from the list you gave me."

"Veronica Martin? I know. Her mom declined to give a sample. It's okay."

"I know about Martin. You told me about that last night. It's Lauren Fletcher. I don't have a sample from her."

The news caught Serena completely off guard. Riley had gone to the Fletcher's house. In fact, she was pretty sure he'd said he was at their house when she'd arrested Norton.

"Riley didn't drop it?"

"Nope. Nothing."

"Let me get back to you, okay?"

After searching Riley's desk and checking with Jake and Hayley, Serena finally broke down and called Riley. Though she tried both his house phone and his cell, she received no answer.

Frustrated, she sought out Jake, who was sitting in the conference room drinking coffee and staring at the murder board.

"Did Riley tell you anything about going to the Fletcher's for a sample of Lauren's hair?" she asked.

Jake met her eyes in confusion. "Are you still doing that hair thing? I mean you got Norton, right? What do you need to process the hair for?"

The response was answer enough for her purposes. Riley always thought he knew better than her. It didn't matter that he'd promised to stop by the coach's house; it didn't matter that they'd agreed to pursue this avenue. All that mattered was they had a suspect in custody, and infallible Riley was certain he had to be their guy.

~ 63 ~

Serena was muttering to herself, considering what exactly she was supposed to do about Riley when she pulled up to Coach's house.

In the driveway were two cars; one was the Fletchers' and the other was Riley's. The sight drove her blood pressure even higher. She didn't delude herself into thinking he was actually doing his job and collecting the hair sample. Riley was probably sitting with his feet up, having a beer with Coach.

Without any hesitation, Serena marched up the front walk and rapped sharply at the door. Processing the hair samples was going to take forever as it was. She didn't want to waste another day waiting for a hair sample she knew would be easy enough to obtain.

It took longer than it should have for Coach Fletcher to open the door. He looked odd, tired. She thought of Norton's gossip about Lauren's health. It was certainly looking like he'd been right.

"Good afternoon, Sheriff. What can I do for you?" There was a broad smile on Fletcher's face that Serena figured was supposed to conceal the other emotions that were so obvious. It didn't work.

"Can I come in, Coach? I'd like to talk to you about a couple things."

Serena kept her voice even, but she wasn't liking what she was seeing. The room behind Fletcher looked very dark, as if the blinds were drawn. She wished she'd been paying more attention on the walk up.

Fletcher shuffled his feet a bit, but then stepped aside. "Sure, of course, come on in."

The door opened into the spacious living room. Serena had been right. The blinds were drawn. Stranger still, Riley wasn't in the room.

"Where's Riley?" she asked.

Coach closed the door behind her and walked toward the kitchen. "Can I get you an iced tea?"

Serena shook her head. "I'm fine. Why don't we just sit down?"

He poured a glass for himself and then joined her in the living room. He took a seat in a well-worn recliner. The chair was next to a small reading lamp, which provided the room's only light.

Serena took a seat on the couch opposite him and tried to assess the room without looking obvious. There was a glass of iced tea on the table in front of the couch. Most of the ice was melted, but not all of it.

"Where's Riley?" she repeated.

Fletcher looked at her oddly, and then said, "Oh, of course, his car's out front. He's upstairs with Lauren. I'm sure he'll be down in a minute."

"How is Lauren? I haven't seen her around much lately," Serena asked.

Fletcher sipped his iced tea absently. Without meeting her eyes he said, "She's been sick, but I think things are starting to get better."

Realizing she might be missing the obvious explanation, Serena asked, "Is the light bothering her?"

He only stared blankly.

"It seems a little dark. I was wondering if the light bothered her."

Fletcher fidgeted with a small paperback that was on the table under the reading lamp. "Of course. I forgot about that. Yes, she's been getting headaches from the bright light."

There it was again, the feeling. Something was wrong. Something more than Norton's stupid gossip. Something was very wrong.

Fletcher kept talking, giving her time to think. "Riley says you arrested Norton for the murders. You must be relieved to have all that over."

Serena wondered how best to answer the question. It was one she'd be asked a lot in the coming days. Coach Fletcher wouldn't be her worst audience, so this was as good a time as any to try the truth.

"We arrested Norton Finwick last night, but not for the murder."

His head bobbed up. "Not for the murder?"

"I really can't get into it too much, but he's been arrested for stalking and some related offenses."

"Not the murder?"

Serena felt more than a little uncomfortable under the weight of his stare. "No. I still have some loose ends to tie up. I'm not ready to close the case yet."

"Riley sounded pretty confident."

She hated the tone. It was the same tone that had been used when the locals were calling for Clay's head just because he was new in town.

"Riley's not the sheriff." Her voice had more bite than she'd expected. Softening her tone, she continued, "We have more than enough to hold Norton for a good long time. There's no need to rush into an arrest before we're sure. I just want to be thorough."

Coach nodded and turned his attention back to the paperback on the table.

It seemed like it was time to bring up the reason she was there in the first place. "Actually, I was stopping by to tie up some loose ends. I just wanted to follow up on Riley's visit from last night."

The coach seemed more comfortable talking about Riley. "Yeah, he stopped by last night. We had a great talk. You know, it seemed like he might have had something official to get down to, but he got a call from the station before we could get to it. I think it was when you arrested Norton."

Serena felt a little bad that she'd assumed Riley had just blown the whole thing off. He was probably talking to Lauren right now about the hair.

"Maybe I should join Riley upstairs," Serena suggested.

"No," Fletcher said with more vehemence than was appropriate. Then, more calmly, he added, "They wanted to talk. Lauren's very fond of the boy. I wouldn't want to interfere."

"Sure, that's fine. I'll just wait then. I was hoping to talk to Lauren myself."

The coach stood and walked very calmly over to the bookshelves. He stared at the books pensively for a moment before he spoke. "You know, I have my doctorate. I've studied ancient cultures my entire life. I must have a thousand books here on these shelves and on the shelves in my study."

Serena simply stared. Her gut feeling that something was wrong was turning into a certainty. She was starting to think Riley might not be okay.

Fletcher continued on, not meeting her eyes, surveying the books. "They had the keys to so much. Information that modern science cannot even hope to understand. We disregard a lot of it as religious zealotry and superstition, but it was more than that. Often when science evaluates the practices with an open mind it sees the truth. But it's rare that we look to the past with anything but disdain."

He spun on his heel and faced her directly. "You never respected the past. Never took the time to understand. Always so focused on science. You didn't have time for my classes."

The rage on his face was bizarre and irrational. Serena could only stare.

"I really thought you'd miss it, but you didn't," he continued. "I thought you'd rely on the state labs, bring in the state police. I didn't think you'd do it this way."

"Coach, just tell me what's going on," she said, her voice calm, despite everything. She was alone here. There was no way to call for backup. And she was pretty sure she needed it.

He shook his head. "Your father would understand. Liam would understand. But you? No. You just won't understand."

"Try me," she suggested. Serena considered drawing her gun, but she couldn't. This was Coach Fletcher. She didn't need a gun to talk to him. That wasn't possible.

When he turned back to his books, Serena used what little she knew. "Lauren's sick, isn't she? She's really sick."

He didn't seem to hear her. His eyes were fixed on his books. When he finally spoke, his voice was distant.

"Did you know Lauren and I started dating in high school? I got a scholarship to play ball for the University. I was afraid I'd lose her if we went to different schools, so I proposed. We were married the week after graduation."

Serena wasn't sure where he was going with all of this, but the more he talked, the more time she had to assess the situation.

Fletcher pulled a book from a shelf and sank onto the window seat.

"She could have gone to college, you know. She was a smart girl, smarter than I ever was. But all she wanted was for us to be together, to start a family. She told me that children were what mattered. They were the reflections of our best selves. They were our legacy."

Coach shifted and met Serena's eyes. "When she committed to a life with me, she committed to that life of being a wife, being a mother. That was the path she chose. The rest of it passed her by."

Serena could see the agony in his eyes. The deep, desperate pain.

"Of course, you know, we never had those children. It was us. Just us. It always broke my heart to know how much she gave up for a dream that was never meant to be."

Fletcher turned his attention back to the book in his hand. "When she got sick it all came back to me and I just knew. I knew I had to act. I had to do something. She was the kind of woman who was supposed to leave a mark in the world. A legacy. I could not let her leave until she had that chance."

"Coach," Serena said, calmly, "it's going to be okay. Why don't we go upstairs? We'll sit with Riley and Lauren. We'll talk this through."

His eyes only darkened in response as he stood. Turning his attention back to the bookshelves, Fletcher slid the book back into place, running his hand down the spine.

He spoke more softly now. "I think the answer has to be in the history of the Aztecs and the Mayans. So much of what they did focused on eternal life."

"Didn't you say it was the Mayans who would present the heart as a plea for eternal life?" Serena asked, slowly beginning to comprehend, desperately wishing it wasn't so.

He turned to her and a small smile spread over his face. It was not unlike the look he would have given her when she'd answered a question right in class. "Exactly. And it was the Aztecs who would use the blood they drained from bodies to give them increased life and strength."

Serena suddenly saw it all. The reality was so much worse than any scenario she'd concocted in her head. "Whose heart is it, Coach?"

He cocked his head to the side. "Isn't it obvious?"

Serena felt sick to her stomach. This was so much worse than Riley's deceit or Norton's stalking. "Lauren? Did you kill her?"

There was no emotion on his face. No pain. No sorrow. No anger. Just nothing.

He shook his head. "I couldn't. I should have. Maybe that's why it isn't working. But I couldn't do that to her, even if it meant failure."

She watched as his eyes glanced quickly back to his chair. It was then she saw it. The book, on the table. It wasn't one of his old texts on history. It was a medical reference book about blood. Tucked inside the book, clearly marking a page, was the wrapper from a syringe.

In her mind's eye she could see Clay telling her about the hemorrhage, telling her about his ridiculous theory. Not looking so ridiculous now.

"You have to explain it to me, Coach. I imagine the Mayans and Aztecs weren't cutting out their own hearts to gain eternal life."

He ran a hand over his neck. "Of course not. But that was the problem, you see. I had to think it through, consider the big picture."

Serena knew the truth. When he paused, she continued, "Her body had failed her. So you offered up her heart, and drained her body of blood."

Fletcher looked at her with surprise. "You always were a smart girl, Serena. See what you can do when you learn your history?"

"But then you needed a new vessel?" she prodded.

He sighed. "Daisy seemed like the perfect solution. What a waste of a life. But it didn't work."

Serena stood. "Where's Claudia, Coach?"

He didn't seem to hear her. "There are stories in the old texts. Not many, but some. The references to reincarnation, but it was more than that. They would join the blood of the departed soul with the blood of the living soul and they believed the living soul would *become* the person who had gone."

"The blood type was wrong," Serena suggested.

He nodded vaguely. "They always did it within families. Makes sense. The blood types. Of course that would be a problem."

"Did you give Claudia a transfusion?"

Fletcher squinted at her, not understanding why she seemed to know what had happened, but simultaneously not caring enough to ask for clarification. "She's sleeping. It won't work with her because she's always sleeping."

"What do you mean – sleeping?"

When Coach turned away from her, returning his attention to his books, Serena knew she needed to act.

"I'm going to call the station," she said calmly. "Jake and Shane can join us. Jake was one of your best students, wasn't he?"

Fletcher didn't respond.

She used her phone and kept her voice low. Dropping her head to muffle the sound she said, "Hayley, I need Shane and Jake at Coach Fletcher's house now. I've found Claudia. We need Dr. Drayton too. And send some ambulances. Riley may be hurt."

Hayley's shock permeated the phone as she shrieked several questions all at once.

In a low growl, Serena said, "I can't repeat it. Now. Get them here now."

She was lifting her head to face Fletcher when she glimpsed the shadow. Though she only had a second, she managed to dodge the blow. The iron fireplace poker came down across her shoulder, instead of her head where it had been aimed.

He swung again, this time missing her completely and splintering the table next to her.

Regaining her balance, Serena drew her gun. "Step back, Coach. Step back. I don't want to hurt you, but I will."

Her arm shook as she pointed the gun at him. It was painful to raise it. Fletcher must have done something to her shoulder when he'd hit her. The pain was searing, and just surprising enough that Fletcher was able to take advantage. He swung the poker again, and she hesitated. She couldn't help it. This was her high school history teacher. She couldn't shoot him.

When the poker smashed into her wrist and knocked the gun from her hand, Serena was almost relieved. Before he could raise the poker again, she grabbed it and wrenched it away. She moved instinctually, dropping him to his knees like a drunk who needed to be sent home.

She had him on his stomach and cuffed in an instant.

She started to lift Fletcher, but as she did, she was reminded of the pain in her shoulder and wrist. She dropped him to floor and demanded, "Where is Riley? What did you do to him?"

As Coach shook his head, refusing to say another word, the front door burst open. Jake and Shane looked surprisingly competent with their guns drawn.

"It's okay," she said, gingerly raising her hands against the pain. "I have to find Riley. Hold him."

Figuring that Fletcher's lies were based on some kernel of truth, Serena rushed upstairs calling Riley's name. As she reached the top of the stairs, the smell told her she was about to find Lauren Fletcher's body.

Serena headed straight for the door at the end of the hall and the source of the smell. Inside she found a king-sized bed with a floral quilt, and a woman lying in the middle, under the sheets. If not for the smell, she might not have immediately realized what she was seeing.

She was walking toward the corpse cautiously, when she saw what she was looking for. Riley was sprawled face first on the carpet. The blood drizzling down the back of his neck told her that he hadn't managed to avoid Coach Fletcher's fireplace poker. The steady rise and fall of his chest told her that he was still alive.

Before she could turn Riley over, Clay's voice filled the room, "What the hell is going on in here?"

Turning to face him, she explained quickly, "It looks like Riley took a hit to the head. I'm pretty sure that's Lauren Fletcher in the bed. There's nothing you can do for her at this point."

Clay grabbed her arm. "What happened to you? You're bleeding."

Serena shook him off, but even as she did, she felt the blood running down her back.

"I'm fine," she said impatiently. "Check on Riley. Do what you need to do, but hurry. I'm going to need you downstairs in the basement."

Clay looked baffled.

"Claudia has to be down there. Deal with him. Please hurry," she ordered, as she pushed by him.

The pain was getting worse and there were occasional spots in her vision now. But she didn't even consider stopping. She took the stairs as quickly as she could, hurrying past Shane and Jake. As she headed to the back of the house, she heard the sound of an ambulance pulling up out front.

Like most houses in Whitefield, the Fletchers' basement stairs were off the kitchen. Serena rushed down into the stuffy basement. Smells of waste and maybe even death assaulted her nostrils as she descended. In a back corner of the room was a bed and what looked like an old-fashioned chamber pot.

On the bed, eyes closed, arms folded, was Claudia. Her hands and feet were bound and there was a gag in her mouth. Not unexpectedly, she was not as passive as Daisy had clearly been. Her face was bruised, but a check of her pulse revealed she was alive.

Serena quickly checked both arms for needle marks. She found no obvious signs of a transfusion, no tape residue. But there was a used syringe next to the bed with an empty vial. Serena could only assume it was a sedative.

Serena thought of Fletcher's comments – *she just sleeps*. She wondered if his ceremony required some kind of participation from the victim. While Daisy Roman might have been pliable enough to be forced into participation, Serena suspected it would have been a cold day in hell before Claudia Daly aided her captor.

The next few minutes passed in a flash. The medics took Claudia away. Jake took Riley to the hospital. And Shane wrestled the coach into his patrol car to be taken to a holding cell. All of her deputies had a thousand questions on their faces, but Serena could answer none.

She returned to the basement and sat on the cot. Thinking. Wondering. Processing the truth.

Clay's voice startled her. "Are you okay?"

She looked up. "You're still here?"

He ignored the question. "Can I please look at your shoulder now?"

Serena did nothing to stop him as he unbuttoned her shirt, revealing the tank top she wore underneath. She didn't look. She barely even noticed how much it hurt when he poked at her shoulder.

"It's a nasty gash. We need to get you to the hospital to clean it. You're going to need stitches – a bunch of them. Based on where you were hit, I'm concerned about your shoulder. Can you lift your arm?"

Serena tried to lift it, but about halfway up Clay stopped her. "Yeah. I've seen enough. We're going to the hospital."

She considered protesting, but realized she lacked the strength. Actually, she thought she lacked the strength to even stand up.

"Sheriff?" Clay was staring at her and she wanted to talk, but she couldn't find the words.

Placing his hands on either cheek, he looked more deeply into her eyes. "Serena," he said, his voice softening.

"I'm okay," she said, hoping somehow the words would make it so.

He seemed satisfied with her response. Smiling a little himself, he said, "Then you need to stand up. You need a hospital. And unless you want me to carry you out of here, you'd better get your ass up. I gave you time to clear the scene. That's it. You're done."

She inhaled the foul air and rose unsteadily to her feet. Clay offered a guiding hand as she rose. He walked cautiously behind her up the steps, helping her regain her balance more than once. At the top of the stairs, she almost ran into her father.

William Marlowe had her in a hug so tight it took her breath away. If the sharp pain in her shoulder wasn't enough to tell her there was something wrong with her, the spreading warmth down her back told her Clay was certainly right about the stitches.

Her father stepped back. Looking between her and Clay, he said, "She's bleeding. She needs a hospital."

Clay stepped forward. "We were heading there right now."

They each took a side and walked with Serena toward the door. Before they reached it, she heard the buzz of the crowd outside. Patting them both on the hand, she dug deep into what little reserves she had left. This needed to be dealt with. To their credit, both her father and Clay seemed to understand.

Clay shot her a stern look before he let her leave. "I'm saying this as a doctor – five minutes. That is it. You need to get to the hospital. More than five minutes and I'm going to take you there by force."

The look she received from her father told Serena that Clay would have some backup to help him with that plan.

She offered them both a smile and stepped outside. She had a job to do.

Keep Reading for a Preview of....

~ ~

The Prophecy

By Elizabeth Flaherty

~ ~

Coming in 2017

◇◇◇

An Ending

◇◇◇

Deb Pendleton woke with a scream on her lips. Heart pounding, muscles taut, she waited.

First she waited for the men to come. The men from the dreams. The men who came every night. The men who would not rest until they had tortured her to the brink of death.

Then, as her mind cleared, and the dream faded, her panic only rose. Over her own ragged breath she strained, listening for sounds in the house. Sounds that would tell her that help was coming. Help that she did not want.

But with each pulse of her heart in her ears, she realized that the scream was only in the dream. She hadn't cried out.

Her best friend still slept in the room down the hall. She wouldn't be coming.

For an instant, Deb realized she almost wished Lindsay had heard her struggle. That she had come to see if she was alright. Because there was some small solace in knowing she wasn't alone in this.

Deb sank back into her pillows. It was only then that she saw it. A smear of blood against the light blue sheets.

It was her arms, she realized. Both of them. The abrasions were mostly superficial, but there was one that was bleeding freely.

The images came immediately back. She was running through the woods. She could hear the sound of their heavy boots on the frozen ground behind her. But still she ran. These were her woods. She knew them better than the men did. The branches slashed at her arms, shredding the thin fabric she wore. Another snapped back, hitting her in the face. But it was the root that finally tripped her. A long gnarled root of an old oak. She fell hard. Unable to get her hands out fast enough, her forearm took the brunt of the blow. Pain shot up her arm and through her elbow.

Deb shook off the dream again, turning on the light next to the bed. She told herself that the light would reveal the truth. There were no scratches from the trees. No gash from the rocky ground. It had been a dream. It had only been a dream.

But the light revealed the dark truth. Her arms were both scratched. In the middle of one forearm was a gash that was bruised and bleeding.

This was real. She didn't know how it was possible, but it was real.

And she was doubly glad that she hadn't cried out. That Lindsay hadn't come to make sure she was okay. Because then she would have learned the truth, she was not okay. Not by a long shot.

<><><>

Lindsay Smithwick woke with the sun. She was usually an early riser, but today it was excitement that had her out of bed before her alarm clock buzzed her awake. Today was her last final. In mere hours three years of law school would be complete. A decade of tending bar and scraping together every spare cent she could had led to this moment. One final test.

She was ready for whatever her criminal procedure professor had in waiting for her, but that didn't mean she wasn't planning a few extra hours to review before she headed in for her ten o'clock exam.

Grabbing her robe, Lindsay headed across the hall to the bathroom. That was when she noticed the light under the door.

Deb wouldn't be up yet. She had only a ten minute drive into work and she wouldn't head in until much closer to nine.

So the light meant something else entirely.

She'd lived with Deb for almost their entire friendship, she knew her better than she knew anyone else in the world. And she knew the only thing worse than the constant nightmares was the insomnia. Deb could endure the nightmares, managing push aside the pain and panic that was so clear on her face when she woke screaming.

The times when the screaming grew quiet were the problem. Because it meant Deb wasn't sleeping, at least not in any effective way. It had happened only twice before. Both times ended in hospitalization.

The light under the bedroom door told Lindsay there were problems brewing. Serious problems.

<><><>

Fran McTigue watched intently from her office. Deb was standing in front of the coffee machine, reading a file and absently pouring the thick black substance into her oversized cup. There was nothing odd about her behavior. It was what she did every day. What they all did. But Fran knew there was something wrong. Social work has one of the highest burnout rates of any career. As the boss, it was Fran's job to watch for the signs, to catch problems before they got out of control and began affecting a person's work.

In the past week things had gotten bad enough with Deb that it didn't take a Ph.D. to realize her best social worker was on the fast track to a breakdown. Something had changed. Deb was thin, she always had been. But she looked like she'd lost ten pounds off her already thin frame in the past couple of weeks. The weight loss made her usually pretty features seem awkward and oversized. The black circles under her eyes had become so dark that Fran was wondering if she was sleeping at all.

She'd scanned Deb's cases, trying to isolate if there was one particular file that was troubling her. She kept hoping there would be an identifiable source for Deb's troubles, something that could be fixed by a case transfer. But there was nothing there. It just seemed the stress of the job had finally gotten to her.

For years she'd worried this day would come. She'd hoped Deb was one of the rare people who could outlast this job and make a career of it. For five years Deb showed no signs of the strain. No signs the horrors were outweighing the joys. In fact, Fran had so come to trust her endurance that she gave her many of the tougher files in the office.

When there was a family or child that seemed to be at that make or break point, it was Deb that Fran relied on. Her instincts were impeccable. She had a knack for sniffing out lies – drug use, abuse, neglect. Fran couldn't think of a time the girl had been wrong. And it wasn't because she didn't go out on a limb on a regular basis. It was as though she just *knew* things. Deb was so good that if you'd told Fran she was a closet psychic, she wouldn't have been the least surprised.

She took a deep breath. She didn't want to do this. But she knew it was for the best. Maybe if she convinced Deb to take some time off she would be able to shake whatever was bothering her and return to the fold in a couple of weeks. If not, Fran had no idea what she would do. It was going to be impossible to replace her.

She approached slowly, hoping the girl would see her coming. The fact that she didn't notice her approach only confirmed Fran's suspicions.

She placed a soft hand on Deb's shoulder. She jumped a little in surprise, but then slowly turned around. There was only darkness in her eyes, a brooding sadness that made Fran wonder if she'd somehow missed earlier signs. The pain looked too deep to be new.

"Come on honey," she said in a voice that she usually reserved for the mournful parents she dealt with almost every day. "We need to talk."

Deb nodded and took her coffee and the file she'd been reading. Fran could see the recognition on her face. She knew what was coming, but she didn't have the strength to fight it.

<><><>

Her mind felt clear. Cleansed. It was as if a dark veil had been lifted. There was a peaceful town. A shining lake. Friends. There were women all around her. But whenever she tried to focus on them, they seemed to disappear. It seemed she could only see them out of the corner of her eye.

The women were talking softly among themselves. The sounds seemed to be words, but they were too muted and indistinct to really hear. From the soft blur of the women, a figure began to come into focus. Another woman. Dark brown hair. A gentle smile. And the most familiar grey eyes...

Deb woke slowly. It was nice to dance at the edge of sleep, instead of being jolted awake by a nightmare. The peace was blessed and glorious. Like a tall glass of lemonade on a scorching day. She felt rejuvenated in a way she hadn't experienced in a long time.

The television was on in the room. Some talk show. Ellen, maybe. A woman with a polished voice was answering questions about her newest movie and her difficult relationship with the paparazzi. Something about meeting the love of her life in a hotel in Arizona.

Though she didn't turn her head to look, Deb could feel Lindsay's presence in the room. Her tests were over. Law school was over. But nothing suggested to Deb that Lindsay was celebrating that accomplishment. Her silent entry to the room and decision to let her sleep told a different story.

Hoping she was wrong, Deb turned her head to face her friend, and asked, "How was the last exam?"

Lindsay almost jumped at the sound of her voice. "How long have you been awake?"

"Just woke up. How was the exam?" Deb repeated, hoping to avoid discussions about nightmares and forced vacations.

Lindsay gave a half smile at the question. They'd known each other too long for her not to realize the obvious delay. "It was fine. Four essays. Pretty much the type of multipart hypotheticals the professor told us to expect. I think I did okay."

Deb was pretty sure she'd done more than okay. Lindsay had worked too hard for too long to settle for okay.

"That's a pretty half-hearted response. You're done. Law school done. Graduation upcoming."

Lindsay shook her head. "Studying for the bar exam is what I have upcoming. Graduation is just a party for a bunch of twenty-five year olds who don't have enough life experience to understand what real accomplishment is."

Deb laughed. "It's a real accomplishment, Linds. Give yourself a little credit."

Lindsay only shrugged. "I'll just be happy when I can settle into a full time job that has nothing to do with reciting the day's specials and asking if you want another cup of coffee with your dessert."

"Speaking of which, when is your next shift?"

"I'm working tonight and tomorrow, but I'm off for a week starting on Sunday."

Deb sat up straighter at the comment. Lindsay had three weeks before her bar prep courses started. This was the time for her to load up on shifts at the restaurant. Taking time off was completely out of character.

"I talked with financial aid last week. They set me up with a pretty substantial loan to get me through until after the bar exam," Lindsay explained.

Lindsay had managed to make it through three years of law school only using loans to pay a part of her tuition. She'd taken classes, worked at the restaurant, and even taken on the internships necessary to get a job. Taking a loan now had to mean she was going to cut down on her shifts at the restaurant, which really didn't make sense.

"Are you really that concerned about the exam?" Deb asked.

Lindsay shook her head. "It'll take work, but I'll be fine. I know that."

Lindsay paused, and gave her old friend a closer look. "I think maybe it's time we talked about why you're home in the middle of your usual work day."

The realization hit like a punch to the gut. "This is about me? That's ridiculous. You can't possibly…."

Lindsay held up a hand. "Seriously, stop. You need to talk to me. You need to explain what's really going on with you. I'm worried, like really actually worried. When was the last time you got a full night's sleep?"

"I'm fine," Deb insisted.

Lindsay closed her eyes a moment, seeming to try to gather herself. When she opened them again, she didn't look angry, but she did look determined. "Why are you home?"

Deb sighed. "They've asked me to take a leave of absence."

"Did they say why?"

Of course, it was the same reason that Lindsay was worried, but Deb was helpless to tell anything other than the truth.

"She thinks work is starting to wear on me. She thinks I look tired. That the strain is causing me to lose sleep and eventually it'll affect my work."

"Do you think there's any connection between work and the nightmares being worse lately?" she asked. There was no hope in her voice. She knew the truth as well as Deb did.

"I really wish it was that simple." Deb's voice was less bitter she'd expected it to be, which helped her to ignore the distressing tone of resignation. "Though, I have to admit, I had the greatest nap down here this afternoon. Maybe she was right."

Lindsay seemed to almost physically brace herself before she asked, "The nightmares have been a lot worse lately, haven't they?"

Deb couldn't meet her eyes when she answered. "They get bad sometimes. You know that. They'll ease up soon."

"Maybe you need to talk to someone again?"

Deb rolled her eyes. "Linds, come on, it doesn't help. It never helps."

They'd known each other almost a decade. In that time Deb had tried therapists, sleep experts, medications. Nothing had helped. The dreams cycled. They always cycled. There were good times. There were bad times. Lindsay knew that. Unfortunately, she also seemed to know the truth that Deb was trying so hard to hide. It had never been this bad before.

"You aren't sleeping. From the look of you, you aren't eating either. You can't live like this," Lindsay insisted.

Since she knew that Lindsay was right, Deb fought back the only way she could. "So your solution is you're going to cut down on your hours so you can take care of me? That's not a solution. That's just stupid."

Lindsay shook her head. "Look, I'm tired. I needed a break. You've seemed tired. I thought we could get away for a week or so. Hit the road. Just head somewhere quiet. I think we both have earned it. I was going to ask you if you could take some time off, but I guess we already answered that question."

"You sound like you're planning something bigger. Something longer term. You don't need a loan to take one week off," Deb replied.

"I'm really not sure that a week is going to be enough for me."

"Enough time for you?" Deb countered.

Lindsay offered a sad smile in response. "For either of us."

"So, what happens if a vacation doesn't do it?" Deb asked.

Lindsay seemed to consider the question. When she finally responded, her voice was soft, concerned. "I'm really hoping that we don't need to find out."

<><><>

Ruth Montgomery woke before the sun. On most nights she slept soundly, only waking to the chirp of her alarm, but for the past week she'd slept fitfully. She felt a nervous energy pulsing through her constantly. The feeling was so intense that she'd cut coffee from her diet completely. If this kept up, sugar would be the next to go.

Fortunately, there was always plenty to do around the Inn. It was spring, so the weekends were busy. There were even a few people who would stay the week to enjoying peaceful walks through the woods, a quiet time fishing on the lake, and all that little Eden, Massachusetts had to offer.

It was a beautiful spot. She knew that. But she still couldn't understand why people would come, why people would stay. She couldn't understand how they didn't sense what was hidden beneath the surface.

But they never did. They only saw the beauty. The serenity. They thought the quiet religious community that populated most of the town was quaint. One person had once told her that he thought it was a perfect slice of a simpler time. Ruth didn't tell him that simple wasn't always good. That religion wasn't always positive. And that evil's best disguise was often a friendly face.

On this early morning she tried to shake dark thoughts from her mind. She forced herself to look out the kitchen window. To sip her herbal tea and focus on the pink light that brightened the sky behind her well-tended rose garden. She'd long ago come to terms with the community in Eden. Come to terms with her role in the bigger picture.

That was why she didn't understand why she suddenly felt so haunted. Why her heart was so full of anger that she could feel it pounding in her chest. She'd let the anger go long ago. Or she'd thought she had. To hate the men of Eden was as foolish as hating the sun for rising. They were nothing more than a product of their ancestry. They'd had as little choice about the role they'd play as she did.

But she could feel the tea cup tremble in her hands and she wondered yet again what was wrong with her. Why she felt like she had to be on alert on watch. She just couldn't help thinking that her role was about to change.

◇◇◇

Ben Cole began his day by bringing in some logs for the fire in the cozy dining room of the Moonlight Inn. He piled the logs next to the fireplace and he got the fire started. It would be a warm afternoon. Bright sun. Cloudless sky. But this morning there was still a chill. A little reminder of the winter that had just passed.

It had been his first winter in Massachusetts. Though Ruth assured him that it had been a mild season for them, he found it hard to believe. Growing up in Virginia, Ben had thought he'd experienced winter. But one season here had taught him how wrong he was. Up here the snow flew and it seemed to stay forever, layering one storm upon the other. It took the warm spring sun weeks to melt.

Ben shivered at the memory and extended his hands toward the now roaring fire. He wasn't sure he had another winter like this in him.

He was staring at the fire, wondering why he'd stayed through this winter in the first place, when he heard Ruth's voice behind him.

"You've gotten pretty good at that."

Ben rose and smiled a greeting. "I've certainly had enough practice. I'm just happy not be shoveling sidewalks."

The smile that Ruth returned wasn't as broad as usual, and he noticed that she looked tired. Though Ben knew that she had to be in her late forties, Ruth typically looked ten years younger than that. But today she looked her years and there was an unfamiliar darkness in her eyes.

Ben considered asking if she was okay, but he felt uncertain about the conversation. Ruth was always friendly, but they really weren't what anyone would mistake for friends. She was his boss. A boss who offered him a job when he had nowhere else to go. Prying into her life didn't seem appropriate.

Instead he asked, "Do you need me to take care of anything in here this morning? I was going to head out to the shed to work on that new porch swing."

Ruth nodded. "Go ahead. I have breakfast ready to layout. It won't take both of us to do that."

Ben hesitated a moment, again feeling like he should ask her if she was okay. But again he reached the same conclusion. He sent a casual wave her way, and headed out to the shed.

The shed was nothing fancy. Just a small wooden structure with some loosely run electrical lines. There was enough power for a small space heater, some lights and the power tools that he needed to work. It was chilly enough that he was glad he had his jacket, but he didn't really mind. It was a small price to pay for the solitude. Solitude was something he craved above all else.

It had been late June when he'd arrived in the tiny town of Eden, Massachusetts. He found the inn at the very edge of town. To call the moment déjà vu would not give it enough credit. It was like coming home. For the first time in a long time, he saw a glimmer. And believed that maybe – just maybe – there was something more for him.

He'd gotten a room. Stayed a week. Then two. He'd been staying at the hotel a month when Ruth had told him about the leaky faucet in the kitchen. She'd made it seem like he was doing her a favor looking at it. There were a couple more jobs like that when she asked if he was considering staying in Eden.

Now, looking back, he felt like he'd been swept up in some greater plan. Like there was some force that had brought him here. Some force that would never let him leave.

The thought should have made him uneasy. But he actually found it reassuring that there was some force at play in his life and that the force had led him to this peaceful place. Because it made him believe for the first time in a long time that life wasn't entirely random and pointless.

◇◇◇

Chip Potter ate a quiet breakfast in the corner booth of the local dinner. He did what he did every day. He waited. Watched. Observed the people around him. Observed the town. And absorbed the story that it had to tell.

At precisely nine am, the same as he had every prior morning, Joseph appeared in the glass doorway. He was a tall man, well over six feet, with narrow shoulders. He would have seemed like a giant, but he walked with a slight slouch, with his head down, as if he was hoping that he could pass through unnoticed. Regardless of his height, there was little likelihood of that. Joseph was one of seven elders who ran the religious sect that populated most of Eden, Massachusetts.

He was silent. Stoic. And, in Chip's view, utterly fascinating.

The owner scurried forward as the glass door opened and immediately handed Joseph the paper and led him to the same seat that he used every day. A waitress arrived at the table simultaneously and poured a cup of coffee. There would be toast eventually. But not right away. Like clockwork, the moment that Joseph turned the paper to the second page, the bread would go in the toaster. It would appear on the table – spread with butter and jam – before Joseph finished the first section of the paper.

This morning, Chip watched closely, hoping to confirm what he suspected.

Though the paper was open in front of Joseph, and his head was lowered in a way that suggested he was reading, Chip didn't think that was the case. The man seemed to be meditating. His eyes were lowered, hard to see, but they seemed unfocused, like he was seeing something that no one else could. On top of that it seemed like it took him an inordinately long time to read the front page of the paper.

The question was – what was the man doing? Why meditate in the middle of a dinner?

Chip was a writer, a creative guy, but he had no explanation for this. No story that made it all make sense. He thought of the stories that people in town told. Stories of a powerful group of men that ran the religious order. Men with fantastic powers. They spoke of the ability to read minds, to heal, transport the mind to another place.

Was that what this was supposed to be? Some kind of impersonation of a man with magical powers? It was all shenanigans of course. Chip knew that. The more interesting question was why did he act like this? It was somehow too subtle. The sort of action that was designed to be discreet. But why exercise discretion? Wasn't the whole point for them to see? To believe? Nothing else made sense.

As Chip considered the situation, Joseph's head rose ever so slightly and he turned around. Joseph's eyes locked on his with a frightening intensity. He wanted Chip to leave. He wished this was such intensity that Chip received the message without words. He received the message so clearly that it was actually difficult to not to comply.

And for just a moment, against every sensible bone in his body, Chip wondered what was really going on in this town.